SIRENS IN THE NIGHT

Michael Bradley

Amberjack Publishing
New York, New York

Amberjack Publishing
228 Park Avenue S #89611
New York, NY 10003-1502
http://amberjackpublishing.com

Publisher's Cataloging-in-Publication data

Bradley, Michael, 1970-
Sirens in the night / Michael Bradley.
pages cm
ISBN 9780692517192 (pbk.)
ISBN 9780692517208 (ebook)

1. Mythology, Greek --Fiction. 2. Detectives --Pennsylvania --Philadelphia --Fiction. 3. Women detectives --Fiction. 4. Paranormal fiction. 5. Fantasy fiction. 6. Mystery and detective stories. I. Title.

PS3602 .R34273 S57 2015
813.6 --dc23   2015950083

Cover Design: Jerilyn Hassell Pool

Printed in the United States of America

Author's Note

One of the challenges with writing a novel that is based in the world of radio broadcasting is the fact that it is necessary to identify a radio station by its call letters. The problem with this is that call letters often come and go at the station management's whim. Stations often select call letters that either reflect the city they are in, or their format. When writing this story, I selected the call letters WPLX because the story takes place in Philadelphia. At the time of writing this story, those call letters are assigned to an AM radio station in Memphis, Tennessee.

This is the long way of saying that this is a work of fiction. Names, characters, places, incidents, and radio station call letters are products of the author's imagination or are used fictitiously and are not construed as real. Any resemblance to actual events, locales, organizations, radio stations, or persons, living or dead, is entirely coincidental.

"The more real things become, the more like myths they become."
Rainer Werner Fassbinder

Chapter One

Samantha Ballard cursed under her breath as she watched the line of cars on South Street remain motionless, just as they had for the past ten minutes. It was a typical Monday morning in Philadelphia with traffic tied up for blocks. She sat in the passenger seat of the Dodge Charger wondering if it would have been quicker to just get out and walk. Glancing out the side window, she took in the scenery, which was mostly brick, concrete, glass, and graffiti. A man, who was carrying a laptop bag, walked along the sidewalk past the car, moving at what seemed like the speed of light compared to her own forward progress. She could see the bus stop ahead at the corner of South Street and Fifteenth Street, with a dozen people waiting for the next bus. Despite having the Charger's windows closed she could still smell the acrid exhaust violating her olfactory senses from the idle cars and trucks ahead. *Someday I'll end up with cancer from sitting in too many of the city's traffic jams*, Samantha thought.

Flipping down the sun visor over her seat, Samantha gazed at herself in the small mirror. With a flick of her hand, she brushed a few stray auburn hairs back into place. Just like every other Monday, her hazel

1

eyes seemed dull and tired. Although she had gotten eight hours of sleep the night before, she still felt like crap. Samantha was no longer the kind to go out and party hard all weekend, and then rise early on Monday ready for another week. Telling herself that she was too old to still be acting like a college student, she had given up most of that life a few years ago. She was only thirty-three, but she knew her limits.

Her partner, Peter Thornton, gripped the steering wheel and joked, "Lookin' to hook up at the crime scene?"

Returning the sun visor to its original position, Samantha glanced at her partner. The tall African-American was five years younger than Samantha, a fresh faced college boy who had "rising star" written all over him. His face reminded Samantha of an inverted teardrop, with a round top covered in dark, close cropped hair, and a chin that formed a dull point. Dark eyebrows matched his hair, and rested above two narrow brown eyes.

Her captain had assigned the homicide division rookie to Samantha as her new partner three months ago, and it had been a long three months. She had never had much patience when it came to "mentoring" her fellow officers. Her previous partner, Eddie Murdock, had retired four months ago with a full pension and plans to move south to get away from the harsh Philadelphia winters. Having been together for five years, Samantha and Eddie had a routine, and they understood each other. It was almost as if they could read each other's minds. It was the rapport that she missed the most. Peter asked too many questions, forcing her to stop doing something that she could normally do with her eyes closed, and actually think it through in order to answer his inquiry. It was driving Samantha crazy.

"Not really into that sort of thing," she replied, turning her eyes to gaze at the traffic before them.

Peter gave a quick snort. "What are you into?"

Samantha refused to look his way. She knew he was just speaking in jest, but she wasn't in the mood. "You've heard the rumors. You figure it out." She gave him a quick glance and a half smile. "Now piss off." Peter chuckled.

The Ford pickup in front of them started to move, so Peter gently inched the car forward as well. Beginning to regret telling her partner to skip the lights and sirens, Samantha went back to staring out the window, and thought of the past. She had been on the Philadelphia police force for ten years, five as a uniformed officer and five as a detective. Even as a child, it seemed that she was destined to be a police officer. Her father had been a uniformed officer in Philadelphia for twenty-five years, until he was killed in the line of duty. Her grandfather, on the other hand, had been lucky and retired from the force after thirty years. By the time she had turned five, her father had already taught her how to fire his department-issued revolver. These days, she could shoot rings around most of her fellow detectives. Before she had turned twelve, she knew every legal move for taking down a perp, as well as a few illegal ones. By her seventeenth birthday, Samantha could recite almost every rule and regulation in the department. It seemed that she had been fated to become part of the thin blue line.

As an old man, wearing torn trousers and a stained t-shirt, pushed a rusted shopping cart filled with trash bags past them on the sidewalk, Samantha felt momentarily nostalgic for her days as a uniformed officer walking a beat on the streets of the city. Patrolling the city had never been easy, but the one thing she loved was getting to know the people who lived and worked along her beat. Whether they were male or female, homeless or millionaires, young or old, she would remember the names of each and every one. It was a trick that her father had taught her. Now, the only faces that she remembered were the ones that had been brutally murdered.

Peter Thornton turned the steering wheel to the right as he guided the unmarked police car onto Broad Street. Traffic was flowing only slightly better, with their progress being a slow crawl as opposed to a complete standstill. As they inched up the busy thoroughfare, Samantha could see their destination ahead indicated by the flashing red and blue lights of two police cars parked in front of the building. Five minutes later, Peter nosed the Dodge into a space between the two other police cars. Samantha glanced at her watch—eight thirty-seven.

Pushing the car door open, she said, "Let's see

what we got."

The crisp, chilly March air forced Samantha to slide her hands into her grey overcoat, and push it closed in front of her. It had been a colder than normal March, and it didn't look as if it would warm up anytime soon. Sidestepping to avoid a puddle of water left from the previous evening's rain, Samantha stepped up onto the sidewalk and surveyed the scene before her. The old six-story brick building was nothing more than a shell. The windows and doors had been removed, leaving nothing but gaping holes between the dark red brickwork. A large green dumpster, filled to the brim with lumber and other construction rubbish, sat to the right of the entryway of the building. Construction workers, most with yellow hard hats pushed back from their foreheads, milled around the exterior of the building talking and laughing amongst themselves. When Samantha strode by, the workers fell silent, some giving her physique their undivided attention, their eyes scanning her from head to toe. Others, however, turned away, avoiding eye contact with the police. Her five foot five trim physique was the result of years of a rigorous fitness routine that Samantha followed religiously. It was expected that every officer on the Philadelphia police force stay physically fit. For her, it was doubly so. Even during these enlightened times, there were still men in her male-dominated workplace that would look for any excuse to get her fired. She didn't smile, or even look in the construction workers' direction, leaving them to watch her pass. She wondered how many of those that averted their eyes had criminal records.

With Peter at her heels, Samantha climbed the three concrete steps that led into the old building. If she had found the exterior to be just a shell, the interior seemed even more so. The floor had been stripped down to the plywood subfloor, and the walls were nothing more than two-by-four studs. A string of bare light bulbs illuminated the interior of the building in harsh white shades of bright incandescent light. A uniformed officer had been waiting for their arrival by the entryway.

"You get stuck in traffic?" the officer asked as they approached.

"No. We stopped to pick up doughnuts for you and your partner." Samantha glared at the officer. "We're nice like that."

The officer gave a mock laugh. "Ha, real funny."

"You reported a triple homicide?" asked Peter.

"Down those stairs." The officer gestured toward a flight of stairs in the far corner. "Sergeant Williams is waiting for you." Pausing, the officer added, "Some weird shit down there. I've never seen anything like it."

Briskly brushing past the officer, Samantha replied, "Lucky you're not leading the investigation then."

Pulling a small flashlight from her coat pocket, Samantha shone the beam down the dimly lit stairwell leading underneath the old building. The concrete stairs were damp and slick, and the two detectives had to tread with care to keep from falling. The chamber below was cold, dark, and empty with the exception of the three figures standing at the far end.

"Over here," said a raised voice.

As Samantha approached, she could see two more uniformed officers and another man standing around the top end of an aluminum ladder, which disappeared into a dark hole in the floor. Sergeant Williams, wearing a white uniform shirt and black trousers, turned and waved to Samantha and Peter. His white octagonal police hat was pushed back on his head, with wisps of dark hair peeking out from under the brim. The dark skin of his pudgy face showed the lines of a twenty-year veteran of the police force. Because of her father, Samantha had known Williams for many years. There were a few officers still on the force who could say they had watched Samantha grow up. One or two had even kept their eye on Samantha after her father had been killed. Williams had been one of those. The other officer, who, she thought, had all the looks of a rookie, was unfamiliar to her. The lanky, young policeman looked ill at ease in his pale blue uniform shirt, and his trousers still had the "fresh from the package" crease down the front.

Extending his hand to Samantha, Williams said, "Sam, good to see you. Got a bizarre one for you." Williams turned, and gestured to the third man. "This is Stanley Henderson, assistant foreman for Rhinehold Construction. He discovered the bodies this morning."

Peter Thornton pulled a pair of latex gloves from his coat pocket, and as he pulled them over his hands, asked, "Where are they?"

Williams pointed toward the ladder. "Down there."

Samantha's feet touched the cobblestone covered ground as she stepped off the bottom rung of the ladder. The fetid air was a musty mix of odors, from mildew to a faint smell of vomit. Clicking on her flashlight again, she swept the room with the beam of light to get her bearings. The walls and low ceiling of the near claustrophobic chamber were lined with rotting timbers held in place with old peg and hole construction. Centered in the floor was a round opening, like an oversized manhole Samantha would have expected to see on any street in the city. An oxidized ring of iron encircled the outer edge of the opening, and must have been, at Samantha's best guess, at least a century or more old. Attached by a crude hinge on one side of the ring was a heavy iron hatch, five inches thick. Embedded into the cobblestone surrounding the opening were eight thick iron hoops, covered, like everything else, in layers of rust and oxidation. A long length of chain, with its metallic links corroded with age, snaked across the floor, ending in a pile in the far corner. Aiming her flashlight into the hole, Samantha discovered a well about ten feet deep by her estimation. It was a narrow shaft with red bricks forming the outer walls. The sandy bottom of the shaft was uneven, and, although she couldn't be sure, appeared to hold the indentation of numerous footprints.

As her light swept to the opposite corner, it froze on the three occupants of the chamber. They were seated on the floor with their backs propped against the wall. The attire adorning the three corpses seemed as modern as anything she would see on the streets above her. Blue denim jeans, grey trousers, white shirt and tie, tan work boots, and even a green Philadelphia Eagles sweatshirt seemed like perfectly normal attire to find on a modern day corpse. What caused Samantha to shudder were the faces and hands of the three bodies. The skin on each face had a color and texture more like dried, cracking leather than human flesh, and had sunken in around the skull, showing a distinctive outline of the underlying bone structure. The flesh on the fingers of each hand had the same leathery appearance as the face, and also seemed to have shrunk around the bones, revealing every joint. The eyeballs looked lifeless and unreal, as if they had been substituted for eggshells. Stepping off the ladder behind her, Peter Thornton turned and followed her gaze.

"Whoa! Didn't expect that!" he exclaimed.

Taking a cautious step forward, Samantha felt uneasy and a little fearful. The scene seemed like something out of a horror film. Between the modern clothing and the dried mummified remains, she couldn't help but wonder if someone was playing an elaborate hoax. She knelt down before the middle corpse to get a closer look, and immediately felt ill. She fought back the bile that was rising from her stomach.

Upon closer examination, Samantha noted that each corpse had hair, which was something that she never remembered seeing on any museum mummy. The first corpse had a full head of dirty blonde hair, which looked freshly washed and styled. The thinning hair on the second corpse was grey. And, although bald, the third corpse had a tuft of dark chest hair peeking out from under the green sweatshirt. A silver watch dangled from the emaciated wrist of one of the bodies, and a gold wedding band hung precariously from the bony knuckle of another. Around the neck of the bald corpse was a silver chain, on the end of which hung a St. Christopher medallion. Standing beside her, Peter summed up his own assessment of the unusual crime scene succinctly by saying, "It's a hoax. It's got to be."

Without responding, Samantha rose to her feet, and swung the flashlight around the chamber once again. The beam halted on the iron hatch, and she studied the reddish orange object carefully. The metal work was crude compared to modern day standards. It was pitted and uneven, with round indentations scattered around the surface. Samantha stepped closer, and peered at the dents. As she focused her flashlight on one of them, she was surprised to see a row of four smaller depressions. Studying the markings, she felt certain they looked familiar.

"Peter, come look at this," she said, using the beam of light as a pointer. "What do you make of these dents?"

Peter gave the hatch a cursory glance. "Solid iron, pretty damn old by the looks of it. Maybe happened when the hatch was forged?"

Silence fell over the chamber as Samantha continued to examine the markings on the hatch. She tilted her head to one side, and then sighed. Making a fist, she looked at her hand for a moment before gently inserting it into one of the indentations on the hatch. The knuckles on her hand slid into the row of small depressions almost perfectly.

Looking up at Peter, she said, "Tell me something. How strong do you have to be to dent iron with your fist?"

———————

The forensics team was just arriving when Samantha and Peter emerged from the dark hole. Sergeant Williams was still standing above with Stanley Henderson and the other officer. Samantha peeled off the latex gloves from her hands, and slid her flashlight back into her coat pocket.

"Who upchucked in the corner down there?" she asked.

Williams smiled. "It's Stoltz's first murder scene." He jerked his thumb toward the young officer. "Couldn't keep his Egg McMuffin down."

"You sure picked a doozy to pop your cherry on," Peter said to the blushing young officer.

Samantha turned to the representative of Rhinehold Construction. "Tell me what happened," she said.

Henderson slid his yellow hard hat from his head, and rubbed his high forehead with his hand. The blonde hair was thinning along the top of his square head. Henderson's muscular arms stretched the fabric of grey t-shirt he was wearing underneath the yellow reflective vest that rested over his broad shoulders. His dark blue jeans, although permanently embedded with stains tracing the history of dozens of construction sites, looked freshly laundered, and his tan steel-toed Timberland boots appeared to have been recently cleaned, showing only a faint coating of construction dust around the toes.

"We were preppin' to pour a new floor down here. Friday morning, I had a couple of guys breaking up the old concrete with jackhammers. One of them broke open that hole." Reseating the hard hat on his head, Henderson added, "A lot of these buildings, they're built right on top of older ones. It's, uh . . . not unusual to find hidden rooms and stuff. Happens all the time in this city. Our foreman, Steve Rafferty, climbed down to check it out." He gestured toward the hole. "He found that hatch sealed and all chained up. When we find shit like this, our standard operating procedure is to call the historical society."

"Why?" Peter inquired.

"It's an agreement we have with 'em. Keeps us from damaging anything important. A pain in the ass is what I call it. They come, check it out, and give us the okay to keep workin'." Henderson paused for a moment, watching as two forensics officers began to climb down the ladder into the hole. "Nobody could come out 'til Saturday morning. We don't work weekends, so Steve agreed to come down and let 'em in. Me and my guys got here this morning, found the job site open . . . and those things down there."

"Who opened the hatch?" asked Samantha.

Henderson shrugged his shoulders. "Don't know."

Peter Thornton asked, "Where's Steve Rafferty? Can we talk to him?"

Henderson fell silent for a moment, trying to maintain control of his emotions. His voice cracked as he replied. "Down there." He gestured toward the ladder. "He's the one in the Eagles sweatshirt."

Samantha glanced at Peter, and then back toward Stanley Henderson. She noticed the pained lines on his face. His quivering lips hinted at an emotionally charged frown, which seemed to balance perilously between anger, sadness, and confusion. Samantha said, "If this is some kind of joke—"

"I swear! That St. Christopher medal around his neck? He always wore that. His kid gave it to him a few years back."

Samantha gestured back toward the dark hole. "Hang on a sec. Those bodies got to be at least six months old. You can't possibly tell me that one of them was alive last week."

Henderson became agitated as his careful balance of emotions began to crumble. "Look, I can't explain it. Steve hasn't been seen since Saturday morning. Call his wife if you don't believe me!"

Trying to calm the assistant foreman, Peter Thornton replied, "I know you may think that's the body of your friend, but Mr. Henderson—"

Henderson's voice rose with emotion as he interrupted, "I've worked with Steve for eight years. I know him when I see him. It's the same bald head, same necklace, and same wedding ring. I don't know how, but one of those things down there is Steve Rafferty!"

Chapter Two

The clock on the bedside table beeped loudly as its alarm blared throughout the small bedroom. A man-sized lump buried under the sheets and blanket of the king-sized bed slowly shifted, inching its way toward the source of the obnoxious noise. A hand crept out from under the sheets, and smacked at the bedside table until it found the alarm clock. With a gentle swat of the fingers, the alarm stopped. Forcefully kicking the sheets and blanket off the bed, Jack Allyn stared up at the ceiling of his bedroom with glazed, sleep-filled eyes. He let out a long sigh, and then glanced at the glowing numbers on the alarm clock. Seven thirty-five at night. Jack sighed again, and went back to staring at the ceiling. Despite having gone to bed at noon, he felt as if he had gotten no more than three hours of sleep. Even after more than a year, he had still not adjusted to working the overnight shift.

Swinging his legs off the bed, Jack sat for a moment, giving his mind a chance to clear from its sleepy fog. As he did every evening when he awoke, he wondered where things had all gone wrong. His career in broadcasting had been on an upward trajectory for years. He had started working part-time at a small

15

station in Schenectady, New York as a weekend on-air personality. He had been young and eager back then, and his raw talent had shone from the very first day. It hadn't taken him long to be picked up by a Classic Rock station in Allentown, Pennsylvania, working the Midday shift. From there he moved on to Charlotte, North Carolina, working for the number one Top Forty station in the city. "Afternoon Drive" was what those in radio called the afternoon shift from three to seven, and that was where Jack had truly begun to make a name for himself. His witty banter with listeners and fast-paced personality had made him a minor celebrity throughout the Charlotte listening area. When he wasn't on the air, requests for Jack to appear at concerts and events kept him on the go constantly. And his good looks certainly hadn't hindered his chances with his female listeners.

Jack Allyn was naturally tall and trim, which was good since he found exercise to be abhorrent. His crisp blue eyes and the shoulder length blonde hair framed a long, sculpted face which helped add to his popularity with the ladies. Whether he was partying at the hottest nightclub or hanging out backstage at a concert, it hadn't been unusual to find Jack out in public with a different woman on his arm each night, making him the envy of many around Charlotte. But to him, every one had been just another in a long string of meaningless flings. He had spent several years in North Carolina, and had even been nominated for a Marconi Award, the biggest accolade in radio broadcasting. He didn't win, but just to be nominated was enough for him.

Although he enjoyed his time in Charlotte, Jack Allyn had larger aspirations. When the number one Top Forty station in Dallas came calling, Jack didn't hesitate to make the move, taking the Texas radio market by storm. He quickly established himself as the dominant afternoon on-air personality throughout the city. As in Charlotte, his popularity in Dallas brought with it a string of blondes, brunettes, and redheads, who he rotated in and out of his life with nonchalant ease, his brief liaisons never lasting more than a few weeks at most.

After three years of working the afternoon drive in Dallas, Sinclair Satellite Entertainment had approached Jack about syndicating his highly successful afternoon show to radio stations throughout the country. Having spent his childhood listening to some of the biggest names in radio syndication, like Howard Stern, Rick Dees, Casey Kasem, and even Shadoe Stevens, the thought of joining their ranks was a dream come true.

He didn't know how it had happened. Between his professional success and apathetic attitude toward his personal relationships, Jack had become arrogant and a bit conceited. He often wondered if there was perhaps some truth to the old adage of pride coming before the fall. The negotiations with Sinclair Satellite Entertainment had gone better than he could have expected, and they had promised a contract by the end of the week. It had been a Wednesday, and Jack had felt like he was really in the groove that afternoon on his show. Somehow, between punching up songs on his studio computer and talking dirty to a female listener on the phone, Jack broke one of the cardinal rules of broadcasting. He said "fuck" on the air.

He was pulled from the Dallas airwaves within a half hour, fired within ninety minutes, and Sinclair Satellite Entertainment stopped returning his calls. With the utterance of one word, he had gone from being radio's golden boy to a pariah. Word travels fast in the broadcasting business, and Jack struggled to find another top forty station that would hire him. Now, a year and a half later, the only job he had been able to find was doing the overnight shift at WPLX, a relatively small Easy Listening station in Philadelphia. Jack often tried to tell himself that he was still working in big market radio, but every time he had to play a Celine Dion song, it felt like yet another piece of him died.

Rising from the bed, Jack crossed to the large window, which spanned an entire wall in his bedroom. He drew aside the curtains, and gazed down upon Philadelphia's South Street. Even for a Monday night, the street was bustling with college students, teenagers, and twenty somethings. The eight-block stretch of the street just past Eighth Street had always been known for its "bohemian" and "punk" atmosphere, with an urban mix of bars, takeout restaurants, sex shops, and retailers that catered to hip hop fashion, punk fashion, and urban culture. Jack's fourth floor apartment building was on the corner of Eighth Street and South Street, placing him just at the transition point between the residential area that was most of South Street, and the more commercial part of the street. Even four floors up, he could hear the horns honking and the revelry of those on the street below.

Realizing that he was standing in the window wearing nothing but his boxers, Jack pulled the drapes closed and switched on the light. He walked into the bathroom and gazed in the mirror. His shoulder length hair had been replaced by a shorter cut, which swooped from the right down over his left eye. His chin retained two days of stubble, which he decided would become three days of stubble by tomorrow evening. He still had his trim physique, a fact for which he was grateful. Sliding his boxers down his legs, Jack stepped into the shower.

———————————

As Jack Allyn closed the door to his apartment, he heard the whine of the motor and the vibration of the cables bringing the elevator car up the shaft at the end of the hall. There were only four apartments on this, the top floor of the building; Jack's being apartment 4A. He turned the key in the lock of his door, gave the knob a quick jiggle to make sure it was locked, and then turned to watch the elevator doors. The apartment building, which was built in the 1920s, had been restored with all the latest amenities. But the owners had tried to keep some of the building's old charm by keeping the old elevator in service. Jack stared at the caged door as the elevator car slowly rose into view, halting with a slight jolt when it reached the fourth floor. He heard the inner door being pulled open, followed moments later by the outer door. With an expensive looking leather laptop bag in his left hand, a tall handsome man with broad shoulders, dark clean-cut hair, and a distinctively chiseled chin stepped out of the elevator.

"Jack!" he exclaimed. "Headin' to the station?"

Jack smiled. "What else do I do at this hour?"

The man laughed. Jason Spinacker lived in 4C, the apartment next to Jack, and had been in residence before Jack moved in. The thirty-two-year-old was wearing a black pinstripe suit and an expensive silk shirt with his tie hanging loosely around his neck. Jason worked for Hildebrand Financials, one of the larger wealth management firms in the city. The two men had met a week after Jack had moved in, hit it off instantly, and had been friends ever since. During the week, Jason and Jack frequently met in the hallway as one left for work and the other returned home.

The two stood face to face in the short hall. "How's the stock business?" asked Jack.

"Up and down more times than a hooker on a good night," Jason replied, with a loud laugh.

"Little late tonight, aren't you?"

Smiling, Jason replied, "One of the senior guys is retiring. We had a little shindig for him." He paused, frowned for a moment, and then smiled once again.

"Well, I say shindig . . . Bad booze. Bad food. Terrible company. It was very painful. Kind of like having a tooth pulled without anesthetic."

Jack snickered at his friend's analogy. Jason always had an odd sense of humor, which seemed to go right along with a wild streak in the well-dressed businessman. For all his fine suits and professional acumen, Jason, at heart, liked a really good party. He also had a taste for the finer things in life—including liquor and women. There had been more than one morning where Jack met Jason's latest "conquest" in the hallway as she was on her way out.

"You jockin' at the club this weekend?" asked Jason.

Jack nodded. "Every Friday night, as usual."

"I'm planning to be there."

"Great," said Jack as the two men parted company—Jack heading to the elevator, and Jason to his apartment.

Walking two blocks down on South Street, Jack stopped before a small restaurant and glanced up at the neon sign above the door. The sign bathed the sidewalk in red and green hues. It should have read "Geno's Pizza", but the "e" wasn't working so the sign read "G no's Pizza". Jack stepped inside the small restaurant, and found an empty booth. The floor was composed of alternating white and black tiles that had a greasy coating on top, which couldn't be washed off with even the most intense mopping. The Formica on the tabletop of his booth was chipped and scratched. The dirt and grime in the small restaurant often made Jack think that the place was moments away from being shut down by the city's health inspector.

A short, heavyset Italian man approached the booth and smiled at Jack. His balding forehead was glistening with a faint layer of sweat, and a stained white apron was tied around his bulging stomach.

"Jack! My best customer! How ya doin'?" the man asked.

Jack returned the smile. "Good, Geno. Good."

"I was tellin' my old lady last night 'bout you." The man wiped his hands down the stained apron. "Told her you were more regular than the cockroaches."

Jack shook his head, and replied, "I'll take the usual, Geno."

"One chicken cheesesteak with fried onions and peppers comin' right up. You want onions rings with that?"

"Of course!" Jack smiled. "Come on, Geno. I'm your best customer you said. You should know that by now."

Geno made a rude hand gesture and a few exclamations in Italian, which Jack was certain he'd be better off not understanding, before smiling and returning to the kitchen to work on the order. Jack sat quietly in the booth and gazed out the window at the people passing outside. Sitting in Geno's had become part of his routine over the past year, just as getting up at seven thirty, or meeting Jason in the hallway had become routine. It bothered Jack to think that his life had become just a long list of routines. He watched as people passed the windows of the small restaurant, many on that Monday night looking like something out of a freak show. There were the shaved heads, the spiked mohawks, and the multi-colored hairstyles. Then there were the ones with so many piercings that Jack wondered how they would ever get through an airport security checkpoint. He had seen his share of odd stuff throughout his years in broadcasting, but he always told himself that some of the stuff he saw on South Street was, by far, the oddest.

At eleven fifteen, Jack Allyn pulled his Harley Davidson into the parking garage of the Osgood R. Flimm Building in downtown Philadelphia, and raced up the ramp past row upon row of empty parking spots. On the second level, he drifted the motorcycle into a spot right by the elevator, which he took to the twentieth floor. Off the elevator to his right was a pair of glass doors with the WPLX logo etched in each. Using his security badge, Jack swiped it through the slot in the security panel next to the door, which clicked loudly as it unlocked. Once through the door, Jack could hear music quietly filling the hallway from the speakers embedded in the ceiling tiles. He cringed at the sound of Roberta Flack's "Killing Me Softly with His Song", and gritted his teeth as he walked toward the broadcast studio. The "On Air" light above the door wasn't lit, so he pushed the door open, and walked on in.

The broadcast studio at WPLX was not a large room to begin with, but once the control console, computer, and other equipment were added, it looked exceptionally cramped. Just inside the door was an L-shaped counter, which covered one wall and extended halfway down another. It was waist high, providing the personalities the option to either sit in the high chair provided, or stand. In his heyday, Jack had always preferred to stand, giving him the freedom to move during his high energy show. But these days, he used the chair because there was no need for high energy during his broadcasts.

Centered on the counter was the broadcast control console, or the "board" as it was called. The console contained a series of sliding controls and buttons on a slightly upward sloping surface, all of which were used to control the sound level of the various audio sources in the studio, such as the studio computer system, microphones, digital editor, and even CD players. Hanging just to the right of the console was a touchscreen computer monitor used to control and play the commercials, music, and station jingles during the broadcast. And, to the left, hanging from a boom clamped to the backend of the counter was the microphone. The Heil PR-90 Pro Broadcast microphone was suspended in the middle of a round frame of thin tubes, hanging from four rubber bands that acted as vibration absorbers. A thin layer of dust had accumulated on the stack of three CD players to the right of the console. With everything digitally recorded in the computer system, the CD players were rarely ever used any more. Next to the CD players sat a Zoom R8 2-track digital recorder, itself looking like a mini version of the control console with slider controls and illuminated buttons.

Sitting at the console with his feet up on the counter was a man with long grey hair pulled back into a ponytail. He was wearing faded blue jeans, a tie-dyed t-shirt, and flip-flops. When Jack walked into the studio, the man's legs dropped to the floor and he quickly rose to his feet.

"Jeez, you scared the crap out of me! Don't you ever knock?" he said.

Jack laughed. "Sorry, Riley. Thought you heard me coming."

"Hell, no!"

Only standing five foot three inches tall, Riley Stevens was the shortest personality working at WPLX. At fifty-two, he had been doing the night show for over five years, and the only aspiration he had was to retire from the station in another ten. With a long career behind him, Riley had little desire to make any more moves, and hoped that he could keep riding the status quo into the proverbial sunset. Having been a rocker for most of his broadcast tenure, his career had even included short stints at Classic Rock powerhouses in New York City and Los Angeles. Now, he just wanted a quiet ending to his long broadcast history, and was content to wind it all down at WPLX.

"Quiet night?" asked Jack.

Riley shook his head and snorted derisively. "The wackos are out in force tonight. I put the phones on hold an hour ago. Couldn't take it anymore."

Jack smiled. Phone calls from listeners had always been a double-edged sword in broadcasting. Every personality loved interacting with the listeners, and it made for great banter on the air. But sometimes the calls just got too weird, especially at night. Jack couldn't help but be reminded of Clint Eastwood's 1971 film, "Play Misty for Me".

"It can't be any worse than last night," said Jack.

Riley reached for a pair of headphones sitting in front of the control console, and slid them over his ears. Pressing a red button on the console, he leaned toward the microphone, and, with a deep, sultry voice, said, "That's Roberta Flack here on WPLX. It's eleven forty-five on this crisp Monday night, which means that I'm just about out of here. Jack Allyn is coming up next to take you through till morning, and he's got music lined up from Elton John, Barry Manilow, and Celine Dion."

With a commercial playing in the background, Riley switched off the microphone and turned to Jack, who had raised his right hand and extended his middle finger.

"You just had to say her name, didn't you?" mumbled Jack.

Shrugging his shoulders, Riley smiled. "Someone requested it."

Chapter Three

Samantha checked her watch as she ran a brush through her hair one last time before the mirror. If there weren't any traffic issues, Peter would be arriving in ten minutes to pick her up. They had plans to head to the city morgue first thing that morning to talk to the assistant medical examiner about his autopsy results. It had been three days since the discovery of the three "Broad Street Mummies", as they had begun calling them, and every new fact that she and Peter had uncovered had simply made the investigation even more incomprehensible. When they had received the autopsy report yesterday afternoon, the two detectives couldn't believe what they were reading. It seemed so insensible that they had decided to speak to the doctor in person the next morning.

Giving her make-up one final inspection, Samantha turned off the bathroom light, and walked into her bedroom. She picked up the black leather holster, which was lying on the bed, and extracted the Glock 9mm handgun. She ejected the magazine, checked the firing chamber, and then slid the magazine back into the weapon. It was a routine she followed every morning like clockwork. It was just another thing her father had taught her; always check your weapon before leaving the house each morning. Samantha returned the firearm to the holster, which she then clipped to her belt just above the right hip. Brushing a little lint from her navy trousers, Samantha gazed across the room at the framed photograph hanging on the opposite wall. It was of her father, wearing his Police Department dress uniform. A faint smile appeared on her face, as she thought about the day that it had been taken.

"I miss you, Dad," she said quietly.

Staring at the photograph, she wondered what her father would have said to her if he were alive. Would he have been proud of her? Would he have been happy to see his daughter reach the level that she had on the force? How would he feel if he knew what she had done two years ago? Would he have understood the guilt that had hung over her head ever since?

The doorbell rang, shaking her out of her brown study, and indicating that her partner had arrived. She grabbed her badge from atop the dresser and headed to the front door. When Samantha stepped out of her townhouse, Peter Thornton was standing on her top step, holding two steaming cups of Dunkin' Doughnuts coffee.

"I thought you might need one of these," he said.

Wrapping her hands around the cup, Samantha smiled. "Perfect. Thanks."

In the car, Peter steered his way through the

city streets toward the Medical Examiner's office on University Avenue. Samantha took a sip from her coffee cup, and realized that something was missing.

"Did you get sugar packets?"

Peter shook his head. "No. Sorry."

"No worries," she lied, thinking that Eddie Murdock wouldn't have forgotten to get sugar packets.

She turned the past few days over in her mind. After spending the whole of Monday morning at the old building where the bodies had been discovered, Samantha and Peter had headed over to question Steve Rafferty's wife. Betty Rafferty had confirmed what Stanley Henderson had already told them. Her husband had left the house at nine-thirty on Saturday morning with every intention of being home by lunch. He never returned. Betty stated that she had repeatedly tried to call her husband's cell phone, but it kept going straight to voicemail. By then, she had left over a dozen messages. When Peter asked what her husband had been wearing when he left the house, Betty had simply stated, "An Eagles sweatshirt".

Tuesday morning was spent at the historical society, questioning the office manager who was overly distraught by the news that her two bosses were missing. Thomas McKay and Robert Crosse had arranged to meet Steve Rafferty on Saturday morning to evaluate the potential historical significance of the find at the old building site. Thomas McKay, an older man with thinning grey hair, had a long career with the historical society, starting there in the 1980s as a researcher. Now he worked as the managing director for the small organization. Robert Crosse, on the other hand, was a young man with sweeping dirty blonde hair who had recently joined the society as a new researcher. According to the office manager, both men had left the office on Friday evening with plans to meet the next morning for breakfast before heading to meet Rafferty at the construction site.

Interviews with the families of McKay and Crosse brought about similar answers as those from Steve Rafferty's wife. They had both left early Saturday morning, and never returned. McKay's wife had been frantic all weekend trying to reach her husband, and Crosse's live-in fiancé had been calling all of their mutual friends trying to find Robert.

The early forensic report had been delivered on Wednesday, along with the initial autopsy reports. There had been very little found at the scene of the crime. Fingerprints from the three men had been identified on the ladder, along with a large number of smudges of unknown origin. According to the forensics team, a number of footprints had been found on the dirt floor, which made things even more unusual. Besides the shoe prints of the three dead men, forensics had found three sets of distinctive prints of bare feet. And, judging by the size and shape, the forensics team had postulated that they were the prints of three different women.

Peter interrupted Samantha's train of thought when he said, "Hookers. They were using the underground chamber to meet some hookers."

Turning to glare at him, she replied, "Seriously? That's all you've got? Hookers?"

Peter jerked the steering wheel to the left to avoid a bus pulling away from the curb, honked the horn, and then said, "It explains the women's footprints."

"Right, and exactly how did the hookers kill three men, and then mummify their bodies? Oh, and without leaving a trace?"

Peter shrugged his shoulders. "I hadn't figured that out yet."

"I'm still not convinced those were our three missing men." Samantha shook her head. "It doesn't seem possible."

"Radcliffe confirmed the identities. It was all in his report."

Samantha turned her head to gaze out the car window. "McGregor called me this morning."

"What'd the Cap'n want?"

"The feds have already called to offer their assistance. They're chomping at the bit to get in on this one," replied Samantha.

"Shit!"

Samantha said, "He's going to hold them off as long as he can." She rubbed the sides of her forehead with her fingertips. "This case is already giving me a headache."

The unassuming, tall brick building, which was

the home of Philadelphia's Medical Examiner's Office, was located on University Avenue; across the street was Our Lord of Mercy Cemetery, a fact which lead to a never-ending string of jokes about extremely short trips from the slab to the grave. The building itself lacked any unique characteristic that would make it stand out over any of the other brick buildings in the surrounding area. It was a simple brick and glass structure, reflecting either a lack of imagination on the part of the architect, or a desire for significant cost cutting by avoiding any sense of style or adornment.

The two homicide detectives took the elevator down to the basement, and, when stepping out, could feel a distinctive drop in the temperature of the atmosphere around them. Samantha, who had been down to the morgue more times than she could count, had grown accustomed to chilly air. But Peter, who lacked the same level of experience as his partner, shivered at the cold.

"Damn! It's cold down here."

The wide hallway was just as cold and uninviting as the air in it. The whitewashed cinder block walls and concrete floor looked sterile and unwelcoming under the bright illumination from the fluorescent tube lighting. Down the hall, they found a set of swinging double doors which led into the morgue. Pushing their way through, the detectives stepped into an odorous mix of antiseptic and death. The room which they had entered was narrow but long, culminating at the far end with wall-to-wall stainless steel. A single large door was centered in the steel covered wall, which, Samantha knew, led into the refrigeration unit used for storing the recently deceased. Down the length of the room sat four stainless steel autopsy tables. Suspended from the ceiling above each table was a hexagonal light fixture attached to a self-balancing arm. The four bright halogen bulbs embedded in the lights illuminated only one of the tables. Upon that single table lay the naked body of young man whose arms and chest were covered in tattoos. His flesh had the grayish blue hue of death, and his chest contained three distinct bullet holes.

Looking up from the body as they entered, a tall, scrawny man in his mid-forties crossed the room to greet the two detectives. He was wearing a long white surgical gown, elbow length surgical gloves, and a disposable face shield. He drew off the face shield to reveal a long, narrow face with deep set eyes, a long hawk like nose, and a tuft of disheveled black hair atop his head.

"Detectives Ballard and Thornton, it's a pleasure to see you. May I assume that your visit is about the autopsy report I sent over yesterday?" he asked, with his usual air of pomposity.

Dr. Spencer Radcliffe was the assistant Medical Examiner for the city of Philadelphia, a position that he had held for over twelve years. As far as forensic pathologists went, Radcliffe was well known for being one of the best on the east coast. Despite being offered the Chief Medical Examiner's position twice, he was content to stay away from the politics of being in charge, and preferred his work in the field and the morgue. Samantha had worked with Radcliffe for several years, and could never shake the idea that he looked like the quintessential Ichabod Crane from Washington Irving's *Legend of Sleepy Hollow*.

"Yes," replied Peter.

"Are we interrupting?" asked Samantha.

"No, no. That gentleman on the slab is just another poor victim of gang infighting. He's in no hurry." Dr. Radcliffe smiled. "He'll happily wait for me."

"I'm hoping you could elaborate on your report a little bit. I'm having a hard time believing that those three . . . mummies, for a lack of a better term, are Rafferty, McKay, and Crosse," said Samantha.

The doctor peeled the surgical gloves off his hands. "Ah, I don't know if I'd call them mummies. Based on the condition of their bodies, I'd say our victims are more like . . . beef jerky."

Samantha shook her head. "Seriously?"

Dr. Radcliffe snorted loudly. "Just a little morgue humor, but not very far from the truth. Practically every drop of moisture was removed from the bodies. Blood, plasma, water, urine. Every drop, gone. Just like you get when you dehydrate beef to make jerky." Radcliffe, with his hands behind his back, began to pace back and forth in front of the two detectives as if he were delivering a lecture to students. "I've marked the official cause of death as extreme dehydration, but that's just a guess on my part. I suspect dehydration's more of a result than a means. Your victims endured something—either naturally or artificially induced—that rapidly dried out the cells in their bodies, resulting in their deaths." He stopped and glanced at the two detectives to ensure that they were still listening. "The human body is anywhere from 50 to 75 percent fluid. Over time, a corpse will lose moisture as part of the process of decay, and eventually end up in the same state as your three victims. Just looking at the bodies, I'd have sworn those three men had been dead for six months, possibly longer. It's like something hyper-accelerated the rate of decay. Dental records were the only way I could identify them."

"Are you certain about their identities?" inquired Peter.

Radcliffe nodded.

Samantha asked, "What about a fire? Could that have done this?"

"No. Far too much heat would be required. There would be residual signs of charring on the flesh."

"Your report mentioned something about pin holes," said Peter.

The doctor's face lit up with excitement. "Ah, yes. I'd almost forgotten about that. Give me just a second . . ."

Radcliffe hurriedly made his way to the far end of the autopsy room, opened the heavy steel door of the refrigeration unit, and disappeared inside. As the detectives waited, they watched as wisps of vapor drifted out from the door to create a low lying fog across the floor. Samantha could see a body, covered with a white sheet, resting on top of a gurney. A pale foot, with a tag attached to the toe, stuck out from under the sheet. Moments later, Radcliffe rushed out of the doorway pushing a stainless steel gurney with a white sheet draped over its current occupant. The doctor kicked the door to the refrigeration unit closed with his foot as he passed.

"I'd like you to take a look at this," stated the doctor as he pulled the sheet back, revealing one of the leathery bodies from the other day. Pointing to the corpse's neck, he said, "Look closely at the neck."

Samantha leaned forward and examined the area indicated by the doctor. She could just make out dozens of almost imperceptible holes in the skin; smaller than the smallest pin she had ever seen. The holes were located along the side of the neck, and extended up along the lower jaw. As she studied the markings, she began to realize that they formed a familiar shape: a human hand. She straightened up, and muttered, "A handprint?"

Dr. Radcliffe was smiling. "It gets better. Look at the other side."

Samantha moved around to the other side of the table, as Peter leaned in to get his first look at the markings. She leaned forward, and was astonished to find the same marks on the left side of the neck as well. Just as with the opposite side, they formed the shape of a human hand, with the palm and four fingers on the neck, and the thumb along the lower jaw line. Stepping back from the table, she shook her head in amazement.

"What is it?" asked Peter.

Radcliffe pulled the sheet back over the corpse's face and said, "I don't know. But they're on the necks of all three victims. I've never seen anything like it. But I'll tell you this. Whatever killed your victims, happened through those holes. The question remaining is how."

Samantha's head was spinning as she tried to make some form of rational logic out of what Radcliffe had just explained. The two detectives had come to the morgue hoping to make sense of what they felt had been an insensible autopsy report. But, if anything, she felt like they simply had more questions to add to their growing list. In Samantha Ballard's five years as a homicide detective, she had seen enough to not be surprised by the ingenuity of the human race to find new ways to inflict death upon one another. Shooting, poisoning, stabbing, hit-and-run, and even good old fashioned lynching weren't unusual in her line of work. She had seen beatings so brutal that DNA testing was required for a positive identification of the body. Two years ago when she was leading the Society Hill Serial Killer investigation, Samantha thought she had seen it all as she tracked down a serial killer who tortured his victims before killing them and butchering the bodies. It had been a long and grueling investigation, which had left its lasting mark on her; but she wondered if this new investigation might end up eclipsing it. She hoped it wouldn't. Samantha wasn't sure if she could go through it all again.

She shook her head and said, "It doesn't make any sense. None whatsoever!"

Shrugging, Dr. Radcliffe replied, "I just do the autopsies around here. It's your job to figure out the who, how, and why."

Chapter Four

The arrival of Friday morning meant the start of Jack Allyn's weekend. His shift at WPLX ended at six in the morning, as the "Breakfast Club" went on the air. The "Breakfast Club" was the name of the morning show on WPLX, hosted by Ron Michaels and Dana Brooks. Jack had listened to the show once, and, thinking that it was four hours of inane jokes, goofy sound effects, and stupid contests that even the dumbest listener could win, never listened again. Ron Michaels, an overweight forty-six-year-old, had a long mediocre career in small-to-midsize radio markets before coming to WPLX. Ron had been the previous occupant of Jack's overnight shift until the station's morning host was arrested on child pornography charges. Unable to find anyone else to take over the morning shift at a price they were willing to pay, the management of WPLX, as a last resort, allowed Ron Michaels to take the reins of the most coveted shift in radio—Morning Drive.

Dana Brooks, on the other hand, knew radio only through her experience at WPLX. She was a quiet twenty-something with short blonde hair, cropped just below her ears. She had started as an intern six months before Ron Michaels took over the morning shift. The new morning show host, feeling that his position warranted additional perks, began asking the young intern to get him coffee, doughnuts, and any other food that suited his fancy each morning. As a joke, Ron put the shy intern on the spot by telling her a joke on the air. To everyone's surprise, Dana Brooks' personality behind the microphone was a far cry from the shy young lady that everyone had become accustomed to. Station management hired her to become the second member of the morning show. However, when not behind the microphone, the young Dana would instantly revert to her former shy self.

Ron wrestled his girth into the studio chair behind the control console while Jack gathered his coffee mug, newspaper, and copy of Rolling Stone magazine. Glancing at the back of Ron's shirt, Jack shuddered at the damp patches of sweat soaking through the cloth.

"Where's Dana?" he asked.

Ron Michaels plugged his headphones into the control console. "She's picking up coffee. She'll be back in a few minutes."

Jack shook his head and thought, *It's been over a year and you still make her get your coffee, you lazy bastard.*

"You working at Pulsar tonight?"

Jack nodded. "As always."

Stepping out of the studio, Jack Allyn made his way down the hall and pushed open the door to the production studio. Similar in size and shape to the broadcast studio, this one was used for producing audio elements that were used on the air, such as commercials, jingles, and promotional announcements. Although this studio had the same control console, microphone, and studio computer system, it also contained an eight-track digital recording system. Jack checked his mailbox, and found three requests for production voiceover work. Within an hour, he had recorded the three commercials, and loaded them into the studio computer system, marking them available for use.

On his way out of the station, Jack passed Dana Brooks in the hallway, juggling a box of a dozen doughnuts, and two coffee cups. He said hello to Dana, who muttered a quiet reply with her head down, avoiding eye contact. Watching as she walked down the hall, awkwardly struggling with the burden in her hands, Jack shook his head and smiled. He didn't offer to help, knowing that Dana would mumble something about being fine and not requiring assistance. Glancing at his watch, he noticed that it was closing in on eight in the morning, and realized that he should be on his way before anyone else arrived in the office. Early in his time at WPLX, Jack had made some comments resulting in most of the station staff labeling him as nothing more than a cynical asshole. It was an assumption that he didn't feel compelled to correct. There were only a few members of the radio station staff to whom Jack regularly spoke: Riley at night, and Ron Michaels and Dana Brooks in the morning being the three most frequent. It was a situation that was acceptable to him, so he didn't see the need to change it.

Penn's Landing, the waterfront area of Philadelphia's Center City, stretched between Spring Garden Street to the north and Washington Avenue to the south, and was mostly cut off from the rest of the city by Interstate 95. The area, almost completely covered in concrete, had become a family-focused entertainment venue over the past fifteen years, and included the permanent mooring of several historical ships, an outdoor concert venue, two casinos, and even an outdoor ice skating rink. One of the latest additions to the area was Pulsar, a nightclub that had transformed one of the old riverside warehouses at the far end of Penn's Landing into one of the hottest nightspots in the city. Open only on Friday and Saturday nights, Pulsar, with its multi-level dance floors, six bars, and elaborate laser and lighting effects, had quickly become the premiere nightclub by which all other nightclubs in the city were judged.

Jack Allyn had been lucky enough to land the job of Pulsar's resident disc jockey on Friday nights, a title which he found to be a bit archaic considering that, like the studio at WPLX, all of the audio at Pulsar was digital, and controlled by a computer system. There were no discs for him to jockey anymore. Although he was paid well for the eight hours he spent providing the musical atmosphere for the club, he didn't do it for the money. Jack used it as his opportunity to rebel against the stagnation he felt in his broadcasting career. It was a weekly respite from the five-day-a-week hell that was his nightly shift at WPLX.

Arriving at Pulsar at five in the afternoon, Jack Allyn rang the doorbell by the side entrance designated for employees. He waited patiently, leaning with his back against the wall, until the steel door swung open. Stepping through the doorway, Jack was standing in the small hallway in the business offices of the nightclub. The red carpet ran the short length of the hallway, the walls of which were painted a pale blue. Ahead of him, two doors, one on each side, opened into the hallway. Jack spent very little time in the business offices, but had been there long enough to know that each door led to an office of grand proportion and extravagance. One of the two offices was frequently used, but Jack knew that the second had been rarely occupied since Pulsar's inception a year ago. The owners of Pulsar were wealthy men, one from Philadelphia, and the other from New York. Jointly, they owned Pulsar in Philadelphia, and a smaller club in New York City called Nebula, which, although smaller than its Philadelphia sibling, was just as impressive. Jerry Rickett, the owner from Philadelphia, spent every weekend in his office overseeing the weekly operations of Pulsar. His partner, Anderson Bock, spent most of his time in their New York club.

Jack glanced over his shoulder at Jerry Rickett as he pulled the exterior door closed. Jerry, in his early fifties, always looked as if he was trying too hard to fit in with the younger crowd that came to his club. His shoulder length hair, which Jack knew to be grey, was regularly dyed black and slicked back with hair gel, giving it the always wet look. Jerry maintained a two-day growth of stubble on his face, and he was wearing faded denim jeans, a black silk V-neck shirt, and a black and white plaid sports jacket. He had pushed the sleeves of the jacket up his arms to just below the elbows. Jerry always tried hard with getting his "look" right, but Jack thought it looked too forced every time. It also didn't help that Jerry had developed a bit of a paunch as he grew older, and his choice of outfits weren't always very flattering for someone of Jerry's shape and size.

"Jack! You're gonna rock the house tonight?" Jerry asked, just as he did every Friday afternoon.

Smiling, Jack replied with his usual cliché answer, "Yep, I'm going bring the house down."

That always made Jerry happy, and that night was no different. The club owner smiled, gave Jack a pat on the back, and said, "That's my boy!"

For Jack to get to the club's DJ booth, he had to traverse a series of hallways that ran along the outer perimeter of the club, and ascend a long flight of spiral stairs. The booth hung out from one wall over the multi-level dance floor. Because of its position, its occupants had a perfect view of almost every part of the club through the booth's large window. As Jack entered the booth, the lighting engineer, Brad Colburn, was already there. The interior of the booth was a showcase of high tech electronics and computer systems. The wall opposite the door was covered from floor to ceiling with rack mounted control modules for the amplifier system installed in the club. The control boards and computer systems for the lights and audio were centered at the base of the window. Brad Colburn was testing the lights for the dance floor as Jack entered the booth.

"What's up?" asked Jack.

Concentrating on the lighting transitions in the club, Brad replied, "I've got a bulb out above level three. I can't get it changed before we open."

Brad, who was in his early twenties, was wearing jeans and a Metallica t-shirt. His head was cleanly shaved, and a brown goatee hung from his chin, trimmed to a downward point. Black horn-rimmed glasses were perched on the bridge of his long, narrow nose.

"Can you compensate?"

Without looking up from his work, Brad replied, "I'm working on that now."

Jack smiled, knowing that Brad could easily reprogram the lighting system matrix to compensate for the loss of half the bulbs in the club. One burnt out bulb would be a piece of cake. Tapping at his keyboard, Jack began compiling his music playlist for the evening.

By ten o'clock that night, the dance floor of Pulsar was packed with bodies, all moving to the pounding beat, which could not only be heard, but also felt throughout the building. The thumping rhythm permeated every inch of Pulsar, even causing liquor inside the bottles at the bars to vibrate to the beat. On the dance floor, men and women were packed in tightly, swaying, grinding, and sweating to the music. The atmosphere smelt of a convoluted mix of perspiration, alcohol, and fog machine chemicals. The bartenders at the six bars around the club were feverishly rushing from one side of their respective bar to the other, filling and refilling drinks. The liquor was flowing freely, fueling the gyrating mass on the dance floor. The lights and lasers flashed and blinked in an extravagant show designed to dazzle and inspire awe.

Jack, watching from the booth, estimated that the headcount was close to two thousand people. From his vantage point, he could see Jerry Rickett standing by one of the bars on the opposite side of the club. Jack smiled as he watched Jerry's head sway out of rhythm to the beat. The night was going well, and he felt like he was in his groove with the music. Brad had been feverishly programming and reprogramming the lights and lasers to increase the intensity on the dance floor. Programming the next fifteen minutes of music into the computer gave Jack a chance to relax and watch the festivities below.

The crowd below him was a mix of ages, ranging from those in their early twenties to those in their forties. He found it interesting to watch the different age groups segregate themselves in the club. The twenty somethings would alternate between the bar and the dance floor, seeming as if they could never get enough of either. The female thirty somethings would spend a lot of time on the dance floor, while their male counterparts would gravitate to the bars. It was easy to pick out the forty somethings because they would spend most of their time sitting in one of the many small lounge areas scattered along the edges of the dance floor. They would make occasional trips to the bars, but would stay clear of the dancing crowd altogether. Jack had made it his hobby to study Pulsar's urban wildlife, as he called it, from his perch high above them all.

As he gazed down upon the throng below, his eyes were drawn to a woman who had just entered the club. Normally, he wouldn't give much attention to any single individual, no matter how attractive that individual might be. But there was something about her that made it difficult to pull his eyes away. Her hair was golden blonde, and fell alluringly onto her shoulders. Her face radiated a beauty that Jack was certain could melt an iceberg. She looked to be in her early thirties, and when she crossed to the nearest bar, the head of every man turned. As she walked, the tight red dress clung to her body, bending around every curve and flexing with each movement. For the first time in his tenure at Pulsar, he actually wished that he were on the dance floor. There was something sexy and sensual about every move she made. Just the act of breathing seemed to have animalistic undertones. From high above the dance floor, Jack watched as heads turned in her direction all over the club.

At the bar, she ordered a shot. When her drink arrived, she jerked back her head and downed the shot instantly. Jack could see her slowly moving her head from side to side, scanning the crowd around her. He leaned over, nudging Brad with his elbow, and gestured in the blonde's direction. Like most of the men on the floor below, Brad became instantly mesmerized. She continued to scan the crowd, until it seemed as if she had found what she was looking for. Jack watched her move effortlessly through the crowd onto the dance floor. She seemed to be homing in on one man, who, oblivious to the sudden attention, was dancing with three twenty somethings. The blonde moved in toward the man, as if she were a wild animal stalking her prey. She slowly circled around through the crowd, inching her way toward him. Sliding up next to him, she began to provocatively gyrate her hips to the beat of the music, instantly attracting his attention.

The three twenty somethings the man had been previously dancing with seemed irritated by the new arrival and, feeling that they were being ignored, moved off to dance somewhere else. The man, who was broad shouldered with black hair and a matching goatee, turned all of his attention to the newly arrived blonde. Jack wondered if they knew each other, because it wasn't long before their bodies were rubbing and grinding against each other, generating a sexually charged atmosphere between them. The fact that they were in the midst of a crowded dance floor didn't seem to matter to the couple as they continued their alluring motions.

For the next two hours, the couple never left

the dance floor. They had continued their tantalizing dance with no sign of slowing down. Suddenly, Jack saw her lean in close to the man's ear. Nodding his head in response, the woman took hold of his hand, and they rushed off the dance floor toward the exit of the club. Jack laughed as he watched the couple disappear out the door. Figuring they were heading out to the parking lot, probably to the back of the man's SUV or whatever car he had, Jack decided that it was just another one-night stand.

Chapter Five

S amantha was pissed off when she lifted the yellow police tape and ducked under it. Not only was it Saturday morning, but the police dispatcher had called her at six fifteen to tell her about the body that had been discovered. She had dressed quickly, cursing the entire time, and left her town house. It had not been a good night, and Samantha was running on three hours of sleep. She had difficulty shaking the images of mummified corpses, making it difficult for her to close her eyes. She feared that the nightmares, which had been gone for close to a year, might return, bringing with them the guilt that she had worked so hard to suppress.

The dispatcher had given scant details about what had been discovered. She had simply told Samantha that a body had been found in an alley next the nightclub at Penn's Landing called Pulsar. Although she knew of the club, Samantha had never been to it. The club scene wasn't really her style. However, the dispatcher had made one comment that gave Samantha reason to pause.

"The captain thought it'd be best to assign it to you since it might be related to another of your cases," the dispatcher had said.

The only active case on which Samantha was working was the three mummified corpses from earlier in the week. She told herself that this couldn't possibly be related to that case. Yet it nagged at the back of her mind all the way over to Penn's Landing. And, as she stepped through the cordon at the crime scene, she had a faint feeling of nausea as she saw the shriveled corpse leaning against the exterior nightclub wall. The victim, with its back against the wall, was seated with its left leg outstretched and the right folded under the buttocks. The skin of this body had the same leathery texture as the three that Samantha had seen on the previous Monday. The eyes were wide open, gaping at some unseen terror, while the mouth was frozen in a silent scream, with the white teeth peeking out from under the prune-like lips. The black hair on the head was disheveled, probably caused by the wind that had been blowing in from the river all night. The victim was dressed in black trousers and a white silk shirt, which had been torn open with such force that the top four buttons had popped loose from their threads. Due to the dehydration, the skin of the chest and abdomen had tightened around the rib cage, forming a distinctive outline of each and every bone.

Kneeling beside the corpse, Samantha gazed closely at the neck, and could just make out the small pinpricks forming the shape of a human hand on either side. *If I hadn't known to look for them, I would have missed them*, she thought. Sighing, she looked up and down the alleyway. One end led to the front of Pulsar, while the other ended at the edge of the pier on which the club was built. The structure providing the wall on the other side of the alley was a parking garage owned by the city's parking authority. The alleyway itself was narrow, not even wide enough for a car to fit down. At each end, Samantha observed, was a security camera mounted on the club wall about twenty feet above the ground.

As she rose to her feet, Peter Thornton approached, having just arrived moments earlier. He stood behind Samantha, and surveyed the crime scene.

He said, "Another beef jerky corpse."

Samantha gave him a long disapproving look, to which he shrugged his shoulders, and said, "Just following Dr. Radcliffe's lead."

Pointing to the security cameras, Samantha said, "I want to see the footage from those cameras."

"Got it."

As Peter walked away to fulfill her request, Samantha approached the young uniformed officer standing nearby. He had been watching silently from a short distance as the detectives made their initial survey of the scene.

Glancing at the officer's name badge, Samantha asked, "Officer Hardy, did you discover the body?"

He shook his head. "No, ma'am. I was on patrol early this morning, up along Spring Garden Street, just across the interstate." He pointed in the general direction of interstate behind them. "I patrol that area a lot. There's a couple of homeless folks that I know up there. One of them—Roger, don't know his last name—flagged me down this morning up on Spring Garden. Said he'd been down here about an hour before and saw the body. I guess that's what you'd call it." The officer paused momentarily to look over Samantha's shoulder at the mummified body, and then continued, "Anyway, Roger said he wasn't going to report it, but when he saw me coming up the street, he had a change of heart."

"Do you know where we can find Roger? I'm going to need to talk to him," Samantha said.

Officer Hardy shook his head. "I don't know where he stays. I just see him on the streets occasionally."

Samantha replied. "If you see him again, pick him up and bring him in."

"Yes, ma'am."

Turning away from the officer, Samantha gave her full attention to the corpse and the surrounding crime scene. She knew that it would take a miracle for forensics to find any footprints on the hard asphalt surface beneath her feet. She peered at the body, which looked as if it had been resting on the ground in that very spot for centuries. There didn't appear to be any signs of violence, although she wondered how one could tell on a body in this condition. Samantha was careful as she circled the corpse to not step on the four small white buttons lying on the ground where they had landed after popping their threads. The shirt was of particular interest to the detective as she once again knelt alongside the body. The front of the victim's shirt had been neatly tucked in his pants, but the back had become untucked at some point, possibly when the body had slid down the wall during or after death. Samantha made a mental note to have forensics look for fiber traces on the brickwork above the corpse's head.

She rose to her feet, and started to slowly move down the alley toward the river, scanning the ground carefully as she walked. Reaching the end of the alley, Samantha stood near the chain link fence, which served as a barrier along the edge of the pier. The fence was six feet high, and looked like it had seen far too many years of service. The posts were rust-covered, and even the chain links were heavily corroded with oxidation. Samantha examined the fence, looking from right to left as well as up and down. She didn't know what, if anything, she was looking for, but she had learned long ago to look in even the remotest areas. In most circumstances her browsing, as her previous partner had called it, didn't come up with anything. But sometimes she found something. This was one of those times. Along the top edge of the fence, Samantha's eye caught sight of a small piece of cloth flapping gently in the morning breeze. It was only a small fragment, and she couldn't be sure that it was related to the corpse in any way, but Samantha planned to send the forensics team down to do a thorough sweep of this end of the alley. She momentarily gazed through the links in the fence, and watched the dark waters of the Delaware River churn in the morning breeze. Samantha could hear the faint sound of the water crashing against the concrete pylons that supported the pier on which she stood.

Someone calling her name suddenly interrupted her thought process. She spun around to see her partner, Peter Thornton, waving to her from the other end of the alley. Retracing her steps, Samantha quickly headed back toward Peter.

"You wanted security footage? I've got security footage," he said with a smile.

"That was fast," Samantha remarked.

"The club owner is working in the office this morning. He's waiting for us."

With his clothing wrinkled, Jerry Rickett looked as if he had spent the night sleeping on the leather sofa in his office. Samantha noted that his hair looked as if he had tried in vain to remove any trace of his "bed head" look. The bags under his eyes gave away the fact that he had not gotten much sleep the night before. But, despite his condition, she was grateful for his cooperative attitude. There were few club owners in the city that would welcome the police into their facility, let alone share security footage with them.

"There's thirty-four cameras in total set up around the club, both inside and out," the club owner explained. "Everything's recorded, and I mean everything, to a DVR. After a week, the oldest footage is erased to make room for new stuff."

Peter said. "Thirty-four? That's a lot of cameras."

"I'm in a business where it's best to protect yourself as much as possible," Rickett explained. "When there's two thousand people crammed into a building like Pulsar, anything can happen. That's why I spared no expense when it came to the security system. Top of the line burglar alarm, security cameras, and even fire detection. If someone lights up a cigarette in the john, I'll know about it."

Leading the two detectives into a small office, Jerry Rickett flipped on the lights to reveal a large desk against the opposite wall. Hanging above the desk were thirty-four square computer monitors, each showing a different camera angle of the interior and exterior of Pulsar. Samantha could see the empty dance floor from at least a dozen different viewpoints. She caught sight of the cameras she had earlier identified in the alley, showing the arrival of the forensics team. She had to admit that it was an impressive arrangement. The owner of Pulsar hadn't been lying when he said he had spared no expense.

"Everything's time stamped. What time do you want to see?" asked Rickett.

"Not sure yet. Can we skip around without watching hours of footage?" Samantha inquired.

Jerry nodded. "I can jump to any time you want."

Samantha thought for a second, and then replied, "Start by checking the top of each hour for the past twenty-four. Once we find the right hour, we can dig deeper."

Jerry Rickett slid into the chair in front of the desk, and tapped on the keyboard. The screens went dark momentarily before they all began to play video in sync. The timestamp displayed on the screen was from the previous morning.

Peter pointed to the monitor displaying images from the camera in the rear of the alley. "No corpse."

Jerry Rickett tapped again on the keyboard. "Ok. Next hour."

This cycle continued as the club owner skipped the video footage ahead hour by hour. They caught a brief glimpse of a delivery truck arriving with the club's alcohol order, the postman delivering Friday's mail, employees arriving for work, and then patrons as they began to arrive the previous evening. But they had not yet seen a corpse appear in the alley. The alleyway had remained the one constant image throughout all thirty-four screens. No one seemed to give the alleyway even a second's glance. However, when Jerry Rickett brought up the video for one in the morning, the persistent image changed. Suddenly, leaning against the wall was the mummified corpse, alone in the alleyway.

"There it is!" exclaimed Samantha. "Can you rewind back to the previous hour?"

Jerry Rickett tapped on the keyboard, and all of the screens began to show the midnight hour footage. They watched as the throng of people on the dance floor swayed to unheard music. The lights on the dance floor blinked and flashed, but were not anywhere near as impressive in the black and white security footage. The alleyway was still empty. The two detectives observed people approaching the bars, placing their orders, and walking away with their drinks. The alleyway remained empty. Then, at twelve forty, the security camera that covered the front of the club caught a couple staggering out of the building tightly clasped in each other's arms. They paused outside the main club door, and embraced with their lips locked in a passionate kiss. The man in the video spun the woman around and gently pushed her back against the wall beside the door. They continued to kiss as his hands groped up the woman's tight dress. Lost in the heat of passion, the couple didn't even notice as two other couples exited from the club.

Samantha was feeling uncomfortable watching the security footage, as if she were some kind of voyeur. The couple seemed oblivious to the fact that their every action was being videotaped. After a moment, a large bulky man stepped out of the club, and approached the couple.

"That's Harry. He's my doorman and bouncer," explained the club owner.

The large man seemed to speak briefly to the couple, which moments later walked out of view of the camera. The bouncer turned and re-entered the club. But it wasn't more than a few moments before the couple reappeared in the alleyway, apparently having felt that it was a safe place to continue their passionate activities. Samantha and Peter watched as the couple locked in another long passion-filled kiss. The brief interruption from the bouncer didn't appear to have dulled any of their fire, as the man and woman groped and fondled each other with growing intensity. With sudden aggressiveness, the woman pushed the man back against the wall, kissing him deeply and lustfully. The video showed the woman's hands reaching for the man's shirt and tearing it open, exposing his bare chest. The two detectives watched as the woman's hands roamed freely across the man's chest in rampant passion. They kissed again as the woman's hands slowly slid up his chest until they reached his neck. With one hand firmly planted on either side of the man's nape, the woman arched her head back, and gazed up toward the sky.

Stunned speechless, they watched the video screen, as the man's head jerked back suddenly in agonizing pain. Samantha gaped at the screen as she watched the man's body writhe, contort, and shrivel away into nothing more than mummified remains. The video was far from perfect, but it was good enough to observe the skin shrink around his bones. Samantha could see the tightening of the man's flesh on his flailing hands. It had been quick, but, even in the grainy black and white security footage, it was plain to see that it had been far from painless. When it was over, the woman guided the body down to the ground, and then, glancing to the right and the left, fled down the alleyway toward the river, disappearing from view.

The small room was silent for several minutes as the three occupants absorbed everything that they had just seen. Samantha suddenly realized that she had been holding her breath during the horrifying video, and she let out a long exhale. Jerry Rickett had slowly slumped down in his chair, staring in disbelief at the video monitor, while Peter remained motionless, in shock at what he had just witnessed.

Regaining her composure, Samantha said, "Mr. Rickett, I'll need a copy of that video."

"Uh, yeah," he stammered.

"I'll have one of the forensics team come in and get it from you," she said.

Jerry Rickett slowly spun his chair around to face the two detectives. "Does this mean I can't open the club tonight?"

Samantha replied, "I don't know yet."

Chapter Six

Stepping out of the elevator into the parking garage, Jack Allyn slid a pair of Oakley sunglasses onto his face and he walked to his motorcycle. He had just relinquished control of the WPLX studio to Ron Michaels after finishing his shift. After his night at Pulsar, Jack had returned to his apartment, and slept most of Saturday away, rising late in the afternoon. He had spent Saturday night in a small bar on South Street called the Philly Brewing Company. With its locally brewed beers, it had quickly become his favorite weekend haunt. Being a friend of the bar's owner, Jack ended up remaining until well past closing time, playing five-card draw in the bar's back room. Sunday had passed with Jack in deep slumber through most of the daylight hours. He was back in the WPLX studio Sunday night to start another week of overnight shifts.

With the first of his five nights on the air over, Jack was feeling hungry. As per his usual routine, he mounted his Harley Davidson, and headed to Monk's Cafe on the corner of Broad Street and Washington Avenue. Jack once told Jason Spinacker that it would take an act of god to keep him from going to Monk's Cafe for breakfast every morning after work. The small restaurant had two reputations throughout Philadelphia. On the one hand, it was known as dive, which had been closed on several occasions by the Philadelphia Health Department. On the other hand, it was reputed to serve the best breakfast in the city. Jack Allyn ate there every weekday morning.

He slid into his usual booth in the far corner and patiently waited. It was only a few moments before the young, petite waitress approached, giving Jack a wide smile. A red and white checked apron hung from her neck, covering her black denim jeans, and black t-shirt. Her hair was as black as tar, with a white streak down the left side.

"Howdy, Jack. You havin' the usual?" she asked.

"Yeah, Meg. Hook me up. Extra crispy bacon this time," he replied.

As Meg went off to arrange for his meal, Jack reclined in the booth, enjoying the peace and quiet that came with being the only patron in the restaurant. He knew it wouldn't last long. Checking his watch, he calculated that he only had another five minutes of solitude before the breakfast rush started rolling in. As the first customer stepped through the door, Meg returned carrying a large white plate with two eggs sunny side up, crispy bacon, hash browned potatoes, and two pieces of white toast. The mixture of aromas was heaven to his nostrils, and reminded Jack of just how hungry he was.

Eating slowly, Jack watched as people came and left Monk's Cafe; some stayed to eat, while others got something to go. Despite its reputation, the little restaurant had a good breakfast clientele that were regular as clockwork. Jack recognized many faces; some even recognized him. It was as if they were all part of a secret club, and Monk's Cafe was their secret handshake. With the occasional nod of his head, Jack would exchange a quick greeting to the nameless faces that were daily visitors.

It was close to nine in the morning when Jack paid his bill and strolled out into the March sunlight that bathed Broad Street in springtime warmth. He slid into the seat of his motorcycle, perched his sunglasses on the bridge of his nose, and hit the starter. The engine ignited with a loud rumble, and Jack sped off up Broad Street. As he made his way through the streets of Philadelphia, Jack was forced to admit that he could be in worse situations. He had a job in the field of his choosing. He was making decent money. It wasn't as much as he once made, but it was enough for him to live comfortably. Granted, he worked at a station that played a music format that he despised, but at least he was still in broadcasting. He had known a few radio personalities in his time that had been drummed out of the business for saying far less on the air than what he had said. Ever since Nipplegate, when Janet Jackson exposed her breast during the Super Bowl, the Federal Communications Commission had been cracking down hard on broadcast obscenity. Many television and radio stations simply wouldn't be willing to take the chance on someone who already had made a mistake. He ended up being lucky in the long run.

His mind wandered to his early days in broadcasting, as it often did during his morning ride home. He could still see her face, and almost imagine she was riding on the back of the motorcycle, her arms wrapped around his waist. Jack still carried her photograph in his wallet, even after all these years. He wondered if things would have been different . . . if only he hadn't—

His thought, however, was interrupted as a maroon Ford Focus pulled out in front of him, causing Jack to slam on his brakes and skid to a halt. As the car sped away, Jack raised his middle finger as high as he could as he shouted a long line of disparaging words in the direction of the departing driver. Moving on, Jack thought, *I hate this city.*

Outside his work at WPLX and Pulsar, Jack Allyn had only one guilty pleasure. It was the one thing on which he would allow himself to spend big. Every few weeks, he would trek into Center City to indulge in his passion. The bell overhead jangled as Jack pushed open the door to his favorite comic book shop, Den of Heroes. For Jack, comic books weren't for reading, and he wasn't one to simply buy any comic book off the shelf. He was a collector of rare comic books. His collection had grown significantly over the past ten years, but he rarely read the comic books that he collected. He'd sealed them in plastic and stored them away. Jack had invested a good deal of money over the years, but he had seen some of his collection show decent growth in value. Among others, Jack had been lucky to get his hands on a mint copy of the issue of Amazing Fantasy in which Spider-Man had originally been introduced to the world. He had bought it for ten thousand dollars nine years' prior, which, at the time, his friends said was crazy. But, the last time he had checked, it had more than tripled in value. He also had a copy of the first Fantastic Four comic book from 1961, which was worth an easy five figures. However, most of his collection was worth far less but, like most investments, Jack knew it took time.

The small comic book shop was brightly lit, with three long tables spanning from one wall to the other. Lined up along the tables were rows of cardboard boxes, each stuffed with comic books. Hanging from the ceiling were large replicas of spaceships from various science fiction films and television programs. Most of them Jack didn't recognize, but he knew some of them as spacecraft from Star Trek, Star Wars, and he even recognized the blue police box from Doctor Who. To the left of the door was a glass display case, which ran along the wall. In it were various sized figurines of comic book superheroes, alien monsters, and film and television characters.

Jack paid no attention to the comic books in the boxes. His interest was in the far end of the glass display case. That was where the more valuable comic books were kept, and Jack made it a point of stopping in every so often to see if anything new had arrived in the shop. Behind the glass display case stood a young man in his mid-twenties, with wavy brown hair on either side of his square face. Bryan Salisbury broke the mold of what Jack had always thought a comic book storeowner should look like. Bryan's physique was trim and muscular, and he was always well dressed. He had bright, intelligent-looking eyes and, although his jaw held some prominence on his face, Bryan was a good-looking man by all standards. It was a far cry from what Jack had been accustomed to with comic book shops in the past.

"Hey, Jack!" Bryan said.

Jack reached across the glass display case and shook Bryan's hand. "How's it going?"

Bryan smiled. "Same old, same old."

"Get anything new in last week?"

Bryan shook his head. "Probably nothing that would appeal to you."

"Try me."

Bryan pointed at the glass display, in which sat several comic books, each wrapped in a protective plastic sleeve. "I got the final issue of the original Star Wars series from Marvel Comics. It's not as rare as the other stuff you're looking for, but worth three figures."

Jack shook his head. "Nah. Not my style. Any leads on Detective Comics, Issue 140?"

"The one with the Riddler's first appearance against Batman?"

Jack nodded.

"Nothing. But I'll keep my ear to the ground," replied Bryan.

Jack glanced around the shop, taking in the

poster-lined walls in amazement at how comic books had changed since he was a kid. Comic books weren't only about superheroes any more. He could remember the day when the two biggest comic book publishers were Marvel and DC. Now, he noticed posters from a dozen or more different publishers, representing titles he had never even heard of. *Gone are the days of Batman and Superman getting top bill at the newsstand,* he thought.

"I heard what happened at Pulsar the other night, that murder," said Bryan.

Jack, puzzled, looked at the young shop owner. "What murder?"

"You didn't hear? The cops found a body in the alley next to Pulsar," Bryan explained.

"When?"

"Saturday morning. Word on the street says there was some funky stuff going on with the body."

Jack responded, "Funky stuff?"

"Yeah. Rumor has it that the body was dry as a bone."

"Bled to death?"

"No. Everything. All that was left was a dried up husk," explained Bryan.

"You mean like a mummy?"

"Yeah, but it wasn't wrapped in any bandages. Just bone dry," said Bryan.

Jack simply replied, "Hmm."

"Jack, there's only one thing that can do that to a body."

Jack asked, "What's that?"

Bryan walked into a small office to his right and returned momentarily carrying a large paperback book. He set it down on the display case, and Jack saw that it was from *Demons of the Myst*, a popular role-playing game. Bryan flipped through the pages until he found the one he wanted. Spinning the book around, he pointed to a picture and said, "There."

Jack leaned forward and gazed at the picture and text. The picture was of a semi-naked woman, with flowing auburn hair. She had large breasts covered in a thin veil of cloth, which flowed over her body in thin folds. The artist had added long shapely legs, which were visible through slits in the translucent cloth. Her beauty seemed to jump from the page, and every curve had been accentuated by the stroke of the illustrator's pen. But there was something else in the image that seemed to make the woman's beauty take on a sinister air. A man was kneeling before this beautiful goddess, with his face filled with terror. With her hands on each side of his head, the beautiful woman seemed to be taking pleasure in the man's agony. The caption below the image read, "A Seirene drains the life from her victim."

Jack looked back up at Bryan. "You're kidding, right?"

"If one of those is loose in the city, we're all in trouble."

Shaking his head, Jack said, "I've known you for almost a year, and yet I never realized you were delusional."

"No, I'm serious. Have you ever heard of Homer?"

"Simpson?" joked Jack.

"Don't be a dick! I mean Homer, from the *Iliad* and the *Odyssey*," Bryan said.

Jack nodded. "Yes, I know Homer. I had to read the *Iliad* in high school. But, Bryan, that's all fiction."

"I know that. The Sirens, as Homer called them, were just creatures of Greek Mythology. That's all they were." Tapping the page of the still-open book with his finger, Bryan added, "But they're based on these creatures. Believe me, these are far more sinister than anything Homer ever wrote about."

Shaking his head, Jack replied, "Look, Bryan. I like you. You've got a great little store here, and I'm even willing to call you my friend." Picking up the paperback book from the counter, Jack waved it in front of Bryan and said, "But you need to get your head examined if you think this shit's real."

———

Pulling his apartment door closed, Jack gave the knob a quick jiggle to ensure it was locked. He glanced toward the elevator, and then in the opposite direction. He walked down to the door of the apartment 4C and, leaning against the jamb, rapped on the door with his knuckles. Moments later, it swung open, and Jason Spinacker stood in the opening, wearing black workout pants and a sweaty t-shirt.

"Jack!" he exclaimed.

"Just wanted to make sure you were alive. You were a no show on Friday night. I assumed you got a better offer," explained Jack.

Jason's face broke out in a mischievous grin. "Oh, I did. I hooked up with this gorgeous redhead from our HR department, and—"

Jack put up his hand and interrupted his friend. "I don't need to hear any details."

Smiling, Jason replied, "Let's just say we violated a number of HR policies."

"Too much information, Jason."

"Did I miss anything, or should I say anyone, on Friday night?" inquired Jason.

"There was this one woman. She came in a few hours after we opened," began Jack, as he thought back to the blonde who he had seen. To his own surprise, he found himself saying, "I don't think I've ever seen anyone so beautiful."

Jason shook his head. "I don't go for beautiful. I only go for hot. And, when I say hot, I mean smoking."

Jack thought back to that Friday night. "Trust me, she turned every man's head. You would've been putty in her hands." He paused. "And you should have seen the way she danced. She hooked up with some guy, and they were bumping and grinding like they were the only ones in the club."

"Hm. I might have to make an appearance on Friday. Maybe she'll come back," Jason said.

Almost as an afterthought, Jack remarked, "Oh, and they found a body in the alley between the club and parking garage on Saturday morning."

"What?"

"I don't really know anything about it. Someone mentioned it this morning."

"That's just insane," replied Jason.

Glancing at his watch, Jack said, "I gotta go. Just wanted to say hello."

"You heading into the station?"

Jack nodded.

"I'd say that I'll be listening, but I can't stand that music," joked Jason.

Jack shook his head. "You and me both."

Chapter Seven

Samantha hugged her overcoat tightly to her body as a cold wind raced down Thirteenth Street and caused her to shiver. The whole of Tuesday morning had been colder than normal, and even though it was approaching eleven thirty, it had not warmed up more than a degree or two from when Samantha had first walked out of her front door. The overcast skies above heaved their grey undertones across the city of Philadelphia. Despite the fact that it was two hundred years old, the colonial townhouse before her looked pristine, with bright white trim around the door, windows that looked freshly painted, and red brickwork that looked as if it may have been cleaned just hours before Samantha's arrival. Even the stained glass, which filled in the arch over the door, seemed to glisten as if it had just received a vigorous washing with a cloth and a bottle of Windex. Two police cars and a black van from the medical examiner's office were parked in front of the townhouse, blocking traffic along the narrow street. Yellow police tape had been stretched from lamppost to drainpipe to handrail, creating a flimsy barrier which flapped in the wind. The maroon door stood open, and framed within the doorway was Peter Thornton.

"No sign of forced entry," he said.

Samantha nodded her silent reply and gazed at each of the first floor windows, which framed the door on either side. Black wrought iron bars had been fastened to the outside of the windows to serve as a deterrent for would be thieves. It was a common sight in the city, and Samantha was not surprised to find them on such an immaculately maintained home. Glancing at the second floor, a pair of windows, perfectly matched with those below, looked as undisturbed as those on the first floor. Maroon shutters matching the front door flanked each window, and looked just as fresh and clean as the rest of the townhouse. Above the second floor windows, the roof sloped back from the front facade, and two small dormer windows protruded from out of the grey shingles.

"How about around back?" she asked.

Shaking his head, Peter replied, "Nothing back there either."

"Whoever did it was let into the house."

Samantha climbed the three white stone steps toward the door, and, as Peter stepped aside, she strode into the house. The aroma of stale potpourri penetrated her olfactory senses as she crossed the threshold. The narrow hallway beyond was covered with a dark, highly polished oak floor. A small brass chandelier hung from the ceiling of the hall, casting a golden incandescent glow over everything. The walls were an off-white, and held a collection of family photographs in black frames.

At the opposite end of the hall, Samantha could see a brightly lit kitchen with cabinets the color of honey. Along the wall to her right was a narrow staircase with an intricately carved white bannister and dark stained wood treads leading upward to the second floor. An archway to her left led into a spacious living room, furnished in an eclectic mix of modern and antique furnishings. Stepping into the living room, Samantha saw an oversized beige leather sofa being flanked by two end tables that were fashioned from old sewing machine tables; the word "Singer" was framed in black cast iron above the old pedal underneath. An antique casual chair sat across from the sofa, the seat back covered with four rows of buttons forming diamond patterns in the aged brown leather. At the opposite side of the room was a tall distressed ebony bookcase filled with leather bound volumes. Samantha glanced at the titles, seeing classic works from Alexander Dumas, Edgar Allen Poe, Jules Verne, Herman Melville, and Robert Louis Stevenson. Despite the presence of four other police officers in the room, the old grandfather clock, which stood in the corner, could be clearly heard ticking away the passing of each second.

Samantha knelt beside the corpse that was seated in the leather chair; she was startled by how similar the skin of the body was to the distressed leather. The long, flowing brown hair had a touch of grey along the sides, and gold hoop earrings dangled from the withered ears. The mouth was open, revealing two rows of sparkling white teeth. A pair of turtle shell reading glasses rested precariously on the tip of the emaciated nose. Dressed in an oversized housecoat, the skeletal body seemed to drown amidst the floral fabric, and Samantha guessed that the dead woman must have been a bit more overweight in life than she now was in death. Noting the oversized diamond ring on the left ring finger of the victim, she said, "I doubt robbery was the motive. No thief in his right mind would leave that ring behind."

Samantha rose to her feet, walked to the other side of the room, and knelt beside the second corpse lying on the floor beside the bookcase. This body was smaller than the other, but just as horrifying. Dressed in white shorts and a pink tank top, the cadaver was the size of a child, perhaps in her early teens, by Samantha's judgment. The honey-colored hair was cut short, and the teeth were just as white as the adult corpse. A pair of Nike tennis shoes, which may have fit the wearer once, now hung loosely from small withered feet. The arms and legs were contorted and sprawled across the floor, giving the impression that it had not been a painless death. Samantha glanced back at the other corpse, and then returned her gaze to the child. Their killer, whoever it may be, was not discriminative.

"What do we know?" she asked.

Peter flipped his notebook open. "The house belongs to Dr. George Hardwick. He's a fertility specialist with an office over near Thomas Jefferson Hospital. He's married with one child, a girl. His wife's name is Susan, and their daughter's name is Kelly.

Presumably the bodies are the wife and daughter."

"Any sign of the doctor yet?"

Peter shook his head. "None."

"Who found them?"

"The doctor hasn't shown up for work since last Thursday. His receptionist, Nicole Greenwood, couldn't get any answer at the house, or on the doctor's cell phone. She called us and asked if we could check on the family. Officer Macklin found the front door unlocked."

Samantha rose and stepped out into the hallway. She gazed down the hall toward the kitchen, and then looked up the stairs. "Kitchen's in the back? Bedrooms upstairs? Anything of interest?"

"Not at first glance. But I've only taken a cursory look so far."

Samantha glanced back in at the two corpses in the other room. She wondered what kind of man Dr. Hardwick might be. Could he have killed his wife and child? Could he have killed the other victims as well? After having seen the security video footage from Pulsar over the weekend, Samantha and her partner had been working under the assumption that their killer was a woman. Now, she was reconsidering that assumption. A doctor might have specialized knowledge, Samantha reasoned, of drugs, substances, or methods for rapidly drying out a human body. Could he have dressed like a woman, and lured Saturday's victim out of Pulsar? Could he have dressed convincingly enough to fool another man? Samantha had seen enough in the city of Philadelphia to know that female impersonation was almost an art form. She had met transsexuals who, when dressed for a night out on the town, could have easily taken in even the most astute man.

Turning to gaze at the row of photographs on the wall, Samantha asked, "Is Hardwick in any of these photos?"

Peter pointed to a large photograph framed in black. At first glance, the portrait showed a family of three, seemingly happy to be together. But a closer look told Samantha that things might not have been all that they seemed. The backdrop of the photo was a cloudscape, not unlike that which Samantha had seen in dozens of photographs before, usually victim photos. The three individuals had been arranged by height, with the young daughter in front. Samantha guessed that the daughter must have been ten or eleven when the photograph was taken, making it at least two years old. Her hair was slightly longer than that of the corpse in the other room, but had the same honey color. The wide smile revealed the same bright white teeth, as well as a pair of sparkling blue eyes. The young girl's round face beamed for the camera with a childlike charm. Standing over the girl's shoulder was an older woman, who, Samantha thought, was in her mid-forties. The brown hair curled up under the chin of her pudgy face, a slight double chin beginning to show. Despite the smile, her forehead held lines of worry that seemed to run deep. The blue eyes matched that of the daughter's in intensity, and Samantha noted that the woman had worn the same earrings for the photo that were currently dangling from her dead ears.

Towering above the girl and woman was a gaunt man with a rectangular face and chiseled chin. His narrow hazel eyes peered down the bridge of a long, thin nose, and his greying hair was still thick on top, but receding up his forehead. He had large ears, which jutted out from the sides of his head, and his smile seemed forced. He stoically stared at the unseen camera with a certain level of pomposity, and with an eager sense of wishing to be somewhere else. The three in the photograph made an interesting trio: the beautiful young daughter, the overweight worrisome mother, and the distracted father. Samantha wondered about the root of the father's distraction and the source of the mother's worry. Could they have been related? She allowed her mind to theorize, with the usual scenarios surfacing in her thoughts. Financial troubles at home? An affair with another woman? Dissension in the marital bed? It could be just about anything.

Looking at Peter, Samantha said, "I'd assume that a doctor—even a fertility doctor—would have enough knowledge to know how to drain the fluid out of a body."

"Doctors and undertakers. They both spring to mind," replied Peter.

"Yeah, but no undertakers have disappeared, leaving behind their dead family. Hardwick wouldn't be the first doctor to crack and start killing people."

Peter shrugged his shoulders. "It's possible, but it doesn't explain the woman in the security footage."

Samantha glanced back at the photograph of the doctor and his family. She peered at his face, studying the hard lines in his cheeks, and the deep crow's feet around his eyes. For a moment, she wondered if the doctor could have disguised himself as a female, but she let the idea pass.

"No one would've fallen for him disguised as a woman," she said. "Certainly not enough to get frisky in an alley. But we should add him to our suspect list."

Peter smirked. "I didn't know we had a suspect list."

"We don't, but it's time to start one. And Dr. Hardwick is at the top of that list."

"I'm no medical practitioner, but I can't see how he could have done this without some pretty advanced equipment," said Peter. "We both saw that security footage. There was nothing there." Pausing, he added, "When I was in college, I took a course on ancient Egyptian history—"

"Really? Why?" interrupted Samantha.

"I needed an elective," replied Peter with a smile. "But I remember a lecture on how the Egyptians mummified the Pharaohs. It was a long, time-consuming process. Even with modern day equipment and methods, there's no way to do it quickly."

"Pull together a description of the doctor, and put out an APB. I want to talk to Dr. Hardwick," ordered Samantha.

"Then what?"

"We'll search the house, and head over to Dr.

Hardwick's office. I want a word with his receptionist."

The sun had set hours before Samantha finally crossed the threshold of her townhouse. Tossing her keys on the table by the door, Samantha flicked on the light in the foyer and stood still for a moment, listening to the silence in her home. She heard nothing. With her hand resting on the grip of her holstered gun, Samantha tread softly into the kitchen and turned on the light. She glanced around the room, and found everything in its place. Down the hall, she did the same in the living room with identical results. She made her way through each room of the house, turning on the lights, and giving each space a cursory glance before feeling safe enough to lower her guard. A year ago, she would have followed this routine religiously every night. It had been at least three months since she had felt it necessary, but tonight, she felt an overwhelming urge. It made her feel safe. Cursing under her breath, Samantha realized that she had just undone what had taken a year of therapy to fix. It was just another habit that she had been fighting for the past two years.

Removing the leather holster from her hip, Samantha returned to the kitchen and poured a glass of wine from the open bottle that had been chilling in the refrigerator. She and her partner had searched Dr. Hardwick's home, finding nothing to indicate the whereabouts of the missing physician. In fact, there had been nothing out of the ordinary in the home, apart from the two withered corpses. When they had left the Thirteenth Street townhouse, two attendants from the Medical Examiner's office were loading the victims into their van, and the forensics team were busy "bagging and tagging" anything that remotely resembled evidence in the home.

Peter and Samantha had made their way across the city to Dr. Hardwick's office on Walnut Street. Their interview with the receptionist had been short and uninformative. Nicole Greenwood had only been employed in the office for about four months, and was still getting to know all of the staff. She had stated that the doctor had last been seen the previous Thursday evening when he left the office. He had not been heard from since. She had made several attempts to call the doctor, both at home and on his mobile phone.

While Peter interviewed the doctor's partner and the other members of the office staff, Samantha had made preliminary search of Dr. Hardwick's office, finding little of interest. From all accounts, Hardwick had been a hardworking, well-respected fertility specialist. "No, he hadn't been acting strangely," "As far as I know, he loved his family," and "I'm not aware of any patients that might have held a grudge against him" were the answers they received from everyone they spoke to in the doctor's office. With nothing more than a list of Dr. Hardwick's patients, Samantha and Peter headed back to their office, feeling no closer to finding the culprit of this latest string of deaths. When Samantha had left the office that evening, Peter had been still sitting at his desk, studying the doctor's patient list.

"Don't stay too late," Samantha had said on her way out the door.

Sitting in her living room, Samantha sipped her wine and considered all that had happened over the past couple of weeks. None of it made any sense, and she had a creeping feeling that things were only going to get worse before she and Peter made any headway. With that final thought, she swallowed the rest of her wine in one gulp, set the glass on the coffee table, and headed to bed.

Chapter Eight

The tires of the dark blue Mercedes were perfectly aligned less than an inch from the curb, which Samantha found to be quite a feat to accomplish on the streets of Philadelphia. There were no scuffmarks on the tires themselves, so the driver was apparently very skilled at parallel parking on the city streets. Samantha was standing on a street in the prominent Society Hill neighborhood, which consisted of a long block of townhouses, all of which would have cost six times her annual salary. The brick buildings were a mix of old and new architectural styling. The more traditional townhouses clung to the styling that was common among many of the old colonial buildings in Philadelphia: large shutters for each symmetrically placed narrow window, lantern-styled porch lights, and a decorative trellis surrounding the front door. In between those were the more modern homes of brick, steel, and glass, looking as if they had forced their way into the neighborhood like some kind of rogue architectural experiment. The more modern style townhouses along Delancey Street were more appealing to Samantha, but she had to admit that they looked out of place with their large multi-floor bay windows, stylized brickwork, and double door entries.

She walked around the Mercedes, looking carefully at every aspect of the exterior of the automobile. Peter Thornton followed a few steps behind, taking notes in a small notebook. After rounding the vehicle twice, Samantha stopped on the sidewalk and shook her head. Two uniformed police officers were busy stretching yellow police tape from one light post to the other, cordoning off the street and sidewalk. The spring-like weather over the city meant that Samantha could soon expect more than the usual share of gawkers that Wednesday afternoon. There were those who would simply appear at the perimeter of a crime scene to watch, hoping to catch a glimpse of a body. She despised people like that. Samantha knew, with the nice weather, that they could add the curious walkers and joggers to the list of those showing up to stare, observe, and snap pictures with their smart phones.

The two detectives had received the call about the corpse shortly after they had finished lunch. On the drive over, Samantha was dreading what they would find in the parked car in the Society Hill section of the city. But the dread was caused by more than just for what they might find. She had spent far too much time in the area during the Society Hill Serial Killer investigation to ever want to return again, especially as part of another investigation. She had closed her eyes for a moment on the ride across town, and she could see the bloody message as clear as day in her mind. The words were always the first memory to return, and it was always the hardest.

Slipping a pair of latex gloves over her hands, Samantha said, "Let's get this done and over with."

She walked around to the driver side door, and lifted the handle. Peter did the same on the passenger side. A faint odor of cigar smoke wafted out as the doors opened. Samantha noted that the vehicle's ashtray held the ash and the stub of a cigar, the plastic wrapper of which was resting amidst the ash. A smart phone was propped up in one of the cup holders between the two front seats, while a blue and silver striped tie lay in a ball on the passenger seat. The driver's seat had been pushed back as far as it could go, and reclined to its full extent, placing its occupant into a partially supine position. The occupant of the driver's seat was wearing a pinstripe suit, and white silk shirt, the top three buttons of which were undone. The egg-shaped head was topped with thinning white hair, and some matching tufts of chest hair peeked out from over the collar of a white t-shirt. Samantha gazed momentarily at the face before turning away. The skin, like that of the other victims, was dry and withered. His eyes were open, and stared forward with unblinking resolve. The lips formed an almost perfect circle, frozen in the state of a final scream.

Pointing to the large gold wedding band on one of the bony fingers, Samantha said, "He's married."

Peter, gesturing to the man's undone trousers, added, "I'm guessing his wife didn't do that."

Samantha struggled, without success, to suppress a smile. She glanced out the front and back car windows to make sure no one had seen her smile, and then returned to the task at hand. She checked the ignition switch, and found the keys still hanging from it. Carefully, she pulled open the man's suit jacket, and checked the inside pockets. Finding a leather wallet, she slid it from the pocket and flipped it open.

She read aloud the name on the driver's license. "James P. Seymour."

Gesturing toward the back seat, Peter added, "There's a briefcase back there."

Samantha pulled back the collar of the dead man's shirt and looked at the neck. The hand-shaped pinpricks, which had become increasingly familiar, were faintly visible.

Looking across the car at her partner, Samantha whispered, "Hardwick's handiwork?"

Peter shook his head and muttered, "Don't know."

While the forensics team began the meticulous process of combing the Mercedes and surrounding area for clues, Samantha and Peter opened the briefcase they found in the back seat. The case itself was made from expensive black leather, and had gold latches and locks. Not knowing the combination, Peter pulled a pocketknife from his pocket, and used the blade to pop open the latches. Inside, they found three stacks of papers, which Samantha recognized as legal briefs, bundled together with paper clips. Besides the papers, the briefcase also contained half a dozen pens, and a business card case. Peter opened the small gold case to find business cards with the dead man's name emblazoned on them.

"I thought I recognized the name!" exclaimed Peter. "He's a lawyer with an office downtown. Mostly works on wills, trusts, and stuff like that. They put together my parents' will."

"His address is just a couple blocks from here. If he wasn't in the car with his wife then he was taking an awful risk. Any of his neighbors could have walked past and seen him. Hell, his wife could have walked by."

"He could've been by himself. You know, shaking hands with the man downstairs?"

Samantha turned toward her partner and asked, "What?"

Embarrassed, Peter tried to explain. "You know . . . Um, slapping the weasel? Rubbing his genie?"

"If you're asking me if I think he could have been sitting in his car masturbating, then my answer's no. He didn't give himself those marks on his neck. And he sure as hell didn't dehydrate himself," retorted Samantha.

Feeling a little chastised, Peter replied. "Sorry. It was a ridiculous theory. Shouldn't have said anything."

Samantha shook her head. "No, I'm the one who should apologize. I'm just frustrated. Look, Peter. You and I both saw that security footage. And we've seen six other bodies just like this one. This whole thing is insane. People just don't die like this."

"Seven's enough to call it a serial killer," uttered Peter.

Serial Killer. The two words made Samantha cringe. Since she had joined the homicide department, there had only been one known serial killer in Philadelphia. It had been a long and grueling investigation, on which she had been the lead investigator. The Society Hill Serial Killer had killed eleven times over a span of five months before he was arrested. The killings had been brutal, the crime scenes had been horrific, and the press had been absolutely ruthless. Every officer who was involved had been stretched close to the breaking point, Samantha most of all. Although she had maintained a tough, callous exterior, the toll that the investigation had on her was immense. The nightmares had lasted for months, and she had only recently been able to start sleeping without her loaded firearm under her pillow. Of the eleven deaths, one had been particularly hard on Samantha, leaving her grief-stricken and guilt-ridden ever since. The thought of going through it all again, and especially with such a bizarre series of deaths, was something that filled her with utter dread.

"I sure as hell hope not," she said. "What have we got? Two suspects, a video of one of the killings, and no other clues at the crime scenes. We can't find either suspect. We're spinning in circles and getting nowhere."

"A good photo of her face would be helpful," said Peter.

Samantha agreed with her partner. After three

days with the security footage, the forensics team had reported that they had not been successful at finding a single clear image of the woman's face. In every second of footage from outside the club, her face had been either turned away from the camera, or obscured from view.

The shrill ringing of her mobile phone interrupted Samantha's train of thought, forcing her to frown as she extracted the device from her coat pocket. She placed it to her ear and answered with a gruff "hello". As she listened, Samantha's frown grew deeper, and she began to shake her head. Peter stood silently watching her expression turn from one of annoyance to disgust, and then finally anger.

When the call was over, she slid the phone back in her coat pocket, and said, "The feds are sending up a profiler from D.C., and two agents from the Philly office are on their way here right now."

Peter grimaced at her news. "What do we do now?"

"We divide our resources and get out of here before they show up. Take one of the uniformed officers with you and go see the family. I'm going to go to Mr. Seymour's office," commanded Samantha.

The offices of Haskell, Seymour, and Meyers were on the twenty-fifth floor of the Independence Capital building in downtown Philadelphia. Samantha sat in the small conference room waiting for Fredrick

Haskell, the senior partner for the firm. The oval table in the center of the room had a grey speckled granite top, and a dark wood pedestal underneath. The far wall contained a floor to ceiling window, which looked out over the city. A large screen television hung from the wall at the end of the table, and the ten chairs surrounding the table were covered in fine black leather. The secretary in the reception area had been hesitant at first to allow the detective to see Mr. Haskell without an appointment, but Samantha had found that her badge and the threat of arrest for obstruction was extremely persuasive. "Mr. Haskell is just finishing up with another client and will be with you shortly," the receptionist had explained as she had pulled the conference room door closed.

Samantha spent the next ten minutes staring out the window at the building across the street. She had a clear view into some of the offices, and idly watched men and women come and go, oblivious to her observation. When the conference room door opened again, an elderly man, in his mid-sixties by Samantha's judgment, entered slowly. He pushed the door closed with a gentle click and then, with deliberate steps, circled the table until he was standing on the opposite side from Samantha.

"My name is Fredrick Haskell. And you are?" he said slowly and precisely, as if ensuring that each and every syllable received equal time on his lips.

Samantha rose and introduced herself. "Detective Ballard."

The elderly man gestured Samantha to return to her seat, which she did. He was a tall, gaunt man with a balding head, lined along the sides with short white hair. His oversized ears protruded out from the sides of his thin narrow face. The crisp, blue eyes were closely spaced above a long, bony nose. His dark suit hung from his meager frame, and seemed almost a size too big.

"Detective Ballard, did you threaten to arrest my receptionist if she did not allow you to see me?" he asked.

Samantha smiled. "No, Mr. Haskell. I merely stated that obstructing a police officer in the pursuit of her duty was a misdemeanor offense, but one that still meant being handcuffed and taken into custody. Just a simple statement to keep your staff informed on police procedure."

Haskell slowly lowered himself into a chair, and stared across the table at Samantha with his cold eyes. "Yes, I'm sure that's all it was. You seem far too intelligent to bandy threats around the offices of a law firm."

"Mr. Haskell, I needed to speak to you as quickly as possible. I'm sorry, but I have to inform you that James Seymour was found dead this morning. I'm investigating his murder."

Fredrick Haskell's cold eyes seemed to thaw rapidly, and the color in his face drained away. He looked down at the table and did not move for several moments. Samantha waited patiently as the shock from her words wore off. When Haskell finally returned his gaze to the detective, the eyes looked sad and tired.

"I'm the one who should apologize. You're simply here to do your job. We're not a law firm that practices criminal law, so we don't deal with the police very often. The firm will, of course, cooperate in whatever way we can," Haskell stated.

"Thank you. I'll try not to be too invasive during the investigation."

"That is appreciated. Are you permitted to give any details about his death?" Haskell inquired.

Samantha replied, "A little. He was found this morning in his car, parked a few blocks from his home in Society Hill."

"Does his wife know?"

Nodding, Samantha stated, "My partner's at his home now."

Haskell shook his head. "Poor Elizabeth. She'll be devastated."

"Mr. Haskell, do you know if James Seymour had any enemies, or any clients that might hold a grudge?"

Haskell again shook his head. "No. We deal mostly with wills, trusts, and legal matters for small and mid-size businesses. Fairly boring stuff, in all honesty."

"How long has he been a partner in the firm?"

"Eight years. But he's worked here for almost twenty. He was one of our staff attorneys," Haskell explained. "Well liked, and had done an admirable job with anything we assigned to him. James was a hard worker, and well versed in business law. Harvard graduate with top marks. He had impressed us for so many years that Andrew Meyer and I finally decided to make him a full partner."

"Was he in the office yesterday?"

Haskell nodded. "Yes, he was. As a matter of fact, he was still here yesterday evening when I left. I believe he had a late client appointment."

"I'd like to get that client's name, if I may. As well as a list of all of the clients Mr. Seymour was working with," said Samantha.

"I can certainly provide you with the client list, but I hope you understand that I cannot divulge information about what we are doing for our clients. I must ask that you respect the confidential nature of our work."

Samantha nodded in agreement. "I understand. If I need to know more information, I'll approach the client for any additional details."

"Thank you," said Haskell.

Her next question, Samantha knew, needed to be asked with a certain level of delicacy. "I realize that this may sound inappropriate, but it needs to be asked. Were you aware of, or would you consider it possible that James Seymour might be having an affair?"

Fredrick Haskell's eyes opened wide as he gazed at the detective. He seemed taken aback by Samantha's question, and momentarily hesitated to answer. "I'm assuming that you have a reason for asking such a question."

Nodding, Samantha replied, "There's some

indication that he wasn't alone in his car when he died. I'm simply trying to cover all the options at this point."

Haskell remained silent for a moment, and then replied, "I see. To answer your question, it is always possible that James could've been having an affair. However, if you knew how dedicated he was to his wife and family, you'd find the possibility to be so remote that it borders on the impossible."

"Thank you. I appreciate your candidness. I won't detain you any longer. If I may, I'd like to have a look around his office before I go, and I'd like to get that client list."

"I'll assume that if I don't allow you to see James' office, you'll simply return with a search warrant," responded Haskell. "So I'll have Jessica let you in, with the understanding that you don't remove anything without first speaking to me. And that you do not extend your search into his files without an official warrant."

Samantha agreed, and then said, "Again, thank you."

Chapter Nine

Thursday brought a torrential downpour into the Philadelphia area, making the morning's commute dreadful. With her raincoat pulled tightly closed around her, Samantha dashed from the door of her townhouse into the waiting car. As Peter stepped on the accelerator, he gestured toward the Dunkin' Doughnuts coffee sitting in a cup holder between the front seats. She picked up the cup, and moaned as she caught the aroma of the freshly ground coffee. She was about to ask about sugar packets when Peter's hand flicked toward her with two sugar packets between his fingers. Samantha smiled. *He was getting better*, she thought.

"I did some cross referencing on Hardwick's patient list. A patient from the list was recently reported missing," explained Peter. "There's also been an uptick in Missing Persons reports over the past couple weeks. There might be more bodies out there that we don't know about."

"Let's hope not. Give me the details," Samantha said as she sipped her coffee.

"Just in the last two weeks alone, there've been five reports filed. Three men went missing, all last seen leaving a gym over on the south side," explained

Peter. "And a young woman was reported missing last week—name's Jessica Sturgis. She was last seen jogging in Fairmount Park. That was four days ago. Her name was on Hardwick's patient list."

Smiling, Samantha said, "Finally we're getting somewhere. If we find the doctor, we'll probably find the girl."

Peter nodded. "It could just be a coincidence."

"A highly improbable one."

"And then there's the missing guys from the gym."

"Hmm, all from the same gym?" pondered Samantha. "Again, it seems too improbable. But how does it all fit together?"

"You haven't heard the best bit yet," said Peter, smiling smugly. "Remember Robert Crosse, one of our first victims? He and his fiancé were patients of Dr. Hardwick. They were having trouble getting pregnant."

Samantha smiled. "Our first link. Good work."

As they inched down the street with the morning traffic, Samantha took a mental inventory of what they knew. The previous day had been a long one, and by the time she had met up with Peter at precinct headquarters, it was well past five. To her annoyance, the two FBI agents and the profiler had already established a presence in the open office space shared by the precinct detectives. She had always despised the way the feds would subtly take over an investigation under the guise of "providing assistance". She had been certain that the two federal agents would have already criticized her handling of the case to her superiors, probably making shrewd references to the way she had left the latest crime scene without waiting for the agents' arrival. "Fuck 'em," she thought. "This is my investigation."

Samantha detailed for them her search of James Seymour's office, which had, for the most part, been a fruitless endeavor. She had found nothing to suggest anything other than loyalty to the law firm, and faithfulness to his wife and family. His office had been tidy and neat, almost to an obsessive-compulsive level. Jessica, the law firm's receptionist, had confirmed that James Seymour was very conscientious about keeping his papers in order. Jessica had also been helpful, by providing not only the promised client list, but also the dates of the last contact that James had with each client.

After the lengthy briefing with the FBI, Samantha, with the client list in hand, spent an hour correlating the names in order of most recent contact, and had found that James Seymour had only met with two clients on the day that he died. One was a Henry G. Faber, and the other was Calithea Panagakos. The latter name had been Seymour's late evening appointment, and, Samantha thought, might be the last person to see James Seymour alive. Before picking up the phone, Samantha had glared at the trio from the FBI, who, deep in discussion, had been paying no attention to her. Certain that she wasn't seen, Samantha placed a call to Ms. Panagakos, and arranged an appointment for Thursday morning.

As he had explained during the FBI briefing

the previous evening, Peter's day had been spent at the Seymour residence in Society Hill. After breaking the news of her husband's death, Peter waited patiently as the grieving widow sobbed uncontrollably. While answering Peter's questions, the Seymours's nineteen-year-old son, Matthew, tried to comfort his mother. "No, he hadn't come home the night before." "Yes, it was unusual for him not to call." "No, he didn't have any enemies." "Yes, James had always been a good and loving husband and father." The answers were all those that one would expect to hear from a Society Hill family. A perfect world, and a perfect family. Those in Society Hill didn't air their dirty laundry in public, and especially not to the police. A quick search of James Seymour's home office turned up little as well. It had, overall, been a fruitless day for both of them.

When Samantha had arrived at home the previous night, she had been utterly exhausted, not just physically, but emotionally as well. She had pulled a bottle of Pinot Noir from the small wine rack in her kitchen and popped the cork. She had poured a generous amount of the ruby red wine into a wine glass and took it, along with the bottle, into her living room. Flopping down on her oversized beige sofa, she took a long sip from her glass. With seven dead bodies, all killed by the same method, it was turning into another serial killer investigation. But she was having difficulty wrapping her head around how the seven victims died. It just all seemed impossible. She had quietly sipped her wine while turning the case over and over in her head, and Samantha assumed that it was the exhaustion that eventually made her start to cry. She couldn't help but see the gruesome images of the victims in her head every time she closed her eyes. What was worse was the way the new images intermixed with the image of another victim from two years ago.

She could still see Peterson's face, fresh from the academy by only three months. And she could still remember the message left by his killer, the crimson red letters forever burned into her memory. The rookie should never have been out there alone. But, in an overzealous moment, Samantha sent him straight into the hands of a horrific killer. The wine helped dull the guilt, but it never truly went away. It always lingered in the back of her mind; a wound that festered and oozed without ever healing. When midnight arrived, she had decided that she'd had enough wine, and she had gone to bed for another sleepless night.

As the rain pelted the windshield, Samantha watched the city pass by her. People dashed down the sidewalk holding umbrellas and wearing raincoats, doing their best to stay dry. She wondered if any of them realized what was out there in the city. Did they know a killer was at large? The newspapers had been cooperative by not publishing the more gory details, as well as keeping the rumblings of a possible serial killer to a minimum. Samantha knew that it wouldn't last too much longer, especially if they didn't start making progress soon.

"What kind of name is Calithea?" asked Peter.

"I'm not sure. She had an accent, but I couldn't place it," Samantha explained.

"What are you expecting her to say?" inquired Peter.

It was one of those inquiries from Peter that Samantha hated. She hated it because there was never a clear-cut answer to the rookie's question. Over her five years of experience, Samantha had learned that you never should expect anything to come from any interview with a prospective witness. As his mentor, Samantha knew she should be educating him with insightful guidance from her years of experience as a detective. After all, that was why he was assigned to her—to learn from her. But she had little patience for his questions. She remembered her own time as a rookie detective under the tutelage of her old partner, Eddie Murdock. She smiled when she thought how Eddie would hang the questions he deemed to be stupid on the bulletin board near their desks for all to see. It had been humiliating at first, but it had helped her grow as a detective. She figured Peter should count himself lucky that he only had to deal with her curt responses.

Samantha didn't know what to expect from their forthcoming conversation with Calithea Panagakos, nor did she know what role, if any, the lady would play in the investigation. Samantha's only concern was that Calithea was the last person, that the police were aware of, who had seen James Seymour alive.

"I'm expecting her to say James Seymour was fine when she met with him on Tuesday evening," Samantha replied tersely.

Peter, who detected the tone in her voice, replied, "Sorry. Dumb question."

Samantha sighed loudly. "Yeah, dumb question."

The silence between them lasted five minutes as they made their way across the city. Samantha stared out the car window, watching the raindrops streak down the glass. She was feeling an overwhelming sense of frustration. Whoever was committing these murders was smart, very smart. Forensics had found close to nothing at any of the crime scenes. There was no connection between the victims that they had been able to find. For all Samantha knew, the person committing these crimes could be standing on the very next street corner. She sighed once again.

Breaking the silence, Samantha said, "Sorry. I didn't mean to snap at you. I'm just feeling frustrated with this case. Too many dead bodies, and no idea how they died or who did it. We're lucky the media has kept their coverage low-key, but that won't last much longer."

Calithea Panagakos lived in the penthouse suite at the top of a newly constructed fourteen-story luxury apartment complex in the Logan Square section of the city. Samantha had remembered reading about the new complex a few months ago in the Philadelphia Tribune, one of the city's oldest newspapers. The property management firm who had built the complex had touted the long list of amenities, including a 24-hour concierge, top-of-the-line fitness center, a resident clubroom, bicycle storage, and even a rooftop deck. However, the list of amenities had not caused the rush of prospective renters that the management firm had hoped for. The last that Samantha had heard, only half of the apartments were currently occupied.

Stepping out of the elevator on the nineteenth floor, Samantha could still smell the faint odor of freshly laid carpet. There were only two apartments on the top floor, both serving as the most luxurious of all of the apartments in the building. The double doors of the two apartments were placed across from each other in the large foyer, with the doors to the left of the elevator being framed on either side with a potted fern. The ferns amused Samantha, as they represented the stereotypical city apartment dweller's attempt at landscaping. The two detectives knocked on the doors to the right of the elevator and waited patiently for a response. Samantha glanced at her watch. They were only five minutes late, which surprised her considering the amount of rush hour traffic they had wrestled with on the way over.

When the door was opened, the two detectives were greeted by what Samantha could only describe as beauty incarnate. The woman appeared to be in her mid-thirties, with long, voluminous black hair, which flowed from atop her head like water cascading downward to form a waterfall on her shoulders. The complexion of her oval face was utterly flawless, without a single freckle, wrinkle, or blemish. Her pert nose was exquisitely shaped and the lips were a deep red, and framed a smile filled with blazing white teeth. Below the narrow chin came an impeccable neck, and a valley of cleavage formed between a pair of ideally shaped breasts. Samantha noticed a perfectly shaped body with curves and proportions that would have taken a thousand artists to sculpt with such perfection. The pale blue dress the woman was wearing clung so flawlessly to each and every supple contour that Samantha was left wondering if it had been painted over her flesh. When she looked back up at the woman's eyes, Samantha found a set of startlingly crystal blue eyes, which were as frigid as ice.

Before Samantha could speak, Peter said, "Ms. Calithea Panagakos? I'm Detective Peter Thornton. I believe you're expecting me."

"Yes," Calithea replied, and then looked toward Samantha, awaiting an introduction.

"I'm Detective Samantha Ballard. We spoke on the phone yesterday afternoon."

Stepping aside, Calithea ushered the two detectives into the apartment. "Please, come in."

The living room of the apartment was sparsely furnished with a generously sized beige leather sofa, two matching lounge chairs, and a pair of brass lamp stands. A dark wood coffee table with a glass top sat in between the sofa and chairs. At the far end of the room was a plate glass floor-to-ceiling window, which looked out across the courtyard below. The sound of their footsteps on the hardwood floor echoed throughout the large space.

"Please excuse the lack of furniture. I'm afraid my apartment must look terribly empty, and quite unwelcoming at the moment," said Calithea, as she gestured the two detectives toward the sofa. "My sisters and I have only just returned to the city, and some of our new furniture has yet to arrive."

Smiling, Peter replied, "Even the emptiest of rooms is made welcoming with just your smile." The tone of his voice sounded different, almost whimsical.

Samantha's head jerked around to glare at her partner, and then back to observe Calithea Panagakos, whose cheeks had taken on a mild pink hue.

"You're too kind. Can I offer either of you some coffee?" the woman asked.

Samantha began to speak. "No, if we—"

Peter interrupted by saying, "No, Ms. Panagakos. We wouldn't dream of inconveniencing you."

"It's not an inconvenience. And please, call me Calithea."

Samantha scowled at her partner as he fancifully said, "Calithea is such a pretty name."

Smiling, Calithea explained, "It's Greek, meaning beautiful goddess. My sisters and I originally came from Greece. We've been here in this country for . . . well, let's just say it's longer than I can remember."

"Yes, I noticed your accent. It's so exotic,"

remarked Peter.

Samantha, who was still trying to wrap her head around what was going on, spoke up. "Look, I'm sure this all very interesting, but I don't want to waste any more of your time than I have to. We had a few questions about your relationship with James Seymour."

The Greek woman turned her attention to Samantha, and replied, "Of course. What would you like to know?"

"You had an appointment with Mr. Seymour on Tuesday evening. Is that true?" Samantha inquired.

Calithea nodded. "Yes. We met for about an hour at his office."

"If it isn't too personal, could you tell us the nature of your business with Mr. Seymour?" requested Samantha.

"He was working on a small legal matter for me. An old family legacy left by some of my ancestors. You could call it an inheritance, if you like. James was finalizing the legal details. As a matter of fact, he'd completed his work on Tuesday afternoon and provided me with the results that evening," came the reply.

Samantha asked, "Did he seem nervous or upset about anything?"

Shaking her head Calithea responded, "No. He seemed very much himself. He was happy to have wrapped up his work for me, and didn't appear to be concerned about anything."

Before Samantha could answer, Peter said, "I don't think we need to bother you with any more questions."

Looking at her partner with a frown, Samantha stated, "I do have one or two more questions to ask."

"Please, ask whatever questions you have. I'm happy to help," directed Calithea.

Taking the cue, Samantha inquired, "This legacy you mentioned . . . how long was James Seymour working on it for you?"

Calithea replied, "Only about a week. As I said, my sisters and I have only just . . . returned to the city after an extended time away."

Peter smiled and said, "Welcome back."

"Thank you. It's been a long time since I've walked the streets of Philadelphia, a very long time." Calithea returned his smile. "I, as well as my sisters, am looking forward to becoming acquainted once again with this city of brotherly love. We are very much looking forward to it."

"How long have you been away?" Samantha asked.

"Oh, longer than I, or my sisters, care to remember." Calithea smiled. "My sisters have done nothing but gorge themselves on the . . . delicacies of the city since our return. I, myself, am more of a discriminating connoisseur. Unlike my sisters, I'm more about quality than quantity. But such is the impetuousness of youth."

As the doors closed and the elevator began its

slow downward plummet, Samantha, infuriated, stood silently next to her partner. Her head was pounding as she gritted her teeth in anger. Samantha could feel her temples throbbing, and fought to hold back an onslaught of fury. Throughout the entire interview with Calithea Panagakos the detective had an overwhelming desire to punch her partner in the face. Samantha wasn't normally prone to violence, but watching her partner toss aside all of his professionalism and self-respect simply enraged her. As the elevator passed floor eleven, she could hold back no more.

"What the hell was that all about?" she exclaimed.

Peter, taken aback by her sudden outburst, stared at her wide-eyed. "What?"

"What? What do you mean what? I'm talking about that dog and pony show you just put on back there!" Samantha responded.

As Peter stared at her dumbfounded, she continued her tirade. "Really? You don't remember telling her how exotic her accent was? Or how her smile makes empty spaces feel welcoming? Oh, and I love this one! How about the way you interrupted me every thirty seconds! Not only did you make an utter fool of yourself, but also you completely disgraced your badge! What the hell were you playing at?"

Peter shook his head as if confused. "I . . . I don't know. I don't know what happened."

Samantha looked astonished by his response. "You don't know what happened? That's your excuse for your behavior? I'll keep that in mind for the next time the captain asks why I shot a suspect! 'Gosh, I don't know!' That'd go down well with Internal Affairs!"

The doors of the elevator opened and Samantha didn't hesitate to storm out into the building's lobby, and then out the front doors. She walked at a rapid pace, neither looking to the right or the left. Peter, with his hands in his overcoat's pockets, followed a few feet behind. Samantha pulled open the passenger door of the Dodge Charger, and slid into the seat. She took two deep breaths, trying to calm herself before her partner entered the car. The more she dug into this case, the more that she hated it. There were too many questions and, up to now, she hadn't found any answers. Samantha couldn't understand why this case was causing her so much grief. She had always been able to keep a cool head with any murder case. Even with the Society Hill Serial Killer, she had been calm and collected during the entire investigation. She would only break down in the privacy of her own home. But this case was getting to her in ways that no other case had before. And it frightened her. *At least this killer isn't leaving messages with each victim for the police,* she thought.

She heard the car door open, and Peter slid quietly into the driver's seat. She said nothing to him. Samantha had said all that she had wanted to say back in the elevator. She wondered if she might have said too much.

"Samantha. I'm truly sorry. I've no excuse for what happened back there. I can't explain it, and I'm not going to try," Peter finally said.

Without looking at him, she retorted, "Don't ever let it happen again."

Chapter Ten

From his vantage point high above the dance floor, Jack saw the bartenders stocking the shelves behind their respective bars with bottles of every kind of alcohol imaginable. That was one thing that Pulsar prided itself on, its selection of alcoholic beverages. Behind each bar were long shelves lined with whiskeys, rums, wines, vodkas, and other kinds of alcohol by almost every major manufacturer. Pulsar also maintained twenty different beers on tap and another thirty varieties in bottles, including a few of the larger local Philadelphia microbrews.

With an hour to go before the club opened, Jack had already completed the programming of his first two hours of music in the computer, and had time to relax. Brad Colburn, on the other hand, was feverishly typing away at his keyboard, frantically trying to program the lighting effects for that evening. Jack smiled at the young man, whose brow was beginning to glisten with a faint layer of sweat. Brad, who normally arrived three hours before opening, had just walked in the door fifteen minutes prior, cursing about traffic on interstate 95 being backed up for miles. The angry young man vividly detailed his inch-by-inch crawl past a serious accident in the right-hand lane involving a jackknifed tractor-trailer and a Chrysler minivan. Now, Brad was rushing to make up for the two hours he had lost.

Jack, once again, gazed out over the dance floor below, lost in thought. It had been another slow week of rising in the evening, working the overnight, and sleeping during the day. He felt like his week had simply been a repeat of the week before . . . and the week before that . . . and the week before that, like he was stuck in some endless cycle. On Wednesday, Jack had toyed with the idea of sending out a few résumés to see if any stations might bite. But Thursday morning he had read in Friday Morning Quarterback, a radio trade magazine, about another Top Forty personality being fired from a Los Angeles station for saying the word "cock" on the air. Jack decided not to send out his résumé.

Feeling that his life was reaching a point of utter banality, Jack began to wonder if it was, as far as his broadcasting career was concerned, simply time to call it quits. At thirty-seven, he wondered if he was just too old to get back into high-paced Top Forty radio. Jack had realized that he was no longer in the age demographic that Top Forty radio was trying to reach, and wondered if that actually made him less appealing to radio stations than his on-air slip of the tongue. *Maybe it was just time to move on,* he had thought on Thursday evening. But what would he do? Radio was his only talent. It was all he ever knew.

When he considered his current circumstance,

Jack had to admit that he was getting paid a decent amount of money to allow him to live comfortably. But he still felt terribly unhappy with his present situation. It took a tremendous amount of effort for him to rise in the evening and spend eight hours a night in the WPLX studios. There were many occasions when, after rising at his customary seven o'clock, he simply sat on the edge of his bed, daring himself to not go to work that night. Jack often wondered what would happen if he simply stopped showing up. Would anyone from the station come and check on him? Would anyone at the station even care? *Probably not,* he thought. After all, he didn't give a damn about them, so why should they give a damn about him?

It never failed that whenever Jack contemplated his career, he started to wonder about other things in his life. Why did his relationships never seem to last for more than a few months? Why had he never married? Why did he never visit his parents up in New York? All three questions had a single common answer. He instinctively reached for the wallet in his back pocket, but then thought twice and stopped himself. He really needed to stop thinking about her as often as he did. He couldn't change what had happened, no one could. Jack knew he had been stupid, and now had to live with the consequences. He found it odd that he couldn't even remember the other girl's name. But he would never forget the look on Emma's face when he told her.

Jack's brooding was interrupted by a shout from the dance floor below. He looked out and saw Harry

Griffith gazing up from the center of the floor. Even if the dance floor had been full of people, it would have been hard to miss Harry. The bouncer's three hundred pound girth along with his broad shoulders, thick neck, and cleanly shaved head made for an unusual sight among the usual crowd of patrons at Pulsar. When the bouncer stood at the center of the dance floor by himself, Jack couldn't help but be amazed at how much Harry looked like a Mr. Potato Head in a black suit.

"Jack!" shouted Harry, in a deep, baritone voice.

"What's up, Harry?"

"A guy at the front door claims to know ya. Jason Spanbaker?"

Jack laughed. "Spinacker! He's a friend. Send him up."

A few minutes later, Jason, wearing acid washed jeans, a pink untucked polo, and an unstructured navy blue jacket, stepped into the booth. Brad glanced up and nodded at Jason, who gave the young man a slap on the back as he passed.

"Nice to see you, four eyes," said Jason.

"Piss off, bean counter!" replied Brad.

Grasping Jack's hand tightly and giving it a hard shake, Jason said, "I've got a feeling tonight's going to be my lucky night."

Jack smiled. "Really?"

"Of course! It's Friday night. I made a killing in the markets this week. And my friend, Jack Allyn, is supplying the mood music as I hunt for this evening's willing partner."

Without looking up from the keyboard, Brad said, "Don't you mean victim?"

"Funny guy!" retorted Jason, raising his hand toward Brad and flipping up his middle finger.

"Should have a packed house tonight. The place has been overflowing since they found that body," said Jack. "Harry's had to shoo a few people away who were back in the alley taking selfies."

"What a bunch of sick bastards!" exclaimed Jason.

Brad looked up from his feverish typing, and added, "Some people get their rocks off to that kind of stuff."

Jack laughed, and said, "They need their heads examined."

"Have you been back there yet to see what all the hubbub's about?" Jason asked.

Jack shook his head. "Nope. It's nothing to do with me. Nothing at all."

Two hours later, the dance floor of Pulsar was packed from edge to edge with bodies as people once again gyrated to the beat that resounded throughout the club. Jack was feeling exceptionally good about how the night had gone. Brad's lighting schemes had worked perfectly with the music that Jack had chosen. And, without trying to sound overly egotistical, Jack had even impressed himself with his own musical mix that evening. Sometimes, there were nights when Jack felt that everything, from the music, to the lights, and even the crowd, all came together to create that perfect atmosphere that Pulsar had become famous for. This was one of those nights. Word had drifted up to the booth that they were turning people away from the club at the front doors. The faint scent of alcohol and human perspiration intermixed in the air to form a unique odor all too well known to Jack's olfactory senses.

Jason Spinacker had remained in the booth with Jack throughout the first few hours of the evening. He would lean over the edge, and peer down at the crowd below, searching for a woman who he felt would be worthy of his attention. Jack, finding Jason's behavior hilarious to watch, would often goad Jason further by steering his friend's attention to those women who would never meet Jason's high standards.

"What about her?" Jack would ask, pointing down onto the dance floor.

Jason would often respond with a running commentary on the flaws in Jack's choice. "The one in the black leather skirt? Are you kidding me? Her nose is bigger than her tits! Plus, she'd be too easy of a lay. That skirt is screaming she'll sleep with the first guy who asks her to dance. I may not have much, but I do have some self-respect. I want to at least feel like I had to do more than just smile to get her panties off."

The banter between Jack and Jason continued well into the nine o'clock hour, with short breaks to allow Jack to program the next hour's music. Brad

Colburn would interject his own suggestions, only to have them severely criticized by Jason. At nine fifteen, as Jason's eyes were roaming the dance floor, Jack gazed in the direction of the club entrance. His eyes locked on the two figures that entered slowly into the foray of the crowded club. One of the two women looked familiar to Jack, with her golden blonde hair being too hard to forget. Even from a distance, Jack would have sworn that every strand of her hair had been made from pure gold. It swayed gently from side to side as she took each step. Her beautiful face was just as radiant as it had been the last time her saw her in Pulsar. The trim, curvy frame of her body once again turned the heads of every man she passed. Jack noticed that she was wearing the same skin-tight red Lycra dress from before.

Her companion was a fiery redhead, with shoulder length hair that curved in under her chin. Her face was just as beautiful as the other woman's, and seemed to radiate a level of sensualism that could easily make her a superstar model. Although slightly shorter than her blonde companion, the redhead had a similar body structure. The tight, strapless black dress she was wearing seemed to defy gravity by clinging to every supple contour of her perfectly shaped figure. Although not certain because of his angle above the dance floor, Jack could have sworn that the sides of the dress were translucent like a chemise. Her legs were muscular, and perfectly toned, without a trace of imperfection. Jack could barely take his eyes away from the two women, and nudged Jason with his elbow.

"Wow!" exclaimed Jason.

Jack watched as the blonde and redhead paused and surveyed the interior of the club. As the blonde seemed to scan the crowd on the dance floor, the redhead glanced up toward the booth. Her eyes locked on Jack and Jason for a long moment, before she gave them both a wide smile, which was overflowing with sexual undertones.

"That's her!" Jason exclaimed. "She's the one! Come hell or high water, I'm taking her home tonight!"

The two women glanced at each other, smiled, and then parted; each going to a separate bar close to the dance floor. Jason gave Jack a slap on the back and said, "Wish me luck." With that, he dashed from the booth and headed down toward the dance floor.

Jack spent the next two hours watching two bizarre mating rituals unfold before his eyes. The blonde had mingled throughout the club, seeming to aimlessly wander through the crowds. To those in among the crowd, the woman's path seemed random, but to Jack, who had a view from above, it was anything but. As she drew closer to her intended partner, Jack could see that she had once again predatorily circled around the man she intended to meet. Once they were face-to-face, the man, who was tall, thin, with short black hair, smiled, indicating that the attraction was mutual. They drifted onto the dance floor and began to rhythmically move to the musical beat in a form of synchronized sexual frenzy bordering on the obscene.

On the other side of Pulsar, the redhead and Jason Spinacker began a quite different form of ritual, starting with drinks at the bar. There had been no predatory stalking; it had simply started with Jason buying her a drink. They talked for an hour by the bar, almost as if they were completely alone in the club. Jack noticed that his friend's gaze seemed transfixed on the woman, and he appeared to be deeply engrossed in his conversation with her. The behavior was perplexing since it was far from Jason's usual approach. Jack's friend had never been known as an engrossing conversationalist. He was much better at getting his intended partner on the dance floor, and wooing her with his smooth moves. For Jason to sit at the bar for an hour-long conversation was way out of character.

Jason and the redhead eventually made their way to the dance floor. Their dancing was far more subdued than that of their counterparts on the opposite side of the dance floor, who at that point were drawing stares from dancers around them who had become irritated by the couple's uninhibited gyrations. If it had not been for the fact that they were still wearing clothing, one might have easily mistaken them for having tantric sex on the dance floor.

Glancing over toward Jerry Rickett, Jack could tell that the couple's moves had attracted the attention of the club owner. As much as Rickett wanted every patron to have an enjoyable experience at his club, there were limits to the kind of behavior he would tolerate. Jack watched as Jerry passed word to the nearby bartender, who in turn picked up a small hand radio from under his bar. Jack knew what would happen next. Harry Griffith would come in from watching the front door, wade through the throng of dancers and quietly escort the couple from the club. It would be quick, quiet, and efficient. That was what Harry was good at. There were few people who were prepared to cause a fuss when being stared down by Harry's girth. Any regular patron knew that to be ejected from Pulsar meant a lifetime ban at the club, at least as long as Harry worked the front door. That was the other thing Harry was good at. He had a tremendously good memory for faces.

As Jack waited for Harry to appear, he saw the sexually charged couple suddenly rush from the dance floor, the man leading with the woman's hand in his own. He followed them as they made their way through the crowds toward the door. Jack could only guess that they had both grown tired of playing at sex, and were ready for the real thing. After they disappeared out the door, Jack turned his attention back to Jason and the redhead. But, as he scanned the crowds, he couldn't find them anywhere. Jack realized that he had been so engrossed in watching the other couple that he had neglected to keep tabs on his friend. He shrugged, figuring that Jason had used some of his smooth lines with the redhead, and they had slipped out to, as Jason would say, make a little sheet music. Jack smiled, and began tapping at his keyboard, programming the next hour of music for Pulsar.

Chapter Eleven

The ringing of her mobile phone stirred Samantha out of a deep sleep. Groggily, she groped at the bedside table in the dark searching for the device, which was blaring loudly throughout the bedroom. When her hand found the phone, she tapped the screen and placed the phone up to her ear.

"What?" she muttered.

"Sorry to bother you, Detective. But we've got another one," responded the distant voice on the other end of the call.

"Damn!" replied Samantha.

"You haven't heard the best bit. This one's still alive."

Samantha suddenly sat bolt upright in her bed. "What?"

By the time she arrived at the Philadelphia General Hospital, it was closing in on four in the morning. It had taken her twenty-five minutes to pull on a pair of denim jeans and the Philadelphia Flyers sweatshirt she had been wearing the previous evening. Her Friday night had been uneventful and ended early when Samantha decided she was exhausted, turned off the DVD she had rented, and went to bed. It was the third time she had rented *The Hunger Games*, and it was the third time that she hadn't finished watching it. A Friday night at home wasn't unusual for Samantha; her lack of romantic involvement with anyone from the opposite sex had led to rumors among a few of her co-workers that Samantha might be a lesbian. They were rumors that she simply shrugged off. They could have their silly little fantasies, she would think. The truth behind her solitary evenings was one that was far different from the innuendo and rumors of her male counterparts. Samantha simply avoided romantic relationships. Having watched her mother suffer for years after her father was killed, Samantha refused to subject anyone to the same anguish. It was a lonely life, but one that she had chosen for herself. No loved ones in life, no one loved ones to devastate in death.

The police dispatcher, who had disturbed her sleep, gave the detective only a brief hint of the details awaiting her at the hospital. Samantha had directed the dispatcher to call her partner, and have him meet her in the Emergency Room. Then, almost as an afterthought, she directed the dispatcher to refrain from calling the FBI. When she entered the hospital, all she knew was that a man had been attacked in the Penn's Landing parking garage, and there were strange markings on his neck.

There were two uniformed officers, one in a pale blue shirt and the other in white, waiting in the reception area of the Emergency Room when she arrived. She knew one of the officers from her early days on the police force. Lieutenant Frank Gellar had only been a Corporal in Samantha's district when she first joined the force. She hadn't seen him in a few years, and was shocked at how he had aged. Gone was the acorn-colored hair to be replaced with a clean-shaven head. And Samantha couldn't help but notice a slight expansion around the waist as well. She extended her hand, which he shook heartily.

"Samantha, it's good to see you again," he said.

"Lieutenant, I'm surprised to see you out in the middle of the night. Last I heard you were jockeying desks these days, and I mean days," said Samantha.

"It's a bit of an unusual situation. I thought I might personally come and oversee things. I'm the one who had you called in," explained Gellar. He gestured toward the other officer and added, "Samantha Ballard, meet Tony Maxwell. He was first on the scene and can give you all the details."

Samantha nodded toward the other officer. "What happened?"

"My partner and I were patrolling down around Penn's Landing area early this morning," the officer explained. "It was twelve fifty-one when we circled past that night club—the place seemed to be really hopping—I don't know if you're familiar with the area, but there's a parking garage right next to it. As we were passing, one of the stairwell doors opened. Out comes this woman, running like the devil. Darts straight out in front of us. She was lucky we were moving slow or she'd have been in the hospital as well."

Samantha interrupted. "Can you describe her?"

"Absolutely. Won't forget that face any time soon. But I doubt it'll do you any good. She was wearing some kind of mask. She had to be. It's the only way I can explain what I saw."

"Go on with your story. We can talk about her description in a minute," directed Lieutenant Gellar.

"So, her hands landed on the hood of the car, and she hissed at us before running off. As we jumped out of the car, the stairwell door opens again, and out comes a guy," Tony Maxwell explained. "He's chasing this woman. He sees us and says that he and his fiancé saw that woman attackin' somebody in the garage. The woman was gone in seconds, so I called it in to dispatch. Then Brad—that's my partner—and I followed the man back into the garage."

"Did you say she hissed at you?" inquired Samantha.

"Yep. That's what it sounded like," Maxwell replied.

"Go on," commanded Samantha.

"So, we get to the third floor, and there's this girl kneeling beside another man. He's in bad shape, just lying there, moaning. Called for a bus, but I wasn't holding out hope that he'd make it."

Samantha asked, "Did you get a statement from

the other man and his fiancé?"

"Yeah." Maxwell pulled a small notebook from his pocket, and flipped it open. "Steve Kinski and Dana Stark. They'd just come out of Pulsar, and they were parked on the third floor. He said they caught sight of this man and woman leaning up against the wall. He thought they were making out. But when they got closer, the man let out a loud scream, and it looked like the woman was choking him. Kinski said he shouted, and the woman let the man go, hightailing down the stairs. Steve chased her out into the street."

"Now give her the description," ordered Gellar.

Tony Maxwell seemed to hesitate for a moment before speaking. "If I hadn't seen her face, I'd have sworn she was a model. One of those ones from Sports Illustrated swimsuit issue. She was all curves, and they were all in the right place—if you know what I mean." Maxwell glanced at Samantha for a moment, and then the young officer added, "Uh, pardon my comments, ma'am." Samantha shook her head, and gestured for him to continue. "Long blonde hair, at least shoulder length. Skin-tight dress. Red, I think. But, her face . . ."

The officer paused, reluctant to continue. "What about her face?" inquired Samantha.

"It would have been the most beautiful face I'd ever seen, but her eyes . . . her eyes were glowing bright red, like fire. And, when she hissed at us, her teeth were . . . were like two rows of sharp spikes. That's the best way I can describe them. It was like staring at some kind of wild beast."

The detective said, "Could've been a mask, like you said."

"If it was, it was a damn good one," came Maxwell's reply.

"You and your partner didn't give chase?" asked Samantha.

Officer Maxwell shook his head. "By the time we had gotten out of the car, she had disappeared."

Samantha glanced at Gellar. "So, why call me? Sounds more like you need Animal Control."

"Come and see," said the Lieutenant Gellar as he led her further into the hospital.

———————————

Pulling the curtain aside, Samantha stepped forward into the small examination area in the hospital's Emergency Room. Before her was an occupied hospital bed, covered with a white sheet. Hanging from a post at the head of the bed were three IV bags, each connected to clear tubing that led down to the arm of the occupant of the bed. A nurse holding a clipboard was making notes while watching the heart rate monitor hanging from the far wall. Samantha gazed in amazement upon the unconscious figure lying in the bed. She estimated that the man was in his early thirties. The black hair on his head was disheveled, and his eyes closed. The flesh on his face had an indescribable dark tinge to it, and appeared taut around the eye sockets and cheekbones. His arms, which she suspected would have normally been muscular, were thin and bony. She was certain that, at one time, he would have been a good looking young man, but now she found it difficult to even look upon his face without a sense of repulsion. It was one thing to see a corpse in that condition, but there was something horrifying about watching a living being in this state. Samantha watched with pity as the sheet across his chest rose and fell with each shallow breath.

Lieutenant Gellar, who stood behind her, said, "I've seen some of the reports about this latest case. Take a look at his neck. Then you'll understand why I called you in."

Samantha knew what she would find before she even looked. These marks, however, looked different than those that she had previous observed. Although the pinpricks still formed the shape of a human hand on either side of the victim's neck, the pinpricks themselves seemed larger and fresher than those on the corpses of the previous victims. The flesh surrounding each hole was slightly raised as if still recovering from some invasive intrusion. Samantha gazed again at the victim's face, feeling a mix of pity and helplessness. Helplessness because there was nothing she could do to stop this insanity from striking again. Pity because this latest victim had survived, and there was no telling what the impact would be on the rest of his life.

"Have we identified him yet?" she inquired.

"Yes. Sean DeMarco," replied Gellar. "He's thirty-one and lives in West Chester."

"What's his prognosis? Is he going to live?"

Samantha asked.

"That depends on whether or not he's left alone to get some rest," came the reply from behind Lieutenant Gellar.

The two police officers turned to face a tall, young-faced doctor in a striped, pale blue shirt and tan Dockers. A black stethoscope hung around his neck, and rectangular metal-framed eyeglasses rested on top of his long, thin nose.

Introducing himself, the doctor said, "Doctor Alex Bock. I understand you've a job to do, but I'd appreciate it if you'd let my patient get the rest he desperately needs."

Samantha and the Lieutenant stepped out of the examination area, pulling the curtain closed behind them. The hectic bustle of one of the city's busier ERs was all around them, with nurses moving quickly from one examination area to another. Heart-rate monitors beeped in an asynchronous rhythm, and voices from the hospital's overhead paging system occasionally interrupted the controlled chaos going on around them. Leading them through a door marked "Staff Lounge," the doctor gestured toward the coffee machine in the corner, and then took a seat at a round Formica-topped table.

"Help yourself to coffee," he said.

As Lieutenant Gellar poured himself a cup of coffee, Samantha slid down into a chair across from Doctor Bock. Glancing around the cramped room, she saw a long row of lockers, not unlike the ones she remembered from high school gym class, lining the far wall. A pale peach-colored vinyl-covered sofa, which matched the chairs around the table, sat along one wall. It looked far from comfortable, and Samantha realized the style matched those that were in the Emergency Room reception area.

Noting her gaze, Doctor Bock said, "It's a leftover from when they refurnished the front waiting area." Gesturing to the chair in which he sat, he added, "So are these charming objects of comfort."

"Only the best for the staff?" joked Samantha.

"You could say that," Bock replied. "They'll spare no expense ensuring the front facade of the building is exquisitely architected, but . . ." He paused, and then said, "Well, you didn't come to hear a young doctor whine about the spending habits of his hospital. You want to know about Mr. DeMarco."

Samantha smiled. "Could you give me an update on his condition?"

"His condition? He's lucky to be alive. That's his condition. I've seen some weird shit come into this ER, but nothing like this."

Lieutenant Gellar inquired, "What do you mean?"

"If I didn't know any better, I'd swear that Mr. DeMarco had been lost in the desert for two weeks," explained the doctor. "He's lost at least twenty percent of his bodily fluid, possibly more. That sort of thing just doesn't happen overnight. Yet, he's dressed like he was heading out for a night on the town." The baffled doctor shrugged his shoulders. "His BAC shows he's had a few drinks in the last few hours. But, based on his condition, he shouldn't have the strength to pick up a glass, let alone dress himself for a party. So I don't know what to make of Mr. DeMarco."

Samantha asked, "What's his prognosis?"

Shaking his head, the doctor replied, "It's hard to tell. He's suffering from extreme dehydration. We're trying to rehydrate with IV fluids, but we've got to be cautious. If we do it too quickly, we run the risk of causing osmotic cerebral edema." The doctor rose from his seat and crossed to the coffee machine. As he poured coffee into a Styrofoam cup, he added, "He's being transferred up to ICU shortly, but it's going to be touch and go for a while. We can't tell what damage his system sustained until we get him stabilized. In all honesty, I'm not even sure he's going to survive the day."

Half an hour later, Samantha was standing at the exterior entrance of the hospital's emergency room, sipping a lukewarm cup of coffee. She breathed in the crisp morning air as the sun slowly began to rise over Philadelphia. The fog that went with not getting enough sleep was slowly fading as she watched a new day dawn. Somewhere in the city before her was a killer, who, for the first time, had made a mistake. It would always happen eventually. Whether it was arrogance or downright stupidity, every serial killer would start to make mistakes. The question would be whether or not Samantha could use the mistake to her advantage before the killer struck again. *I don't want a repeat of the last time,* she thought. *I won't let it happen again.*

Still deep in thought, Samantha watched as a Dodge Charger pulled into the small parking lot opposite her, and slid into the only remaining spot left. She took a long sip of coffee, and then frowned at the taste. She watched as the driver of the Charger climbed from the car, and, in even strides, made his way to where she was standing.

"You're late," she said.

Peter Thornton apologized. "Sorry, couldn't be helped."

"She must have been a really good lay for you to take this long to get here," joked Samantha.

Peter smirked. "If you must know, I was in Jersey staying at my parents' place."

"Sorry to call you back. Looks like we're now on a monster hunt," said Samantha, as she tossed her cold coffee into the waste can sitting just outside of the entrance.

"Monster hunt?"

Samantha replied, "Yeah, just wait till you hear the juicy details."

The next fifteen minutes were spent with Samantha conveying the events of the past few hours. Peter, for his part, listened intently to the details without comment. When Samantha disclosed Tony Maxwell's description of the mysterious woman, Peter raised his eyebrows in surprise, but made no comment.

She finished her narrative with an overview of her conversation with the ER doctor, after which she waited silently for Peter to respond.

"So, are Maxwell and his partner whizzing in a cup as we speak?" he said after several silent moments.

"They're the first eyewitnesses we have," Samantha replied quietly.

Peter shook his head in disbelief. "You don't seriously believe them, do you?"

"No one else has gotten a good look at our murderer."

"Our murderer has glowing red eyes? And fang-like teeth? What are we talking about, vampires? You can't seriously be considering this valid eyewitness testimony!" Peter exclaimed.

"Peter, keep your voice down," Samantha said. "Look. Neither of us knows what's going on here. We've got seven known dead victims, and an eighth that's on the brink. We've got no clues and one missing suspect. What we now have are two eyewitnesses who can give us a description of our murderer." She paused to collect her thoughts, forming her next words carefully. "I don't doubt what they saw. There's probably a reasonable explanation for it. Maybe she was wearing a disguise. Maybe the streetlights reflected off her contact lenses. I don't know. What we need to do now is take their description, minus the glowing eyes and fangs, and start circulating it. Maybe someone's seen her. If this woman really is as attractive as Tony said, she's going to be hard to miss."

Peter responded, "I hope you're right."

So do I, Samantha thought. *So do I.*

Chapter Twelve

Seven thirty on Sunday evening came far faster than Jack would have liked. Like most weekends, this one had been more or less a blur. He had spent another Saturday night playing poker in the back room of the Philly Brewing Company, where he had ended up losing twenty dollars. It was a bit steep considering that they had been playing penny ante. Charlie, the owner of the bar, never allowed the game to grow to anything larger than penny ante for fear that the police would shut him down for illegal gambling. Jack wasn't sure how much of Charlie's concerns were grounded in reality considering that one of the regular players was an off-duty Philadelphia police officer.

Jack had once again slept Sunday away, and now, having risen from his slumber, was feeling bored with his life. He kept telling himself that the endless cycle of tedium would be the death of him if he didn't do something to change it. Thinking back to his college days, Jack remembered the little Mexican restaurant just off campus where he would hang out every weekend. It had a small dance floor in the back room, and a buddy from his college radio station would spin records there every Friday and Saturday night. There had never been a big crowd, but the food was good, and the drinks were cheap. And, most importantly, Emma was there, and they would dance until closing time. That was all that mattered in those days. He recalled the night he had asked Emma to marry him. Neither of them was even old enough to drink, but they were so deep in love that their age didn't seem to matter. "After college," she had replied. That had been good enough for him. But now, as the tedium threatened to encompass yet another week, he sat on the edge of his bed, lost in his memories, and staring aimlessly at the wall. Jack simply shrugged his shoulders in surrender. *It's just another week,* he thought.

The long hot shower washed the sleep from his eyes and brought him back to life. The hot water flowed down his naked body, burning at first, but then soothing not only his body but also his mind. He lingered under the showerhead longer than usual, savoring each drop of scalding water. Deciding not to shave, Jack left two days' worth of stubble on his chin, dressed, and then headed out for his usual Sunday evening dinner.

Before heading to the elevator, Jack made a quick stop at apartment 4C, giving a quick rap on the door with his knuckles, and waited. After a few minutes, he knocked a little harder. There was still no reply. Assuming that Jason was out on the town, Jack shrugged his shoulders and moved toward the elevator. As he listened to the rattle of the elevator cage rising from below, Jack felt a slight uneasiness. It was unusual for Jason to not be at home on Sunday evenings. *Must have been a damn good weekend,* thought Jack.

Walking the two blocks to Geno's Pizza on South Street, Jack hovered outside the door for a few moments. The malfunctioning sign above his head had lost two more letters, and now read "no' Pizza". His eyes drifted down South Street, watching the anonymous faces of those who ventured along the street that evening. There were millions of people living in the city of Philadelphia, and he wondered if any of them knew his name. There had been a time, while he was in Dallas, when he couldn't walk down a city street without someone recognizing him. After all, the radio station he worked for at the time had plastered the listening area with his face on a hundred billboards. Now, the only people who knew who he was were those to whom he had introduced himself. He had become just another anonymous face on the street. He glanced at the door of Geno's Pizza and decided that he wanted something different tonight. *Change is good,* he thought, *even if it is just a little one.*

Finding an open booth in a Greek restaurant called The Acropolis Bistro, Jack ordered a lamb gyro with chips and a cup of coffee. He sat quietly while waiting for his meal, feeling a mild pang of guilt over his decision to eat somewhere other than Geno's Pizza. He had been eating there every evening before work for the past nine months, and he felt as if he were now committing adultery by partaking somewhere else. The restaurant was small, with only ten round bistro-style tables, each covered with a red and white checkered tablecloth and a single lit candle in the center. Three of the tables were occupied, one with a young couple, and the other two by solitary individuals like himself. Photos of Greek landmarks such as the Delphi Theatre, the Temple of Zeus, and the bistro's namesake, the Acropolis of Athens, hung along the walls in a fruitless attempt to instill some sense of connection between the little bistro in Philadelphia and the romantic beauty of ancient Greece. Beyond a brown paneled counter was the kitchen with steam rising from the grill, and the sound of clanging pots and pans echoing out into the dining area. Hanging from the ceiling to the right of the counter was small flat screen television, which was airing another Sunday night drama that Jack didn't recognize. Working the shift that he did made it difficult to keep up with prime time television, so he had given up trying.

As he dined on his meal, Jack watched as people entered the small bistro, picked up their orders, and left. Two young men with jet-black hair and pale faces entered the bistro, both wearing black leather trench coats, and sporting multiple lip, nose, and ear piercings. They picked up their takeout order without saying more than three words to the older man behind the counter. Then an elderly man, with a receding hairline and a single bushy eyebrow that covered both eyes, entered to retrieve his takeout order. Moments later, three teenage girls wandered in, placed a takeout order, and hovered around the counter waiting for it to be prepared. *If nothing else,* Jack thought, *they have a good takeout business.*

Jack had just finished his gyro when he looked up at the television. The local ABC news had come on, and Jack was mesmerized by the caption on the screen. Unable to hear the audio, Jack could only see the news anchor with a caption that read "Attempted Murder at Nightclub". The image switched to another reporter, apparently at the location of the attempted murder. His eyes widened as Jack recognized the background behind the reporter. It was the parking garage next to Pulsar. Frustrated that he couldn't hear anything that the reporter was saying, Jack simply stared at the screen; his eyes took in every image until the newscast flashed a photo of, he assumed, the victim.

"Shit!" he muttered quietly.

Jack arrived at the studios of WPLX at eleven fifty, which was far later than normal. Scott Anderson, a local college student who worked Sunday evenings part-time, was in a state of panic when Jack walked into the studio.

"Damn it, Jack!" exclaimed Scott. "I was getting worried you weren't gonna show up."

Jack didn't like Scott Anderson. He hadn't liked him since the first night he had met Scott. There was simply something about the nineteen-year-old that rubbed Jack the wrong way. He couldn't be sure if it was his overly perfectionist attitude, or the way that Scott blew everything out of proportion. Whatever it was,

Jack simply didn't care for Scott Anderson at all. Jack knew that, as an experienced radio personality, he had a lot to offer Scott in the way of guidance, mentoring, and helpful advice. But mentoring had never been his forte. The tall college student looked emaciated and malnourished. *He's thinner than most bulimic swimsuit models,* Jack had thought when he had first met Scott. A bony face, black horn-rimmed glasses, and neatly trimmed sandy hair projected a studious and conscientious image, which Jack simply couldn't stand. Scott's overblown sense of concern over his supposed tardiness merely fanned the flames of Jack's disdain. Dropping his headphones down on the counter, Jack laughed. "Scott, I've told you before. If I'm not going to make it, I'll call you."

The nineteen-year-old grimaced. "Dude, what if you couldn't get to a phone?"

Jack frowned at the young man's words. He couldn't remember the last time he called someone "dude", but, to his dismay, the word was apparently making a comeback. "Scott, I'm here now. There's no need to panic."

"I was just gettin' worried . . . I've got a big exam tomorrow, and couldn't stay late tonight. If you hadn't shown up, I don't know what I'd have done," said an exasperated Scott, as he stepped away from the console.

Jack plugged his headphones into the console, adjusted the chair to his preferred height, and, deciding to change the subject, asked, "Any idea what happened at Pulsar this weekend? I just saw it on the news, but couldn't hear the details."

Scott ran his hand over his short hair. "Dude, you don't know? Some guy was attacked in the parking garage next to the club. They got him over at Philly General, and he's not in too good of shape. Some young couple saw the whole thing and chased away the attacker."

"Hmm," was all Jack said in reply.

Scott rested both hands on the counter and leaned forward. "It happened Friday night! Dude, it could've been you in that garage. You need to watch yourself. They've been showing the victim's picture all weekend on TV." He paused, and then, wide eyed, leaned toward Jack. "Hey, you were there Friday night! You probably saw the guy! Dude, you might be a witness and not even know it!"

Gritting his teeth, Jack had counted three "dudes" in less than a single minute. He figured one more would be enough to grate his last nerve.

Jack shook his head, and then lied. "No, I can't see anything from up in the booth."

Scott stood back up, and shrugged. "That sucks."

When Scott had left the studio, Jack leaned back in his chair, and thought long and hard about Friday night. He had instantly recognized the face of the victim when it was displayed during the newscast early in the evening. He would know that face anywhere, not because it was a remarkable face by any stretch on the imagination, but because of his dancing partner. He vividly remembered the dirty dancing couple from Friday night, and the victim's face belonged to the man dancing with the blonde woman. The question now weaving its way around in his mind was what to do with his knowledge. There was no way to know for sure that he knew anything other than what the police already did. And, really, what did he know? He knew that the victim was getting all hot and bothered on the dance floor on Friday night with a beautiful woman. He knew that they left together in what appeared to be a sexually charged hurry, with destination unknown. He could probably provide a description of the woman, but that was all he knew. Was it worth bothering the police with that minute amount of information?

The night had gone slower than he would have liked. He wasn't sure if it was an overabundance of slow love songs, or "dreaded love mush" as he often called it, or just his overwhelming boredom with his job. Either way, Jack felt like his shift had lasted decades, instead of six hours. Ron Michaels was in a foul mood when he arrived, and did nothing but complain about everything from the lousy coffee that he got earlier that morning from his local 7-11, to the smell of the studio. After some further prodding, Jack discovered that Dana had called out sick that morning, meaning that Ron had to fetch his own doughnuts.

"Jack, consider yourself lucky. You've got a shift all to yourself. You don't have to share the spotlight with anyone," Ron said. "You have no idea what it's like to work with Dana. She's not been the same since management started paying her to be on MY show. Do you know, she actually refused to go get coffee and doughnuts one day last week? Downright refused!"

Out loud, Jack merely said, "I'm sorry to hear that." Yet in his mind, he thought, *Serves you right, you fat bastard!*

"I heard there was some more trouble down at your little club this weekend," said Ron.

Standing by the door of the studio, Jack replied, "Yep. I heard that too. But, not my club, not my problem."

Before Ron could reply, Jack pulled the studio door opened and exited with his headphones in one hand and his coffee cup in the other.

Two hours later, Jack parked his motorcycle in the small parking garage attached to his apartment building. There had not been any production work waiting for him after his shift, so he left the WPLX offices earlier than usual. Breakfast was served in his usual corner booth at Monk's Cafe, where Meg, knowing Jack's connection with the club, inquired about the attempted murder at Pulsar.

"I heard some guy got jumped in the parking garage. This city's goin' straight into the shitter if one can't go clubbing without getting clubbed!" she had said.

Jack gave a half-hearted laugh, telling her to

keep her day job. The usual Monday morning crowd made their way through the small restaurant and Jack, having finished his breakfast, slipped out quietly, giving Meg a quick wave as he exited.

Everyone seemed to be talking about this attempted murder, and Jack was getting irritated by the fact that they all felt like he should know all the gory details. Just because he worked there didn't mean he kept up on the activities of all the club's patrons. If a man wanted to wander out of the club with a woman, and then let her beat him up, who was Jack to say no?

As the elevator halted on the fourth floor, Jack pulled the old grate door aside and stepped out into what he expected to be an empty hallway. His expectation was shattered when he found three uniformed police officers standing outside of the open door to apartment 4C, Jason's apartment. The officers, who had been talking amongst themselves, had become silent when the elevator doors opened. Jack slowly approached his own apartment door, aware of the fact that three sets of eyes were watching him intently. Sliding the key into the lock, Jack turned the doorknob, and pushed the door open. He felt a faint chill overcome his body as he entered his apartment and pushed the door closed. Leaning back against the wall, Jack was silent as his mind raced through the various reasons the police might be in Jason's apartment. Jack knew that his friend periodically dabbled with marijuana, and Jason had more than once bragged about the occasional bit of insider trading, but none of that ever amounted to much.

He hadn't seen Jason all weekend, and began to wonder if his friend had been in an accident. Jack couldn't help but snicker at the thought. He could remember Jason's frequent jokes about getting so drunk that he needed one of those home medical alert systems because he had "fallen and couldn't get up". But then Jack frowned at the thought that Jason may actually be hurt.

Turning the knob on the door, Jack returned to the hallway. The three police officers turned toward him as he approached. Two of the officers were wearing pale blue uniform shirts, and looked like young, fresh members of the Philadelphia Police force. The third officer, wearing a white shirt, was older with a level of policing experience that showed in his round face.

"Can I help you?" asked the older officer.

Jack glanced at the officer's nametag. "Captain Reynolds, I just wanted to check on my friend."

Putting his hand forward to block Jack's progress, the captain replied, "I'm sorry, sir. This is an active crime scene. I can't let you go any further."

Jack was shocked. "Crime scene? What the hell are you talking about? What's happened?"

Captain Reynolds frowned at Jack. "I'm not at liberty to discuss details with you."

Getting frustrated, Jack replied, "Can you at least tell Jason that I'm out here?"

"Are you acquainted with the deceased?" the captain said, only to regret his slip of the tongue moments later.

"Deceased?" exclaimed Jack.

To the surprise of not only the police officers, but also Jack himself, he charged past the three sentries, sweeping aside their flailing arms. Without thinking, he dashed through the door of apartment 4C, and stumbled past a man and a woman into the living room. He abruptly halted when he saw the corpse sitting on the vintage Chesterfield leather sofa centered along the wall. Jack could barely hear the shouting voices behind him, and he hardly felt the rough hands grabbing at his shoulders and arms. He could only focus on what was sitting before him.

The sofa had been a prized piece of furniture in Jason's apartment. Jack knew that his friend had paid several thousand for it, and it looked worth every bit. The dark brown leather had a distressed, understated look to it that made the sofa seem luxurious. Jack could find no words to describe what sat atop the supple leather cushions of the Chesterfield sofa. He might have called it a corpse, but he had always assumed that the word corpse was reserved for those that were recently deceased. This looked more like something he might find in a museum, or freshly exhumed from a grave. The skin of the body was almost as brown as that of the leather sofa, and had an uncanny similarity in texture as well. The eyes were fixed in a wild stare that Jack could only have imagined in his worst nightmares.

Long, bony fingers rested, palms up, on either side of the body. The face had sunken in around the skull, and white teeth gleamed from the parched and cracked lips. The pink polo shirt and acid washed jeans were the only things that provided Jack with proof to the identity of the corpse lounging on the sofa.

Chapter Thirteen

The Wednesday morning sun reflected brightly off the chrome handlebars of the Harley Davidson as Jack Allyn leaned into a left turn onto Walnut Street as he headed into Center City. For the first time since being at WPLX, Jack had taken a few days off, stating that he required some time to get over the shock of his friend's sudden death. Monday had quickly become a blur as he spent most of the day being questioned by the police. The man and woman who had been in Jason's apartment at the time of his entrance had been quickly identified as Philadelphia homicide detectives. Jack vividly remembered being manhandled out of Jason's apartment, and cuffed in the hallway by the three uniformed officers. Jason's death had hit Jack harder than he would have expected. He spent the first fifteen minutes shifting between sobbing, hyperventilating, and nausea, as well as vomiting twice while sitting on the floor of the hallway.

When Jack had calmed down, the trim, auburn haired detective knelt beside him and introduced herself. Her partner, the tall, dark-skinned man, stood behind her with his hands on his hips.

"I'm Detective Samantha Ballard." She had

glanced at his wallet, which one of the uniformed officers had wrestled out of Jack's back pocket. "Mr. Allyn. Jack. I know you've had a shock. Have you recovered enough to answer a few questions?"

Lifting his cuffed wrists into the air, Jack had replied, "If you'll take these bracelets off . . ."

With a gesture of her hand, Samantha Ballard had signaled for her partner to remove the handcuffs. As the detective inserted the small key into each cuff, Samantha provided an introduction.

"This is my partner, Peter Thornton. I realize seeing your friend's body in that condition was probably unexpected, and you're most likely very confused. But I'm going to need your full cooperation if we are going to discover what happened."

Jack was amazed at how soothing the detective's voice was, and how authoritative it had been as well. Her hazel eyes had met his, and for a moment, Jack felt as if he could trust this woman with anything. Unlike her co-workers in uniform, who were none too pleased to see him out of handcuffs, the detective had seemed more than willing to forget his indiscretion of barging into Jason's apartment. She was simply looking for answers, just like Jack.

As Jack accelerated along Walnut Street, the image of Jason's fossilized body flashed through his mind. It was hard to conceive that the desiccated shape sitting on the leather sofa could have been Jason Spinacker. The face, with its skin that more resembled old parchment than flesh, looked nothing like his friend. Granted, the general shape of the head seemed the same, but the sunken eye sockets and recessed cheeks gave the face a horrifying skeletal appearance, which had made it almost unrecognizable.

When thinking back on Monday, Jack could not remember how he went from being on the hallway floor to sitting on the sofa of his own apartment, but his next recollection was of Samantha Ballard sitting across from him in his living room. The detective had fixed Jack a cup of coffee and had been patiently waiting for Jack to answer her questions.

"Were you and Mr. Spinacker close?" she had asked.

"Close enough. I've only been living here a little over a year, but we were friends."

"Did you see each other often?"

"Our work schedules didn't really align," Jack had replied. "We mostly saw each other in the hall, usually when one of us was coming home and the other was heading out. Sometimes, we'd get together for a few drinks, but that was about it."

"When did you last see Mr. Spinacker?" Samantha inquired.

"Friday night. I'm the Friday night DJ at Pulsar; Jason had come over to the club that evening," Jack had explained, and then paused as the question jogged something in his memory. "He was at Pulsar, like that other guy!"

Samantha had leaned forward in her seat. "What other guy?"

Jack had looked up from his coffee, and stared at the detective. "The guy on the news—the one who was attacked in the parking garage! I saw him Friday night! My god!"

"What? What is it?" asked the detective.

Jack had replied, "Two women came into Pulsar on Friday evening. They were together, but separated once they were in the club. One latched on to that guy I saw on the news—the one that got beat up. The other hooked up with Jason."

Jack had decided to keep his description of the couple's erotic dancing to a minimum, and he simply stated that they had been "dancing quite intimately". He had explained how they had suddenly left the club, and how his friend had vanished from the club with the other woman as well. The detective seemed deeply interested in what he had to say, so much so that she had called her partner into the apartment and asked Jack to repeat his story again.

As he came to the end of his retelling, two men entered his apartment, one in a dark suit and the other in a shirt and tie. The older of the two men—short, with salt-and-pepper hair—introduced himself and his tall, muscular companion.

"Special agent Frank Wilkinson, and this is special agent Steve McCloskey. We're from the FBI."

Jack, for the third time, repeated his story to the newcomers, while struggling to come to terms with what he had seen in his friend's apartment. The FBI agents asked him for a detailed description of the two women, which he provided, and then, after a few more questions, the agents left, with the two detectives following shortly thereafter.

Jack had spent Monday evening in his apartment with a bottle of Jim Beam as his only companion. He couldn't understand why he was taking Jason's death so hard. The two men had only known each other for a little over a year. Jack had not made much effort to make friends since his arrival in Philadelphia. Most of his acquaintances were nothing more than superficial at best. But Jason had been different. The two men had found common ground that had opened up a friendship, which both felt they had been lacking. Jason could often be pompous, arrogant, and a moral reprobate. Jack sometimes found his friend's attitude toward women to be repugnant even by Jack's low standards. But there was also an honest quality about Jason that Jack found refreshing. Jason never pulled any punches with Jack, and that was what he liked about his deceased friend. As much as Jack didn't want to admit it, Jason was his only real friend, and his death was going to take some time for Jack to get over. The last thing that Jack remembered from Monday evening was staggering into the bedroom, and passing out on the end of the bed.

Tuesday hadn't been much better with Jack not rising from bed until close to one in the afternoon. He had found three messages waiting on his answering machine. Two were from co-workers at WPLX, saying that they had "heard about what happened and just wanted to make sure you were okay." He deleted those messages before they had even finished playing. The third message, however, helped snap Jack out of his melancholy.

"Jack? Hey, it's Bryan over at Den of Heroes. I might have a lead on that Detective Comics issue you're looking for. Nothing definite, but a possibility. Give me a shout, or drop by and I'll tell you all about it."

Jack decided that a trip into Center City the next day would be just what he needed. It certainly wouldn't get rid of the overwhelming depression he had been feeling since Monday morning, but it would help take his mind off of what had happened to his friend, for a while at least.

Parking his motorcycle on the sidewalk outside of the Den of Heroes, Jack suddenly felt very conspicuous, as if every eye on the street was watching him. He had a distinctive sense that everyone knew that the police had been questioning him in relation to a murder. Jack knew that he had nothing to do with Jason's death, but with his grief came an underlying guilt, and that had been playing tricks with him ever since Monday. He looked to his left and caught the eye of a tall elderly gentleman, who just happened to be passing. *Was he staring at me?* Jack thought. To his right, he saw a young woman waiting at the nearby bus stop. She glanced down quickly when he caught her eye. He shook his head, telling himself that it was all just his imagination.

Bryan Salisbury was alone in the comic book store as Jack entered. The young man was standing behind the glass display case, flipping through a Batman graphic novel. He looked up at Jack, smiled, and pushed the graphic novel aside.

"I wasn't sure if you got my message," he said.

Jack leaned forward, and rested his elbows on the top of the display case. "I got it. This was the earliest I could get over here. What's up?"

"I found a dealer up in New York who said he could get his hands on the Detective Comics issue you've been looking for," explained Bryan. "But, he's asking for ten grand, and a ten percent finder's fee."

"Seriously? That's almost twice what it's worth."

Bryan shrugged his shoulders. "I know. That's what I told him, but he won't budge."

Jack thought over his options for a moment, and then shook his head. "I'm going to pass. That's a little too rich for me right now."

"That's what I figured. You should have called me. I could've saved you a trip."

Shrugging his shoulders, Jack replied, "I needed to get out anyway. It's been a rough week."

"I'm not surprised with that attack outside the club this past weekend," said Bryan. "You remember that body they found a few weeks ago? There's been a string of those popping up all over the city. All of them just dried husks of who they once were. My police contact's been filling me in."

It was the last thing that Jack wanted to hear that morning. Bryan's words brought a flood of images back into his head. He only half-heard Bryan's words as he fought to subdue his emotions, and force the memories back into the recesses of his mind.

Bryan continued, "I'm telling you, Jack. The only thing that explains it all is a Seirene. That has to be it!"

Snapping out of his emotional haze, Jack gruffly replied, "Don't start with that shit again!"

"I'm serious, Jack! Nothing can strip a body of every drop of moisture like a Seirene. Let me show you."

Bryan reached behind the display case, pulled out a *Demons of the Myst* book, and started flipping through the pages. Jack, immediately recognizing the book, rolled his eyes.

"Bryan, they're just characters in a game. There are no such things as these . . . what did you call them?"

"Seirenes. You don't understand." Bryan paused, took a deep breath to calm himself. "You're right. This is a game, but what makes this game unique is that it's based on the true stories behind the myths. Every myth is thoroughly researched. These Seirenes are the real creatures, and if one is in Philly . . . god help us all," Bryan explained.

"But it's mythology. It's not reality."

"Some isn't true. But don't you understand? All mythology is based on some level of truth. If you believe Homer's version, Sirens were just sea nymphs that lured sailors to their deaths with bewitching beauty and song." Bryan leaned forward, staring at Jack with intensity. "That's all rubbish, of course."

"Oh, of course," Jack responded with a grand wave of his hand as if to dismiss the idea as ludicrous.

"The true Seirenes were far more terrifying. They did have the ability to lure men, but with mind control, not beauty and song," Bryan explained. "They were cannibals, living off the life force of humans, feeding on their victim through their hands. And they're very sensual. It's said that they could take a man to the heights of pleasure and then kill him in an instant."

Jack shook his head in disbelief. "Bryan . . . you're delusional. If this was all true, why did the ancient Greeks make them out to be—what did you call them—sea nymphs?"

"The truth behind the Seirenes was too terrifying. No one dared write about it. Even Leonardo Da Vinci wrote about the Seirenes in one of his notebooks. Let me see, I've got that quote here somewhere . . ." Bryan said as he flipped through the book. Finding a handwritten notepaper clipped to a page, he continued, "Ah, here it is. Da Vinci wrote, 'The siren sings so sweetly that she lulls the mariners to sleep; then she climbs upon the ships and kills the sleeping mariners.'"

"You see, even Da Vinci didn't think they were as bad as you're saying," said Jack, dismissing the storeowner's idea with another wave of his hand.

Bryan continued to vehemently defend his idea. "Jack, there were many stories in old Greece about Seirenes, and of how they would terrorize an ancient city, siphoning off the men, one by one. The people of ancient Greece lived in fear of these creatures."

"Even if I believed that these Seirenes ever existed—which I don't—what makes you think that they're here? We're a long way from ancient Greece," said Jack.

Bryan leaned forward, and began to speak softly, as if in fear that someone would overhear. "There were rumors that a Seirene arrived in Philadelphia sometime in the late eighteenth century. Supposedly, the citizens of the city put up a fierce fight against the beast. I've never had the chance to follow up on it, but I've heard that Benjamin Franklin had written about the incident in one of his diaries."

Jack let out a loud laugh. "Bryan, it makes for a good story, I'll admit that. But it's all bullshit."

Bryan's stare locked with Jack's. "Then how do you explain the mummified corpses?"

The vision of Jason's body flashed again in Jack's mind. He had to admit that he didn't have an explanation for what he had seen on Monday morning in apartment 4C. The police had been far from forthcoming with any explanation, only willing to say that they were investigating several leads. The sight of the hollow eyes and sunken cheeks on the face of his dead friend made Bryan's theory sound plausible. But, if that were true, then there must be two of those creatures in the city. After all, there had been two women at Pulsar on Friday night. *Could they have both been Seirenes?* He wondered. For just a moment, he found himself considering Bryan's theory. But, moments later, Jack's senses returned to him and he laughed again. "No. It's not possible. You almost had me going for a minute, but it's just not possible."

"But Jack . . . my source at the police department said . . ."

Interrupting, Jack inquired, "Have you told your source this theory of yours?"

Bryan hesitantly nodded his head.

"And what did your source say?" Jack asked.

Quietly, Bryan bowed his head and replied, "He didn't believe it either."

"There. You're letting your imagination run away with you."

Jack gave Bryan a quick smile, and then turned to leave the store. As he approached the door, Bryan called out from behind him.

"Jack, be careful out there. If you meet a Seirene, I doubt you'll realize it until it's too late. They say that few people can resist their beauty. Only a heart of the purest intentions can resist them."

Jack smiled. "Well, that rules me out."

Chapter Fourteen

The view from the seventeenth floor of Philadelphia General Hospital was a breathtaking panorama of Center City. Despite the height, Samantha could still hear the sound of horns honking from the traffic below. The faint sound of a distant siren attracted her gaze downward toward the emergency room below her. She watched as an ambulance turned in and disappeared under the canopy by the ER entrance. Looking across the cityscape, she could see the brass statue of William Penn standing tall above Philadelphia City Hall. The Wednesday afternoon sky was bright blue with only a few clouds, which looked like white cotton candy drifting above the city.

Samantha allowed her mind to drift along with the clouds in a vain attempt to forget the horrors of the past few weeks. She had always loved the city of Philadelphia, and couldn't imagine ever living anywhere else. But the string of deaths that she had been investigating had begun to turn that love sour. Samantha wanted nothing more than to pack up and leave town before she had to view any more mummified corpses. Between the Spinacker corpse on Monday and another found on Tuesday in a suite at the downtown

Parkview Hotel, the body count was rolling into double digits. The local city newspapers had finally abandoned their silence and began publishing scathing editorials about the atrocious way the police had handled the case. Editors climbed on their proverbial soapboxes, and, in black and white print, declared the Philadelphia Police Department to be incapable of ensuring the safety of the city's citizens. Those would be the same editors that would be praising the valiant police efforts once they caught whoever was committing these heinous crimes. Samantha sometimes felt utter contempt for the city's fair-weather press.

The FBI had brought in further resources and the FBI Behavioral Analyst had provided a profile of the perpetrator. "A woman with an extreme hatred toward men" was what he said. "A very domineering personality, and probably sexually abused as a child by a male father figure." Samantha had rolled her eyes when the FBI presented the profile. It seemed like every profile she had ever heard from the FBI had some sexual angle to it, making her wonder if the Behavioral Analysts just rehashed the same profile over and over again for every case. Samantha's resentment of the FBI's interference grew every time Special Agent Wilkinson spoke to her. His patronizing manner only served to make Samantha want to keep him in the dark if and when she had a breakthrough in the case.

She was also getting a tremendous amount of pressure from her superiors to make some progress sooner rather than later. She was well aware of the rumblings among some of her male counterparts who thought a man would have better handled the case. There had only been one other time in Samantha's career when she could remember things getting even remotely this bad—the Society Hill Serial Killer case. It had been a long investigation, which had almost ended her career. Not because of anything she had did wrong professionally, but because she had come close to the point of simply not being able to go on any longer. Even four months after the investigation had ended, the hideousness of the crimes and her own personal guilt had been so intense that there had been many nights where Samantha just wanted to eat her gun and be done with it all.

Because of the recent nightmares, sleep had become a distant companion for her, and she was feeling stretched a bit thin. She caught her reflection in the bathroom mirror that morning. The dark shadows under her eyes told the whole story. Even Peter had commented about how tired she had been looking recently. Although she was hoping that the descriptions provided by the nightclub DJ would give them some kind of lead, she wasn't going to hold her breath. The two women described could just as easily be innocent in all of this.

Samantha felt a slight chill run down her spine, and, placing her hands in the pockets of her overcoat, pulled it tight around her body. With little appetite, she had foregone eating breakfast that morning, and barely had much of a lunch. Her sustenance had been three cups of coffee and half a turkey sandwich. When Peter had urged her to eat more at lunch, she'd simply told him to piss off.

Her mind wandered away once again, and she found herself thinking of her father. She remembered the day the police commissioner came to their front door to break the news of her father's death. Samantha had just turned eighteen, and was preparing to graduate from high school in a few months. To her mother's surprise and chagrin, the death of her father had only served to solidify Samantha's decision to become a police officer. Four years in college was followed by her enrollment in the Philadelphia Police Academy, and then she entered the police force with top honors. She threw herself into her new career as a police officer with everything she had, excelling at every step, and being rewarded over and over again for her efforts. Even with all the accolades, she still had to endure an uphill battle to prove she was just as good as her male counterparts. It had been a long, hard struggle, but she knew her father must be looking down on her and proudly smiling. Over the past few weeks, that single thought had been the only thing that kept her going.

Peter Thornton approached her and placed his hand on her shoulder. Samantha, startled by his touch, jumped and spun around to face him. When she saw her partner, she softly sighed. "Sorry, I was miles away. You startled me."

Peter smiled and said, as he gestured down the hall, "The doctor says we can have five minutes with him."

"Only five? Did you tell him this is an ongoing murder investigation?"

Shrugging his shoulders, Peter replied, "He didn't want to let us in at all. The doctor said he's far from stable and he's concerned that any disturbance could be detrimental."

"Fine. If five minutes is all we got, then we better not waste it. Let's go," she replied, as she moved forward down the hall.

The walls of the hospital room had been covered with sterile beige wallpaper with a faint interlaced vine pattern. A plastic mauve-colored handrail lined the walls at waist height. The constant beep of a heart monitor could be heard as they entered the room. Ivory white curtains divided the room in half, providing a meager level of privacy between the two beds. To Samantha's relief, only one of the beds in the room was occupied. Pulling the curtain back from around the far bed, Samantha gazed upon the huddled mass propped up by three pillows amidst the sheets. Sean DeMarco's face, although now puffier than she remembered, still had a distinctive parchment look to it. The color had returned to his lips, and his hands seemed a little less skeletal than they had in the Emergency Room. But his cheeks and eye sockets still seemed sunken compared to the photo Samantha had seen of the young man before his attack. Clear liquid flowed freely into Sean's right arm through a narrow plastic tube connected to an IV bag hanging from a hook at the head of the bed.

When the two detectives entered the room, Sean DeMarco appeared to be asleep. But, as they approached his bed, his eyelids fluttered slightly, and he turned his head in their direction. His lips parted only slightly, and a faint whisper drifted out, forcing Samantha to lean forward to understand what the young man was saying.

"I'm sorry if I look asleep. I can't open my eyes much more than this."

"Just relax, Mr. DeMarco. We won't keep you long," said Samantha.

"Please, call me Sean."

Samantha smiled, introduced Peter and herself, and then explained, "We're investigating your attack as part of a larger series of attacks throughout the city. We're hoping that you can provide us with some detail about what happened."

Trying to raise his head slightly from the pillow, Sean whispered in reply, "I'll try. Things are still a bit sketchy."

Peter said reassuringly, "Whatever you can provide will be a great help."

Sean's eyelids stopped fluttering, and the only motion from him for a minute was his chest rising and falling with each deep breath, as if garnering strength for a pending ordeal. His head turned toward them, and once again his eyelids began to flutter.

"I went clubbing Friday night. It's not something I do very often, and it was a last minute decision," he whispered. "I got to Pulsar around eight thirtyish. Had a few drinks. I was having a pretty good time." He paused for a moment, and took a few deep breaths. "I don't really remember what time it was, but this woman came up to me. She was . . . she was . . . so sexy. So unbelievably sexy. And, ah, she started dancing with me. I mean, she was way out of my league."

Samantha inquired, "Can you describe her?"

Taking a deep breath, Sean replied, "She was blonde. Not a fake blonde. You could tell it was real. Perfect complexion. Maybe five foot four. Said her name was Kallista. Had a funny accent."

"What happened after she started dancing with you?" asked Peter.

Sean's eyelids ceased all movement for a minute, and Samantha noticed that his breathing was becoming shallow. The two detectives patiently waited a few minutes, until suddenly Sean's head turned toward them again.

"Wha . . . what did you ask?"

Peter repeated the question, and Sean's lips parted for another whisper. "I'm ashamed to say . . . I kinda lost control. We . . . danced . . . dirty. Her hands were all over me, and . . . she rubbed her body against mine. It was . . . so erotic. And the more she did it, the more I wanted it. I couldn't control . . . myself."

Samantha noticed his chest rising and falling faster than before; his words faltered, punctuated by his labored breathing. She leaned forward and said, "Do you need to take a break?"

Sean replied quietly, "Just a sec . . . gimme just a

second."

Samantha and Peter waited patiently as Sean DeMarco allowed his head to sink back into the pillows. He seemed to drift off to sleep, and, after a few minutes, Samantha thought they should leave. But, after a long, deep breath, Sean's eyelids fluttered again, and he said, "Ok. Where was I?"

Peter replied, "You said her dancing was erotic."

"It was . . . like getting a lap dance. But I was allowed to participate. She kissed me. Touched me. I kept wondering when we would get kicked out . . . It must have looked obscene. After an hour, all I wanted was to find some private spot where we could screw. She seemed to really want it . . . and I know I wanted it bad. But we just kept on dancing." Sean turned his eyes toward Samantha and added, "I'm sorry. I shouldn't talk like this is front of a lady."

Samantha answered his comment with a smile. "Don't worry. I hear things far worse than this all the time."

"After another hour, I couldn't take it anymore. I had to have her. But, she seemed . . . to know my thoughts. She leaned in . . . asked if I wanted to go find someplace a little more private. I don't know what came over me, but I grabbed her hand . . . and we rushed out of the club," whispered Sean.

"What happened then?" asked Peter.

"Everything's a blur after that. I remember . . . the stairs of the parking garage . . . she kept stopping every so many steps to kiss and grope me. A couple times, I thought we were going to have sex right there in the stairwell . . . up against the wall. I wouldn't have said no if she wanted to." He paused and his head sank back into the pillows again. Then he said, "I was parked on the third level. We half walked and half stumbled toward my BMW. But then . . ." Sean DeMarco paused again. "I was against the wall . . . I remember agonizing pain in my neck . . . a terrible burning . . . searing . . . There was a loud scream . . . a scream . . ."

Samantha leaned forward and touched Sean's hand. "Just rest. We'll come back when you feel better."

The two detectives turned to leave the room. Peter had just pulled open the door when Sean said, "Detective . . ."

Samantha returned to the bedside, and leaned forward. "What is it, Sean?"

"I remember . . . her eyes . . . I remember her eyes."

Samantha quietly inquired, "What about her eyes?"

Sean replied, "They were glowing . . . glowing red . . . like fire."

Standing by the window again, Samantha gazed silently out over the cityscape. Peter stood beside her, patiently waiting for her to say something. The silence between them continued for five minutes until Samantha turned around, and leaned back against the glass.

"It's the same description we got from Maxwell.

Glowing red eyes," she said.

"No need for a drug test, then," joked Peter.

Samantha cracked a brief smile. "What did the doctor say about DeMarco's status?"

"He said it was too early to tell how much tissue and organ damage was caused by the attack. He's not even sure if DeMarco will live to see the end of the week."

"Did you see that editorial in the Post-Gazette this morning?" she asked, referring to one of Philadelphia's daily newspapers.

"The one that called the commissioner a baboon who couldn't find his ass in a wet paper bag?"

Laughing, Samantha replied, "No, I missed that one. I meant the one demanding we let the, quote, professional law enforcement from the FBI, end quote, take over the case."

Peter replied, "Ouch. That hurts."

"The Captain called me into his office this morning. He said he's going to have to do just that if we don't start getting somewhere. Wilkinson's been pushing hard to take over the investigation. The Captain says he'll stall as long as he can, but we need to get our asses in gear."

"At least now we've got corroborating witness descriptions of the woman," said Peter.

"Or women. Don't forget the Spinacker murder. We may be dealing with more than one killer."

Peter gazed out the window, and asked, "Do you think that's likely?"

Turning to follow his gaze, Samantha said, "About as likely as the commissioner finding his ass in a wet paper bag." Peter couldn't stop himself from laughing out loud. Samantha continued, "In all seriousness, there might be two of them working together. I never considered that until this week, but it's a possibility. I'd bet Spinacker died the same night that DeMarco was attacked. And, if that's the case, we've got a good description of our two killers; one's a blonde, and the other's a redhead."

"They seem to be targeting men," said Peter.

"Not necessarily. Don't forget Hardwick's family," Samantha reminded him. "We should get an APB out on them. We've got those forensic sketches from the DJ, along with the grainy CCTV footage, so we at least have a vague idea of what they look like. Plus, let's get someone to scan the city public records to see if they can find anything. There can't be that many people named Kallista in Philadelphia. Maybe one of them will match our description. If she's a resident of the city, there's bound to be a record somewhere." Then she paused, gazing out across the city once again. "Do you know what I hate most about this case?"

Peter replied, "No, what?"

She replied, "Every damn thing."

Chapter Fifteen

Jack Allyn stood in his bedroom window and watched as people on South Street four floors below passed by his apartment building. The Thursday evening sun was setting over the city, bringing a light mist with the darkness. He could see the pavement of the road below glisten from the faint coating of moisture accumulating on its surface. Having been away from WPLX all week long had not helped Jack to deal with the grief and horror of his friend's death. If anything, the solitude had provided nothing more than ample time to think about his tragic loss, as well as ponder the terrifying condition of Jason's corpse. With images of Jason's shriveled face appearing in his mind every time Jack closed his eyes, sleep had been difficult all week. Other than his trip to the Den of Heroes on Wednesday, Jack had not ventured much from the confines of his apartment.

As he stood before the window, he felt an overwhelming need to get out. The walls of his apartment seemed to be closing in on him, and, although he had never been before, Jack was beginning to feel crushingly claustrophobic. The clock on his bedside table told him it was closing in on seven in the evening, and a hunger pain in his abdomen reminded him that he hadn't eaten since breakfast. Jack decided he should go out and find a nice place to have dinner, perhaps some place where he had never been before.

As he pulled on a pair of jeans and searched for a shirt to wear, Jack's mind cast back through the events of the past week, from the gruesome discovery on Monday morning to the police's return to Jason's apartment earlier that afternoon. He remembered hearing the door of the elevator slide open around two, and watched through the peephole in his door as the two detectives from earlier that week passed his doorway. It had been at least an hour and a half before Jack had heard the elevator again, signaling their departure. He had been tempted to go over and ask about their progress on the case. He wanted to know what had happened to his friend. But Jack couldn't bring himself to enter Jason's apartment again.

Out on the street, Jack walked slowly along the sidewalk, barely noticing the people who were around him. The falling mist covered the sleeves of the fleece pullover he had decided to wear to combat the evening chill. Although his strides were steady and straight, Jack had no particular direction in which he was headed. He walked a few blocks down South Street, and then turned left onto S. Fifth Street. Even though he had lived in the area for over a year, Jack had never really ventured far from South Street. It had been his way of saying that his stay in Philadelphia would be very brief, perhaps only a few months. Although a few months had become more than a year, his mind and soul had continued to rebel against the idea of further exploration of his city of residence for fear that it would represent surrendering to his fate.

A few blocks up, he stopped at the corner of S. Fifth Street and Pine Street and glanced around the intersection. An elderly man held an umbrella over himself and his elderly wife at the bus stop near the corner. Jack wondered whom he would hold an umbrella over when he reached that age. Or would he be standing alone at the bus stop, allowing the rain to pour over him? What he needed was a shoulder to cry on. What he wanted was her shoulder to cry on. But she was a long way from Philadelphia, and far too much time had passed. He suddenly felt alone, very much alone.

Crossing the street, Jack continued his aimless stroll along S. Fifth Street. As he walked, he kept his eyes down, watching the toes of his shoes kick up drops of water and scatter them out in front of him with each step. As he crossed over Spruce Street, Jack raised his head momentarily and caught a glimpse of a silhouette stepping out from a narrow alleyway ahead of him. The dark shape paused for a moment to stare into the cloudy sky above, and then turned toward Jack, walking with a determined step along the sidewalk. As the silhouette drew closer, its features became clearer in the dim illumination of the streetlights. Skintight jeans covered her long curvy legs, while a close-fitting sweater stretched over perky breasts. The perfectly curved figure strode forward with confidence and purpose. Jack remained still as she approached in a self-possessed manner that made him wonder if she even knew he was standing along her path. She brushed gently against his right shoulder without even a glance in his direction. But as she passed by him along the sidewalk, her face was momentarily captured in the glare of a nearby street light. The glimpse of her face that Jack received lasted only a fraction of a second, but it was all he needed. Even though he first beheld her face from a distance, hers was one that he could never forget. And even if he had held any doubt, her fiery medium-length red hair was unmistakable.

She continued to walk on, paying no attention to the man who gaped at her departing back. Jack's mind raced in confusion, unable to decide what he should do. Should he chase her? Should he call the police? Weighing his options, Jack decided that calling the detective investigating Jason's death would be his safest bet. His hand slipped into his pocket, and he extracted his cell phone. But he slid the phone back in as he remembered that he had left Detective Ballard's business card in his apartment. She had given it to him, emphasizing that he should call her if he remembered anything else that might help their investigation. He cursed under his breath and then, with a deep sigh, moved forward down the darkened street in the woman's wake.

Jack could just make out her silhouette about

half a block ahead of him. She didn't appear to be rushing, and there was no indication that she was aware of him following behind. Prudence called for a stealthy pursuit, and Jack considered abiding by prudence's request. All he would need to do was to stay back in the shadows, and allow her to guide him to her residence. Then, he could return to his apartment, and call the detective. *It's a piece of cake.*

He took each step slow and easy, to ensure that he was not making an overabundance of noise. The woman walked steadily forward passing Cypress Street, a small side street on the right. With a sudden movement, she stepped out into the street and briskly crossed to the other side. Watching the woman resume her trajectory down S. Fifth Street, Jack stepped into the road to follow.

With his attention focused on her, Jack's only warning of the car's approach was the horn and sound of screeching tires. The Honda Accord's bumper stopped inches from his legs, and Jack found himself staring into the face of the irate young driver, who cursed at him through the windshield.

Ignoring the driver, Jack glanced over his shoulder in the direction of his quarry. The one thing that he didn't want to have happen did. The woman had stopped, and glared at him over the top of a parked car. From her expression, Jack could tell that she now knew he was following her.

Turning toward her, he shouted, "I want to talk to you!"

Her mouth formed an evil grin, and she darted off down the street. Jack sped across to the sidewalk and bolted after her. Although slim and fit, Jack was by no means an athlete, and it wasn't long before his breathing was labored as he tried to keep up. The redhead whipped around the corner onto Delancey Street, and Jack charged ahead to match her move. He turned the corner in time to see her disappear around another corner onto S. Reese Street. Despite the pounding in his chest and the searing pain in his lungs, Jack raced toward the corner, hoping to not lose her. Rounding the next corner, Jack marveled at the distance that his quarry had put between them. *She's got the speed of an Olympic runner,* he thought, as he watched her sprint to the left around the corner of S. Reese Street and Spruce Street. As he followed her onto Spruce Street, the muscles in his legs were on fire. He gasped in desperation for every breath as his feet pounded on the concrete of the sidewalk. Yet he pushed himself forward, knowing that he couldn't lose her.

The mist was beginning to turn to rain as he charged after the woman. Jack could feel the water seeping into his shoes as he splashed through puddles along the sidewalk. He heard someone shout, "Stop!" and then realized it was him. But she ignored his calls and continued to flee. A quick right onto Panama Street, where Jack briefly lost sight of her as she rounded the corner, had followed a left turn onto S. Sixth Street. His head felt as if it was about to burst, and, despite the increasing rain, the sweat from his forehead was burning his eyes.

Turning onto Panama Street, Jack found himself in what was not much more than a narrow alley. To his right was a tall brick building surrounded by wrought iron fencing, and on his left was a long line of residential garages for the townhomes on the opposite road. There were few streetlights burning along the alleyway, and Jack hesitated for a moment. He struggled to see through the darkness, hoping to catch sight of the woman. There was no sign of her and, to Jack's dismay, no sound of running footsteps either. He fought to slow his breathing down as he walked down Panama Street. Standing in the middle of the darkened street, he leaned forward and placed his hands on his knees, trying to catch his breath.

His clothing was soaked with the rain, which had begun to pour down from the sky. The searing pain in his lungs began to subside with each breath, while the rhythmic pounding of his heart was beginning to slow. He cursed aloud, and then he cursed again. He had let her get away, the only link to what had happened to Jason. She had been within inches of Jack, and he had let her get away. He straightened up, and gazed down Panama Street.

When the blow came, he was caught defenseless and buckled at the waist in pain. It was a hard blow that drove all the air from his lungs. He only had time to look up for a moment before the fist slammed into his jaw, sending Jack crashing to the wet pavement. Footsteps moved around him and then, suddenly, two powerful hands grabbed his throat. With his body being lifted in the air, Jack struggled to breathe through his constricted windpipe. His eyes burned from his sweat, hindering his ability to keep them open for more than a second at a time. His body swung through the air—his feet unable to feel the ground below him. The rapid motion suddenly stopped as his back came in contact with the hard brick wall surrounding one of the garages along the street. A spine-jolting pain shot through his body on impact, and Jack feared he would lose consciousness.

With his vision still blurry, he could only feel the hot breath on his face as his assailant came close. One of the hands around his throat slipped off, but the other still had a firm enough grip to hold him suspended in the air against the cold brick.

"Did you want to play, Jack?" said a deep, husky female voice. "Like your friend Jason?"

Jack's lips formed a question, but all that came out was a raspy sound, a pale resemblance of his voice.

"How do I know who you are? Oh, your friend's mind was so open to me when I was feeding," his assailant said. "It's amazing the things I can learn while slowly sapping the life from someone. It's the only time that I can truly see someone's deepest thoughts and memories. It can be so invigorating. But you didn't answer my question, Jack. Do you want to play?"

Jack could feel his assailant's free hand creeping down his body toward his crotch. Despite all of the pain and fear, Jack couldn't help but feel aroused as the roaming hand began to softly cup his groin.

She said softly, "Do you like that?"

Jack couldn't reply. He could barely move as he teetered on the edge of consciousness. His lungs were searing in pain as he struggled for a gasp full of air.

"What about this?" she asked, and then, with a quick motion, squeezed his groin in the tight viselike grip of her hand.

Pain shot through Jack's abdomen, and he felt as if he would vomit. He wanted to scream, but no sound could make it out of his mouth. The iron grip on his groin was released, and the pain subsided only slightly.

Despite the stinging in his eyes, Jack forced his eyelids open to gaze at his attacker. Between his blurred vision and the darkness of the night, it was difficult for Jack to be sure of what he saw.

The face, although beautiful, had left a terrifying impression of evil on Jack. It had perfect skin, and immaculate skin tone, not a freckle or a blemish of any kind. It was a flawlessness that not even the most brilliant artist could ever capture. Her forehead was impeccably smooth, and untarnished by wrinkles. But poised between the perfection that was her nose and forehead were two bright points of light, red as fire, staring back at him. Below the nose were red lips that were so pure in color that they could have been made of true rubies. Between her lips, where Jack expected to see a set of perfect teeth, were two rows of brilliantly white and shockingly sharp, dagger-like teeth.

Between gasps of air, Jack managed to ask,

"What are you?"

She leaned closer to Jack, with her face now inches from his. He felt her hot breath on his face, and saw the saliva glisten on her teeth. The foulness of her breath caused Jack to shudder, and he was certain he would have gagged if it hadn't been for the vise-like grip constricting his throat. She smiled a smile that would have given even the strongest of hearts nightmares.

In her deep husky voice, she replied to his inquiry, "My name's Adonia. It means 'beautiful lady', can't you tell?" She pressed her face even closer to his and taunted, "I'm your deepest desire and your worst nightmare all rolled into one. Did you think you could catch me? Did you think you could stop me? You're such a stupid, puny little man. Did you really think I wouldn't notice you following me? If I was not already satiated on the nectar of man, I might be tempted to devour you."

The hand around his throat suddenly released its grip, and Jack fell to the ground. His feet impacted first, but his legs were too weak to take the sudden load. Giving way beneath him, Jack's legs buckled and he collapsed upon the wet pavement in a huddled mass. He gasped for air, which now flowed freely down his windpipe and into his lungs. He couldn't remember how long he laid there, but when he opened his eyes, he found that he was alone.

The rain was falling steadily down upon him, and his clothing was completely soaked as he struggled to his feet. As he stood up a wave of nausea rushed through him, and he fell to his knees to vomit. His abdomen ached, his throat was raw and sore, and his head was throbbing. He rose again to his feet to find that the nausea had subsided.

Thirty minutes later, Jack stood in the entrance to the narrow alleyway from where his attacker had first exited. The alley had only been a few blocks from where Jack had been attacked, but, still feeling disorientated, it took Jack a while to get his bearings. The dead end alley was dark, but Jack could just make out the figure lying at the opposite end. He slowly stepped forward into the darkness, taking each step with caution. Midway down the alley, he stopped and gazed at the unmoving mass. The pouring rain seemed to bead up and roll off the leathery face. Even with the rain, the face and exposed hands appeared as dry as barren desert.

Jack stepped backward out of the alley, and walked a few paces over to a nearby streetlight. He leaned against it as a car passed by, splashing water up onto the sidewalk near him. Slipping his hand into his pocket, he pulled out his cell phone. He quickly found the number for Philadelphia Police Headquarters and dialed. When someone answered, he said, "I need to get a message to Detective Samantha Ballard. It's an emergency."

Chapter Sixteen

The hot cup of coffee brought mild relief to Jack's otherwise aching body. He sat on the back step of the ambulance and took a long sip from the steaming Styrofoam cup. Flashing red and blue lights from several police cars illuminated the entrance to the alley where Jack had made his gruesome discovery. The paramedic, who had been attempting to treat Jack's injuries, had stormed off in frustration at Jack's repeated refusals. The street, which had been quiet and vacant thirty minutes ago, was now a bustle of activity. Uniformed police officers were busy cordoning off the area with yellow police tape, while Detective Ballard, who had just arrived, was standing at the entrance of the alley surveying the scene. Within moments, the FBI agent Jack remembered only as Wilkinson joined her. He was still dressed in a dark suit, and carried no umbrella, leaving Jack to wonder if the agent's suit was dry clean only. He smirked momentarily at the thought as he watched the duo standing at the alleyway entrance. They spoke for a brief moment, then took a few steps forward, and Jack watched them disappear from view into the alleyway.

He took another long sip from his coffee cup

and felt the warmth radiate throughout his body, taking the edge off the chill he had from the continuing rain. He touched his throat with his hand, and felt a mild twinge of pain. The paramedic had stated that Jack had some bad bruising over most of his neck. His abdomen and cheek were still tender from the attack, and he decided to not tell the paramedic about the aching in his testicles, figuring it would be less embarrassing for all. Running through the details of the attack in his head, Jack wasn't sure if he could honestly tell what actually happened and what may have been a hallucination as a result of the attack. He couldn't deny the fact that most of his body had been bruised and battered, but Jack questioned his memories of his attacker. The strength of the grip that held him against the brick wall had been far greater than he could possibly attribute to the redheaded woman he had been chasing. It wasn't that he didn't think a woman could muster up such strength; she, judging by her size, simply didn't seem to have the body type that could lift a full-grown man several inches off the ground. A fact that he could not dispute was that his attacker must have had enough strength to hold him up with one hand. The ache in his testicles could testify to that.

What was truly up for debate, in Jack's mind, were his memories of the attacker's face. The blazing red eyes and dagger-like teeth seemed to be outside the realm of possibility, making Jack question whether he had even seen them at all. But, when he thought about it, seeing his friend's corpse in a state of utter mummification had also been out of the realm of possibility until earlier that week. He wondered if a lack of oxygen could have caused him to hallucinate. Jack was certain that he had been very close to passing out. Maybe he had passed the threshold of reasonable thought at the time and simply imagined things, he thought.

A familiar voice jogged his mind back to the present. "Mr. Allyn. We meet again." Samantha Ballard was standing before him with her hands in the pockets of a long, grey raincoat. The rain had matted down her auburn hair, and a pair of blue denim jeans and white tennis shoes peeked out from underneath the raincoat. "I hear you're refusing treatment," she added.

Jack nodded.

"Why don't you let me drive you home? You can tell me what happened," Samantha suggested.

As Jack slowly stood up, he looked around and said, "Don't you usually have a sidekick? I thought detectives always traveled in pairs."

"Funny. So you're a comedian as well as a club DJ? Do you have any other hidden talents that I need to know about or should I just put you down as being a jackass?" Samantha responded.

Jack laughed. "Wow. I didn't think cops could talk to people like that."

She returned his smile. "When a person has as many connections to dead bodies as you do, I can talk to you any way I like."

Jack gestured back toward the alley. "What

about your FBI buddy?"

Samantha glanced over her shoulder for a moment. "Him? He's a prick."

Taking a sip from his coffee cup, Jack followed the detective down the street to a white Mini Cooper parked half a block away. A small teardrop emergency light rested on the roof of the small car, and flashed red in rapid succession. As Samantha opened the driver's side door, she grabbed the light from the car roof, and tossed it into the back seat. It landed awkwardly on the leather seat, and the rotating light illuminated the interior of the car in pale red hues every few seconds. Sliding into the driver's seat, Samantha yanked the plug, which was attached to a small wire leading into the back seat, extinguishing the rotating red light. She dropped the plug into the cup holder between the two front seats. Jack, who had slid into the passenger seat, pulled his door closed and stared forward at the mouth of the alleyway up the street. For a moment, his mind flashed back to earlier that evening when he gazed down upon his attacker. The blazing red eyes flared up in his mind, causing him to shudder at the memory.

Samantha found a parking spot two blocks from Jack's apartment building, and the pair walked to the entrance of the building. The ride to Jack's South Street residence had been a short one, and they had not had time to talk much about that evening's events. They rode the elevator up to the fourth floor in silence, and

Jack ushered the detective into his apartment with a brief gesture of his hand.

"Can I get you something to drink? I've got coffee, or if you want something stronger, I've got beer, whiskey, and wine," said Jack, as he took Samantha's soaked raincoat from her to hang on the wrought iron coatrack by the front door.

Samantha toyed with the idea of a glass of wine in her mind. She was wet and cold, and felt that a nice glass of wine would be comforting. But she opted for coffee. Jack's living room was sparsely furnished with a microfiber sofa, which sat across the room from a fifty-inch flat screen television hanging from the wall. Between the sofa and a leather Lazy Boy recliner was a black enamel end table, on which sat several copies of Rolling Stone magazine. As Jack disappeared into the kitchen to fix the coffee, Samantha glanced around the room at the framed artwork that adorned the walls. Among the cheap prints that could have been bought at the local Wal-Mart, Samantha found a framed page from a magazine hanging from the wall. A small silver plaque attached to the bottom end of the frame read: "Friday Morning Quarterback, July 2011". The headline of the article caught her eye, "Jack Allyn Tops Dallas Airwaves". Accompanying the headline was a small photograph of the man who at that moment was making her coffee.

As he returned from the kitchen carrying two steaming mugs of coffee, Samantha turned and gestured to the framed article. "You lived in Dallas?"

Handing her one of the mugs, Jack replied, "Yeah. I did afternoon drive there for a few years."

Puzzled, she asked, "You left Dallas to come work at Pulsar?"

Jack shook his head. "No. I work the overnight shift at WPLX."

Samantha took a long sip of coffee from her mug, and then sat down on the sofa. Jack remained standing across the room from her.

"Hmm. Mr. Allyn, you didn't mention that the other day when we were questioning you."

Jack replied, "I didn't say anything because it didn't seem relevant. And, please, call me Jack."

"Everything's relevant in a murder investigation . . . Jack." She put the emphasis on his name.

He nodded in response, and sipped from his coffee mug. "I'll remember that for next time."

Samantha leaned back in the sofa, holding her coffee mug in her lap with both hands. "Tell me what happened tonight."

"I was out for a walk. Not really going anywhere in particular," Jack explained. "I saw this woman step out of that alley. It was the redhead that Jason picked up at the club. I'd swear to it." He shrugged his shoulders. "What could I do? I couldn't just grab her and drag her to the police station. I decided to follow her. Figured if I found out where she lived, I could tell you, and then you and your partner can do what you do best."

Samantha inquired, "Did she spot you?"

Jack nodded. "Yeah. She ran, and I chased. I could barely keep up with her. I got as far as Panama Street. Thought I'd lost her."

"Is that where you were attacked?"

"I was trying to catch my breath when someone belted me in stomach. Before I knew what happened, someone had me by the throat against a brick wall." Jack's hand instinctively touched his still tender neck. "She called herself Adonia and asked me if I wanted to play like Jason." He paused, reflecting on his memories of the attack. "Then she said something really odd."

Samantha asked, "What?"

Jack was silent for a moment and then replied, "She said she would devour me if she hadn't already had the nectar of a man."

"Nectar?"

Jack nodded, and then paused, unsure whether to say anything more. Then he added hesitantly, "This may sound crazy, and I'm not sure I even believe it myself. But I should probably mention it. I have a friend . . . he seems to think these killings are all the work of—it's so ridiculous, I can barely bring myself to tell you—he's convinced this is all the work of a creature from Greek Mythology called a Seirene."

"A what?" asked Samantha, incredulous.

Jack proceeded to detail for Samantha the theory that had been laid out to him by Bryan Salisbury the week before. As the words flowed from his lips, the theory sounded even more ludicrous now than when he had first heard it. The idea that mythological creatures were running amok in the streets of Philadelphia sounded more like the plot of a bad Hollywood horror film. When he had finished, he stood silently as Samantha took it all in. At one time, she had considered Jack Allyn to be a credible witness, but that belief was beginning to crumble after hearing what he had just said.

"That's just not possible, not in any sense of the word," she replied after a long delay. "Just a word of advice, when the FBI talk to you—and they WILL talk to you—I'd leave the whole monster thing out. It'd be better for all involved."

Jack shrugged his shoulders. "Like I said, I barely believe it myself. I'd never have given it any credence if it wasn't for something I saw tonight."

"What was that?" queried Samantha.

"Eyes, burning with fire, and a row of sharp, spike-like teeth."

Music pumped loudly, and the swirling and blinking lights bathed the dancing crowds in a rainbow of colors on Pulsar's dance floor. Jack stood in the booth above the throng, and observed the moving, sweaty bodies as they swayed and jerked to the rhythm of the music. Although trying not to, he couldn't help but occasionally glance toward the bar where he had last seen Jason Spinacker alive. There was a part of him that hoped it had been nothing more than a dream, and he'd find Jason seated at the bar flirting with a woman. But the faces that he'd glimpse around the bar were those of strangers.

When he had arrived at Pulsar that evening, everyone he encountered commented on his bruised neck and the small scrapes on his face. He didn't tell them about the large contusion on his abdomen. He had explained away his injuries as being from an accident with his motorcycle, but doubted that anyone believed him. He just shrugged off their comments and concerns, stating that it was "no big deal". By the time Samantha Ballard had left his apartment, it had been closing in on four in the morning. Jack had tried to grab a few hours of sleep, but had tossed and turned until finally giving up around six. Now, after nine in the evening, it was coffee and Red Bull that were keeping him on his feet.

His discussion with the detective resurfaced in his mind and caused him to wonder if she had now written him off as nothing more than a nut job. He couldn't blame her if she had. Jack wondered if he should have kept quiet about Bryan's mythological creatures theory and just told her he was mugged. He wasn't sure which was more embarrassing: stating that he believed some fairy story about monsters, or that a woman beat him up.

He smiled briefly as his thoughts drifted to Samantha's prediction, and how it had come true earlier that day. Around ten thirty that morning, a loud knock at his door announced the arrival of special agent Wilkinson and his partner. The conversation had been civil, and focused on the events leading up to Jack's discovery in the alley. Providing the FBI with an abbreviated version of his chase through the city streets, Jack made sure to withhold the more unsavory details. The agents had remained tight-lipped, only acknowledging the fact that they were seeking a woman in connection with the crimes.

But as the conversation continued, he felt very much like a man in a spotlight as Wilkinson asked about his relationship with Jason Spinacker, and his job at Pulsar. The questioning became increasingly uncomfortable as the two FBI agents asked about his relationships with the opposite sex, inquiring specifically about any recent break-ups. Not having dated much since moving to Philadelphia, Jack had little information to offer, a fact that the two agents seemed to find dubious. They had aggressively returned to the subject numerous times, pressing Jack again and again for answers.

Jack's discomfort turned to distress when Wilkinson began to imply that, with everything at Pulsar controlled by computer, it would be "easy for someone to slip away unnoticed for a short period of time". References had been made about Jack's vantage point over the Pulsar dance floor and how beneficial it might be for selecting victims. Their innuendos were subtle but clear. And although there had been no direct accusation made, when the agents had left his apartment, Jack was certain he was on their suspect list, maybe not as a killer, but definitely an accomplice.

Scanning the faces below on the dance floor, Jack wondered if Adonia might return to the club. Contemplating the possibility that Adonia was involved in the other killings, Jack considered the fact that she might be using Pulsar as a sort of hunting ground. Mulling this over for a moment, he realized the lunacy of his thinking. Jack reminded himself that it was none of his concern, and it was better to leave this sort of thing to the police. A faint ache in his abdomen reminded him of how ill-equipped he was for detective work.

Shortly after ten, Jack gazed once again out across the sea of faces, involuntarily examining each one in hopes of finding even the remotest recognition. Pulsar looked like a veritable melting pot for human classification. Drinking at the club's various bars were men in their thirties wearing suits exuding wealth, or at least hoping to look that way. On the other hand, younger college men dressed in edgier attire were more interested in getting drunk, having a good time, and maybe getting laid. Women who looked like they had just come from the office mingled in the crowd, drinks in hand. Their fashions provided a glimpse into the world of business throughout the city. Other women, dressed more casually, provided further contrast of lifestyles and desires. All across the dance floor, men danced with women, women dance with women, and he even caught the occasional glimpse of men dancing with men. Pulsar looked like a microcosm of Philadelphia with different ages, genders, sexual orientations, and financial statuses all represented in one location.

Realizing that he was again searching for Adonia, he shook his head. As he was turning back to his computer, someone at the far side of the club captured his gaze. A woman was standing at the edge of the dance floor, searching through the same sea of faces that had just captivated Jack's attention just moments before. She looked like a goddess, with long, flowing black hair and a perfectly shaped body. She was wearing a pale blue dress, which embraced her supple curves and accentuated the exquisiteness of her figure. Jack admired her beauty from high above the crowd. He spied upon her as she perused the club, her head turning slowly to and fro; Jack found it impossible to turn his gaze away. Suddenly, her gaze turned upward and Jack found himself staring into her eyes. Unable to turn away, he shivered as her stare bore straight into Jack's very soul. His heart began to race, and Jack had the unpleasant sense that she was probing his mind, hearing his every thought. Then she pursed her lips and blew a kiss in Jack's direction. With the spell broken, he watched her step into the crowd and begin to dance.

Chapter Seventeen

At almost three o'clock on Saturday morning, Jack pushed open the employee entrance to Pulsar and stepped outside into the crisp night air. Pulsar had been packed the entire night, right up until closing time at two. The wall-to-wall crowd had danced a lot and drank a lot. Jerry Rickett had been ecstatic over the amount of money brought in at the bars that evening. It was a well-known fact among the employees that Pulsar made its money not on the price of admission, but on the inflated price of the drinks that were served. Getting the patrons to drink more was the priority above all other things. And when Jerry Rickett was happy, it could be relied upon that he would share his happiness. That evening, before everyone left, Jerry handed out a fifty-dollar bill to each of his employees working that night. Jack had just smiled, slipped the bill into his pocket, and headed for the door.

He strolled across the pavement, heading for the parking garage where his Harley Davidson was waiting. He rounded the corner and was startled to see three police cars parked at the entrance to the garage. Their red and blue lights flashed over and over, bringing back memories of the horrors from the previous night. Two uniformed officers were standing by one of the police cars, speaking to a tall dark-skinned man in a long, dark trench coat. Recognizing the man, Jack walked toward the three officers.

"Detective?" he said.

Peter Thornton spun around, gave Jack a quick glance up and down, and, with a look of recognition on his face, replied, "Mr. Allyn? What're you doing here?"

"Just got off work," Jack replied, gesturing toward Pulsar.

"Oh, that's right. You spin the tunes on Friday nights."

Jack glanced around, and asked, "What's going on?"

Peter frowned. "I'm not really at liberty to say. We're in the middle of an investigation, that's all I can tell you."

"My motorcycle's in the garage, can I go in and get it?" inquired Jack.

Peter opened his mouth to answer, but was interrupted as the door to the garage opened. Samantha, with a confident stride, proceeded toward them.

"Oh, shit. Another corpse, and here you are. What the hell are you doing here this time?" she said.

"I just got off work and was hoping to go home," responded Jack.

Samantha asked, "Is your car in the garage?"

"Motorcycle," replied Jack.

"Which floor?"

Jack replied, "Second."

"Peter can escort you up." She paused for a moment, and then, smiling, added, "Unless you want to stick around to see if special agent Wilkinson can pull his head out of his ass when he arrives."

Peter laughed, and gave Jack a nod of his head. "Come on."

With Jack behind him, Peter started toward the parking garage door. They had walked only a few feet before Samantha called them back.

"Mr. Allyn—Jack. You were working at Pulsar tonight, right?"

Jack nodded.

"Can you look at this driver's license, and tell me if you remember seeing this person in the club?" Samantha inquired as she held up a small plastic card.

Jack took the driver's license from Samantha and gazed intently at the photo in the corner. The name on the license was Todd James Williams, which meant nothing to Jack. However, the face in the photo struck a chord in Jack's memory.

"Yeah. He was in tonight," acknowledged Jack.

Samantha questioned, "Are you certain?"

Jack knew he couldn't be more certain. He knew he had seen this man in Pulsar because Jack could vividly recall with whom Todd James Williams had left Pulsar arm in arm.

"I'm certain. And I can tell you who he left with, too."

Peter pulled the car into a parking spot outside of the Logan Square apartment complex and turned off the motor. He turned to face Samantha, who sat silently in the passenger seat. She was silhouetted against the light from the overhead streetlight and had not acknowledged that the car had stopped moving.

"It's awfully early to be showing up at someone's door," he said.

Samantha glanced at her watch; it was three forty-seven in the morning. "I don't care. We've got a witness statement that describes her to a T."

Shrugging his shoulders, Peter replied, "Yeah, the description matches, but it probably matches a dozen other women in the city. It seems a bit feeble to justify barging in on someone in the middle of the night."

"It's the best lead we've gotten, and I don't want to lose it. Did you call for an extra patrol car to meet us here?"

Peter nodded. "What about Wilkinson? He's gonna be pissed."

"Like I care what that jackass thinks."

"What's the plan?" asked Peter.

"That depends on her. If she cooperates and answers my questions, we might not even need to pull her in. If she can't answer my questions, or refuses to . . . well, we'll just play it by ear."

As a police car pulled up in front of the building, the two detectives exited their car and walked to the front entrance. After giving brief instructions to the two recently arrived uniformed police officers, Samantha and Peter headed into the building. The lobby was dimly lit and the security guard, who appeared to be dozing, jumped to his feet as Samantha and Peter displayed their badges for his inspection. The security guard argued momentarily about disturbing building residents at that hour, but Samantha quickly silenced him with the threat of arrest. Shrugging his shoulders, the guard waved the detectives on, while muttering, "I don't get paid enough to deal with this bullshit."

In the elevator, the two detectives silently watched the floor numbers change as they rose toward the top level of the building. In her head, Samantha ran through the questions she had for Calithea Panagakos. Where had she been this evening? Did she know Todd Williams? Could she account for her movements on Thursday evening? For the first time during this case, Samantha saw the first glimmer of hope. In Calithea Panagakos she had a suspect, a bona fide suspect. Not only did they have an accurate description from an eyewitness, they had also found a smudge of ruby red lipstick on the shirt collar of Todd Williams.

When the doors of the elevator opened, Samantha gripped Peter's arm firmly, holding him back from exiting. She turned, placing her body in the elevator doorway, and gave her partner a long, hard stare.

"You're staying here to hold the elevator on this floor. You're not coming in with me," she said.

Surprised, Peter inquired, "Why not? What the hell's this all about?"

Glancing over her shoulder to ensure no one was listening in the darkened hallway, Samantha said, "I don't need a repeat of your behavior from our last visit. Stay here, and if I need you, I'll let you know."

With that, Samantha turned from the elevator and walked across the hall to the well-remembered double doors, leaving her exasperated partner standing in the elevator doorway. With a firm hand, she knocked on the door and then patiently waited for a response. It only took a minute for the door to swing open. Calithea was dressed in a tight pale blue dress that hugged her shapely body. Samantha smiled as she noted that the woman's lips were coated in ruby red lipstick, similar in color to that found on Todd Williams' shirt collar.

Smiling with satisfaction, Samantha said, "Ms. Panagakos, I need to speak to you."

Calithea smiled. "Isn't it a bit late to be calling on people?"

Samantha countered, "Don't you mean early? It is four in the morning." Gesturing toward the blue dress, she added, "You look like you're dressed for company."

"As a matter of fact, I was just about to go to bed," replied Calithea.

"Then it's a good thing I came when I did, or I'd have had to wake you. May I come in?"

Reluctantly, Calithea stepped aside and gestured Samantha into the apartment. The living room looked the same as it had on Samantha's last visit. The lights were dim and cast shadows in the corners of the room. Samantha had the eerie feeling that the shadows were moving, as if they were alive. The air in the apartment felt cold, sending a shiver up Samantha's spine. It reminded her of the cold temperatures in the morgue. Why the morgue was the first place she thought of, Samantha didn't understand. But the apartment, like the morgue, seemed to exude a sense of death and decay. It wasn't like her to get so easily spooked, but she began to regret having left Peter behind at the elevator. She waited until Calithea had taken a seat on the sofa, and then Samantha made a point of idly moving to a place between the woman and the door.

"There's been a murder this evening, similar in nature to that of your attorney, James Seymour," explained Samantha.

Calithea sighed. "That's such a shame. But I don't understand why this news couldn't wait until morning."

Remaining unshaken despite the fact that the shadows in the corners of the room seemed to be stalking her from the darkness, Samantha continued to speak. "You may be surprised to know that a witness provided a detailed description of the last person seen with the latest victim."

Calithea yawned. "Detective, is this going to take much longer?"

Samantha glared at the woman whose condescension was beginning to fray the thin thread that was her last nerve. But, as angry as she was becoming, Samantha couldn't shake the overwhelming feeling that someone, or something, was lurking in the gloom. The shifting shadows seemed to dart from corner to corner, just outside the peripheral of her vision. But when she would glance in its direction, Samantha would see nothing but darkness, settled and quiet.

"That description resembles you, so closely that it even described the neckline of that dress," Samantha added.

Placing her hand on her chest, as if in embarrassment, Calithea replied, "This old thing?"

The shadows seemed to be drawing closer, engulfing the light as they closed in on Samantha. The room was getting darker; she would have sworn it. She drew a deep breath and stood firm, refusing to give in to the rising terror.

"Ms. Panagakos, can you tell me where you were this evening?"

Calithea leaned back into the sofa, and smiled. "Detective, are you accusing me of something? Should I call my attorney?"

"I doubt he'd do you much good. He's dead, remember?" Samantha replied, becoming infuriated with the woman's calm resolve.

"Oh, that's right. Poor James. He died far too soon. He was so full of life . . . such delectable life," said Calithea.

Samantha could have sworn she had seen a pair

of glowing red eyes dancing in the shadows in the far corner. With her heart racing, she took a deep breath and said, "Again, I'm going to ask that you account for your movements this evening."

Calithea remained silent for several moments, staring in Samantha's direction. Her ruby red lips slowly formed a condescending smile and she replied, "I don't feel I should be answering such questions without legal representation."

Samantha could feel a bead of sweat forming on her forehead. The pair of fiery eyes had become two pairs, glaring at her from across the dimly lit room. Her panic had risen to a level that she could barely contain. She glanced down at the woman, and then around the room. With a swift movement, she reached over to one of the two brass lampstand in the room. A brass chain hung down from under the shade, and Samantha grasped it with her fingers and tugged. Light from the incandescent bulb enveloped the room in light, pushing away the shadows and illuminating all of the dark corners. Samantha glanced around, but there was nothing there.

"Detective, you look a little pale. Are you feeling all right?" inquired Calithea.

Feeling her panic subside, Samantha inhaled deeply. "Don't change the subject. Were you or were you not at a night club called Pulsar this evening?"

"Well, detective, I really can't say. It's been a very busy evening, and I just can't recall what I did or where I've been," the woman replied with deep condescending undertones.

"Don't give me this bullshit! Where were you tonight?"

"Detective . . . such anger. If you must know, I had a man for . . . over for dinner this evening. He was such wonderful company. But I don't see why I need to divulge any details about my private life to the likes of you."

"Fine. If that's how you want to play it, fine," stated Samantha. "Calithea Panagakos, I'm afraid I'm going to have to ask you to come with me to the station for further questioning." Samantha paused, and then decided to clarify the point. "When I say ask, I mean you have no choice."

The Greek woman smiled. "Oh, detective. You have no idea who you're dealing with, do you?"

Samantha stepped back to the front door, and leaned out. Peter was still standing by the elevator, holding the door open. When he saw her looking his way, he frowned.

"Go downstairs and ask Faulkner and Anderson to come up. I'd like them to escort Ms. Panagakos to the station for further questioning," Samantha ordered.

Samantha watched the elevator doors close before she stepped back into the apartment. Calithea Panagakos, who hadn't moved from the sofa, was glaring at Samantha with her crystal blue eyes, which seemed as cold as glacial ice. Although the sense of rising terror had subsided, Samantha still couldn't free herself from the feeling that some unseen evil was lurking in the apartment. She had never felt so alone and vulnerable before in her life. It was as if an unseen force was stalking her, circling around her like an animal waiting to attack its unsuspecting prey. She was relieved when she heard the bell on the elevator signal its return to the nineteenth floor.

Moments later, Peter, with two uniformed police officers close behind, entered the apartment. The two officers, Faulkner and Anderson, halted just inside the apartment threshold and gazed in at Calithea Panagakos. Peter moved into the apartment next to Samantha.

"Ms. Panagakos, it's a pleasure to see you again. You're looking even lovelier than I remember," he said.

Samantha threw him an angry look, and then gestured to the two police officers, "Please take Ms. Panagakos to the station. We'll be interviewing her there. Detective Thornton and I will follow you in just a moment."

Officer Faulkner stepped forward and smiled, "Of course. It'd be our pleasure."

Calithea rose from the sofa with a slow and deliberate manner, and then smiled at Samantha. "It seems that I'll not be going to bed after all. I do hope you know what you're about to get into, Detective Ballard."

Samantha stepped forward until her face was inches from the Calithea's. "Your threats don't scare me, Ms. Panagakos. And, unlike my counterparts, I don't get gobsmacked by a set of nice legs and big tits. If you had anything to do with these murders, I'm going to find out. And when I do, I'm going to make sure they lock you away in the darkest cell they can find. You should feel right at home."

As Samantha stepped aside, Calithea smiled and said, "Hmm, I like a woman with balls. They're so much more fun to spar with. But be careful you don't get kicked in them."

Calithea brushed past Samantha as she exited the apartment. Faulkner and Anderson followed along behind her. Samantha and Peter stepped to the apartment door and watched as the woman entered the waiting elevator with the two police officers. Calithea turned and faced the two detectives, smiling as the elevator doors closed.

"You won't forget to lock up for me, will you?" the woman said just as the gap between the doors vanished.

Once they were alone in the hallway, Samantha turned on her partner with a rage-filled glare and exclaimed, "What the hell is wrong with you?"

"Huh? What?" replied Peter.

Samantha never had the chance to respond. Two muffled screams resonated through the closed elevator doors. They were bloodcurdling sounds of utter agony that shattered the early morning peace and quiet on every floor of the apartment building. Each scream was a long, drawn-out cry that faded away in a manner that left no doubt that the end result was death.

The piercing screams shot through Samantha

like two precisely fired bullets, exploding in her mind. She instantly knew what the screams meant, and shuddered at the thought. *Two more,* she thought. *Please, not two more!*

Peter rushed forward, and repeatedly pounded on the elevator button, as Samantha dashed toward a small door marked by a red sign that read, "Exit".

"Come on!" she shouted as she flung the door open and launched herself down the stairs beyond.

Their feet clattered loudly on the concrete stairs as they bounded as fast as they could downward. The sound of their footsteps echoed through the stairwell shaft as they passed the doorway for the eighteenth floor, and then the seventeenth. By the tenth floor, her heart was racing and Samantha gasped for each breath. Peter clamored downward only a few steps behind her. If she had stopped suddenly he would have bowled her over. As they passed the fifth floor, Samantha's shins were burning and sweat was dripping from her forehead into her eyes. Peter had fallen behind her by half a floor.

When the two detectives burst from the door on the first floor, they found themselves in the dimly lit lobby and the doors of the elevator stood open. The security guard was on his knees in front of the door, trying to lift himself up by leaning against a nearby wall. A loud bell was ringing in the elevator, signaling that the emergency stop switch had been activated. The two detectives didn't hesitate as they dashed across the lobby to the elevator. Sprawled on the floor of the small chamber were two bodies, each wearing a Philadelphia

Police uniform. Faulkner and Anderson's corpses had both been reduced to dried husks. There was no sign of Calithea Panagakos.

Chapter Eighteen

Jack Allyn's return to his night shift at WPLX seemed anticlimactic when compared to the events of the previous week. He felt a certain level of relief to have his life return to some degree of normalcy. Ever since Jason Spinacker's death, Jack felt like he had fallen into some other dimension where the rules of sanity no longer existed. Dried up corpses and life sucking mythological creatures had been outside of the realm of his life experience, but they both had seemed to converge on him all at once over the past week. As much as he didn't want to admit it, Jack had begun to seriously consider Bryan Salisbury's theory about the beautiful creatures from Greek mythology that lured and killed men. He would have laughed in the face of anyone that had suggested it before his encounter on Thursday evening, but now he was beginning to wonder if there might be some truth to the idea after all.

The more he ran the events of the attack over in his mind, the more he was convinced that he had not dreamt or hallucinated the fiery eyes and frighteningly dagger-like teeth. His recollection of those moments was too vivid for him to doubt their veracity. He had already convinced himself that his attacker had, in fact, been the redhead who had left Pulsar with Jason. As much as his sense of machismo didn't want to admit it, Jack felt certain that she would have been more than capable of killing him with her bare hands, and there would have been nothing that he could have done about it. The more he thought about it, the luckier he felt he had been. He may be bruised and battered, but at least he was alive.

After Saturday morning's lengthy discussion with Detectives Ballard and Thornton, Jack had decided it might be safer to spend the rest of the weekend in his apartment. Even after the exhausting events of the past few days, sleep eluded him on Saturday and Sunday. Because the events of the past week had unraveled his nerves, Jack would drift off to sleep only to be awakened an hour later by any little sound. He tried watching television, only to find his biased opinions on the fatuousness of the medium to be reinforced. He tried working his way up and down the dial of his stereo, tuning in each FM station in Philadelphia, but they all failed to bring relief to his anxious demeanor. He had even resorted to listening to WPLX for a while, hoping it might put him to sleep. It hadn't helped. Eventually, Jack resigned himself to having a restless weekend. The only thing that seemed to ease his mind was the photo from his wallet—Emma's photo.

Rain came with the arrival of Sunday evening, and Jack returned to his usual routine, starting with dinner at Geno's Pizza. As he sat in the small restaurant, he gazed out at a wet South Street and watched as people passed by, some carrying umbrellas, and other simply getting wet from the rain. Jack had always been amazed by the fact that even the heaviest of rain wouldn't stop the crowds of beatniks, punk rockers, and hip-hoppers from roaming South Street. They seemed oblivious to the rain as they drifted past the pane of glass that separated them from Jack.

As Jack's mind began to wander he felt a faint whiff of warm air across his neck, as if someone was gently blowing on it. He turned his head, but found no one near him. There were three other patrons in the restaurant, all sitting at a table along the opposite wall. They were deeply engrossed in their conversation and were paying Jack no mind. Shrugging his shoulders, he decided it had been his imagination. He gazed out the window again and, moments later, he felt the warmth on his neck again, causing him to shiver. His eyes darted from side to side, sending fleeting looks around the restaurant; once again, he found no one. Rubbing the back of his neck, he tried to convince himself that it must have been air from a nearby heating vent. His eyes returned to the window and his fingers began to tap on the table.

The third time that he felt the warm air on his neck, it was accompanied by a faint whisper calling his name. Jerking his head around, he again found the space around him to be empty. However, his sudden movement had caught the eye of the three patrons at the far end of the restaurant. When Jack looked up, they were all staring at him. He gave them a half-smile, and returned to gazing out the window.

"Jack," came the whisper again.

This time, Jack tried to ignore it. The whisper was very faint, almost inaudible. But it sounded as if the speaker's lips were inches from his ear. His fingers tapped on the table in a random rhythm. Then, it came again.

"Jack."

Closing his eyes, he rubbed his forehead and once again ignored the soft voice calling his name.

"Jack."

Sighing, he continued to gaze out of the window, trying in vain to focus his mind on anything but the whisper. Jack scanned the faces passing the restaurant, hoping to find someone or something that would take his mind off his rising fear. He caught a glimpse of red hair among the crowd, but when he looked again it was gone.

"Jack."

He spun around and loudly said, "What?"

Geno, in his stained white apron, was standing beside the table with his mouth open in surprise at Jack's outburst. The heavyset man timidly lowered a plate with a steaming chicken cheesesteak with peppers and onions onto the table. Slowly stepping away from the table, he said, "Your meal's ready."

Shaking his head, Jack replied, "I'm sorry, Geno. My mind was a million miles away. I lost track of where

I was."

Still unsure, Geno waved his hand and said, "Enjoy."

―――――――――――

When he had parked his motorcycle in the parking garage, Jack sat on the seat for a moment to allow the rain to drip off of his coat before going into the building. Normally, he would never notice the deafening silence in the garage, but that night he was keenly aware of the lack of sound. There were no tire squeals. No running engines. No car doors slamming. Not a sound to be heard. He had never realized before how eerie it was until that moment. And, it was at that moment that he heard it again.

"Jack."

Glancing around, he shouted, "Scott? Is that you?"

The only response was a faint whisper. "Jack Allyn."

Jack shouted, "Scott? I'll kick your ass if I find out that's you!"

He dismounted the motorcycle and walked toward the elevator, trying not to run, but moving faster than normal. The elevator doors opened moments later, and he rode it up to the twentieth floor. Once in the offices of WPLX, Jack furtively approached the studio door, checking over his shoulder with every few steps. Pushing the door open slowly, Jack gazed in through the narrow gap. Scott Anderson, who was seated in front of the control board, looked up from the newspaper he was reading.

"Hello, Jack. Welcome back," said Scott.

Jack looked at Scott, and then back down the hallway behind him. "Yeah, you thought you were funny, huh?"

Puzzled, Scott stared at Jack. "What?"

Smiling, Jack replied, "The voices. Real funny."

Still puzzled, Scott said, "What're you talking about?"

"The voices, out in the parking . . ." Jack's comments trailed off as he began to realize that Scott knew nothing about the whispering voice. "Uh, nothing. Never mind."

At three in the morning, Jack hit the top of the hour station I.D., and went straight into his third hour on the air. Things had been quiet since Scott left an hour ago. The young man seemed to feel compelled to stick around and talk to Jack about the recent killings in the city. It was a topic Jack had tried to steer the college student away from, but Scott had continued to bring the conversation back around to the killings again and again. Curiosity had gotten the better of Scott Anderson, and he had asked Jack repeatedly to talk about the crime scene at Jason Spinacker's apartment. He had also made a point of frequently commenting on the bruises on Jack's face, a fact that had finally driven Jack to sharply tell Scott to drop the subject. After that,

Scott took the hint and had departed, leaving Jack on his own in the WPLX studio.

Preferring the solitude of the night, Jack placed the request lines on hold, and leaned back in his chair. From the speakers hanging from the ceiling came the first few lines of Don McLean's song, "American Pie". It was one of the few songs from the WPLX music rotation that Jack didn't mind hearing. To lessen the distractions around him, he closed his eyes, allowing his ears the freedom to absorb the cryptic lyrics and haunting rhythms.

Two and a half minutes into the song, Jack's head was bobbing to the rhythm of the song and, knowing every word by heart, his lips moved silently with the lyrics. For Jack, a night that contained "American Pie" wasn't a half bad night at WPLX. The other songs were almost tolerable once he got his eight minute and thirty-two second fix of "American Pie". But suddenly, his eyes shot open, and he sat bolt upright in the chair. He had heard something that he knew shouldn't be in the song. Without needing to look around the studio, he knew he was alone. But he was certain he heard it.

"Jack," came the whisper again.

Leaning over the board, Jack turned up the volume for the studio speakers, and tried to return to enjoying the song. The increased amplification, however, didn't help.

"Jack Allyn."

Jumping from his chair, Jack rushed to the door

and pulled it open, hoping to find Scott Anderson standing behind it to tell him it was all a joke, but there was no one there. Returning to his chair, Jack slid his headphones over his head, and tried again to listen as the chorus burst forth from the speakers overhead.

"Can Jack come out to play?" came the faint whisper in his ears.

Ripping the headphones from his head, he began to anxiously pace around the studio. It had to be a prank, he kept telling himself. His co-workers must be playing a prank on him. It hadn't taken long for news to spread around the radio station that Jack had some connection to one of the victims of the mysterious deaths in the city. He wouldn't put it past them to plan some kind of gag for his return. But then he remembered what had happened at Geno's. There was no way that his co-workers could have known he would go to Geno's for dinner. If there was one thing that Jack was good at, it was keeping his private life private. His co-workers knew very little about his habits, hobbies, and life outside of WPLX.

The whisper interrupted his train of thought again. "Jack."

Figuring that the prankster, whoever it was, must be somewhere in the radio station offices, he stormed out of the studio and began a systematic search of each room. He checked the production studio first and, finding no one, moved on to the small lunchroom. No one was there either. Down the hall, he pushed open the door to the radio station sales office and stepped inside. The room, furnished with an open floor plan rather than cubicles, contained twelve desks aligned in three rows of four. File cabinets lined each sidewall and a floor to ceiling window, which looked out over the city, spanned the opposite side of the room. As he walked down one of the rows, he glanced under each desk, wishing that he would find someone under one of them. He found no one. When he reached the far wall, he peered out the window and that's when he saw her.

Knowing that he was on the twentieth floor, Jack had not been expecting to find someone staring back at him from outside the window. She was floating a few feet from the window, without any visible means of support. Her fiery red hair fluttered gently in an unseen breeze, and Adonia's face shone with an absolute beauty he could not turn from. The supple curves of her naked body were utterly without blemish, wrinkle, or deformity. Her breasts were firm and round and, like the rest of her body, seemed to be the epitome of perfection. Her long, smooth legs hung below her, ending with ruby red nail polish on her toes. Her arms were outstretched from her body in an inviting manner. Her blood red lips parted, and she spoke. Yet, her words didn't seem to come from outside. To Jack, it sounded as if she was standing right next to him.

"Can Jack come out to play?" was the whisper he heard in his ear.

With his mouth gaping, Jack was in awe at the effortless way that she drifted before the window. Her beauty was unlike any that he had ever seen, and he wanted nothing more than to touch her silky skin. Without thinking, he stepped forward toward the window, placed his hands against the thick glass surface, and gazed up at Adonia as she smiled down at him. She drifted closer to the window until the only thing between them was a single pane of glass.

"Come play with me, Jack," came a whisper in his ear.

Jack watched as Adonia, hovering before the window, seductively began to caress her own body. Her hands gently slid down her abdomen and around to the side of her smooth thighs. Her erotic touch skimmed back across her stomach and across her breasts. Any sense of logic and levelheadedness in Jack was pushed aside by the eroticism of the moment. Her overwhelming beauty, combined with the sensual way in which she was stroking her body unleashed a carnal lust in Jack that he neither understood nor seemed able to control. His knuckles were turning white, as he pressed on the window, desperate to reach her. She puckered her lips and blew him a kiss, which only fueled the fire inside him. Feverishly, Jack began to bang on the window with his fists, hitting the glass as hard as he could to no avail. Frustrated and in a frenzy, Jack spun around, scanned the room, and then reached for the nearest office chair. Raising it above his head, he turned back to the window. Adonia drifted back from the window, and smiled.

As he prepared to lunge the chair forward through the window, Jack glanced up at Adonia. Her

214

eyes had turned fiery red, and blazed like an inferno. The chair hung above Jack's head as he stared at the two orbs of fire. The piercing bright lights shone through the glass and cast a faint orange hue around the room. Suddenly, Jack's grip loosened on the chair, and it crashed to the floor at his feet.

"Jack, aren't you going to come out and play?" echoed the whisper in his ear.

Speechless and frightened, Jack backed toward the door, never once taking his eyes off the floating image of beauty outside the window. The corner of a desk jabbed into the back of his thigh, but his eyes never wavered. When he felt the doorknob against his back, Jack slowly slid his hand behind him and gripped it firmly. Turning the knob, he heard the latch click, and he inhaled deeply. Then, with one swift movement, Jack flung the door opened, dashed through it, and slammed it closed behind him. Leaning back against the door, Jack's heart raced as he found it hard to catch his breath, and he slowly slid down the door until he was seated on the carpeted floor. Leaning forward, he placed his head into his trembling hands. Then, he suddenly looked up toward the ceiling where a small round speaker was uncommonly silent.

"Dead air! Damn it!" he muttered.

Chapter Nineteen

Traffic in the city was heavier than usual on Monday morning as Jack darted between the line of slow moving cars and those parked on the side of the street. The rest of his shift had gone by uneventfully until Ron Michaels arrived the next morning. Jack had found it difficult to explain to Ron why he had jammed a chair against the inside of the studio door. There had been no more whispering voices, but that hadn't stopped Jack from feeling frightened. The morning show host, getting frustrated with Jack's lame excuses, finally stopped asking questions and took his seat behind the control board, gesturing for Jack to leave the studio. On his way out of the station that morning, Jack had opened the sales office door just enough for him to peek in. The chair was still lying on the floor, but there were no images of beautiful women floating outside the window in the early rising sunlight. He closed the door and hoped that no one would ask what had happened to the chair.

Jack had been relieved to see the sun shining as he exited the parking garage on his Harley Davidson. The crispness of the morning air had helped to revive him as he sped through the empty streets toward

Monk's Cafe. Breakfast had been hearty and satisfying, and Jack had returned home to find a message waiting for him on his answering machine.

"Jack, it's Bryan from Den of Heroes. Look, I know you don't believe me about the whole Seirenes thing, but I've dug up some information you might find interesting. This definitely isn't the first time these creatures have come to Philly. Call me when you get a chance."

He had replayed the message again and then, like a man on a mission, strode out the door of his apartment. Now traffic had become more like he would expect during rush hour, with cars lining the streets in a slow moving gridlock. Being on a motorcycle allowed Jack to be more agile as he darted between and around the cars that lethargically inched through the narrow city streets.

Jack needed to talk to someone about what he had seen over the past few days, and he knew that Bryan Salisbury would be the perfect confidant. The horrifying events of the previous evening had erased any doubts in his mind about the existence of Seirenes in Philadelphia, and he wanted to get as much information as possible. Because he felt that theory was rubbish before, Jack had paid little attention to any of the details that the comic book storeowner had presented earlier. Now he wanted to know everything Bryan knew.

Samantha, with a steaming white ceramic coffee mug in her hand, gazed out the window of her bedroom at the street in front of her townhouse. She had worked feverishly all weekend long, following up leads on the whereabouts of Calithea Panagakos to no avail. Before leaving her office in the early hours of Monday morning, she had sent an email to her Captain informing him that she would be in a few hours late. She knew he'd understand once he saw that the time stamp on the email was from three that morning. Her sleep had been restless, and she drifted in and out of consciousness throughout what had been left of the night. Finally giving up on the prospect of slumber, Samantha had risen at seven thirty and spent the next two hours in her basement workout room. Whether it was residual adrenaline from her long weekend or just a desire to work out some of her frustration, Samantha had doubled her workout routine. She was covered in sweat when she emerged from the basement to the bright sunshine beaming in through her living room windows. After a long, hot shower, Samantha had dressed slowly, trying to drag out her time at home before having to head back into the office.

The first mug of coffee hadn't been successful at taking the edge off of her morning, and the second seemed determined to fail like the first. The traffic outside her window that had rapidly built up through rush hour was now beginning to lighten again. She checked her watch. Nine fifty-two. With another long sip from her coffee mug, she turned from the window and headed downstairs to the kitchen. Pouring the remainder of her coffee into the sink, her eyes remained transfixed on the dark brown liquid as it swirled around the drain of the stainless steel sink. The dull ache behind her eyes had started early this morning; it had not let up, even for the two Tylenol she had taken.

The headaches had started to occur after the discovery of the first three corpses. Each successive corpse only served to increase the frequency until the headaches had become a daily occurrence. She didn't complain about them because she knew that her co-workers would blame them on the stress of the case, and some would even see the headaches as a sign that the case should be reassigned to another detective. It frustrated Samantha to no end to know that because she didn't have a penis and a set of balls hanging between her legs that she had to fight doubly hard for the respect of some of her fellow detectives. She had come out of the police academy with top honors, and had even scored one of the highest scores on record on her civil servant exam when she applied to become a detective. Yet some of the "old guard" of Philadelphia's detective force still viewed her as a usurper. Although her superior officers supported her efforts, she knew those co-workers who still felt the detective force was no place for a woman scrutinized every case. Samantha wasn't the only female detective on the force, but she was by far considered the most successful, which had made her a target. Her aggressive approach to everything she did had become her trademark around the department. But with that trademark came the guilt she had so carefully hidden away. And over the weekend, that guilt had doubled.

Samantha returned to her bedroom, grabbed the holstered pistol from her dresser, and extracted the weapon from its leather encasement. She performed her usual morning check on the firearm, attached the holster to her belt, and slid the gun into its proper resting place on her hip. As her hand reached for the LG mobile phone on her dresser, it began to ring.

Touching the screen to answer, she placed the phone to her ear and said, "Detective Ballard."

"Samantha? It's Jack Allyn," came the reply.

"Jack, what's up?"

There was a pause, and then, "I have something you need to see."

Leaning against the doorframe of the small office in the back of the Den of Heroes comic book shop, Samantha slowly shook her head. It had taken her fifteen minutes to get to the small shop, and another five to survey what she found when she had arrived. She would have classified the small room as more of a walk-in closet than an office. A small desk spanned from wall to wall along the back wall. Cheap shelves had been mounted above the desk five high; they contained a collection of science fiction action figures from a variety of movies, television programs, and comics. A stack of comic books sat on the right-hand side of the desk, each contained in its own clear protective plastic envelope. The screensaver from a grey Dell laptop provided the room's only illumination. Slumped face down on the floor was another mummified corpse with its arms outstretched toward the desk. From its position, Samantha reasoned that the victim must have been trying to reach for the cordless telephone, which rested next to the laptop.

Samantha had been so engrossed in her initial analysis of the scene that she had barely noticed Jack's presence behind her. When he quietly cleared his throat, she turned to face him.

"Did you know him well?" she asked.

Jack shrugged his shoulders. "Not really, but I considered him a friend. I was in here every few weeks."

Brushing past Jack, Samantha paced around the small comic book shop. "I can't really picture you as someone that's into all this crap. You don't seem like the comic book type."

"I'm not. But I collect some of the more rare comics. They're part of my investment portfolio," explained Jack.

"Yet another surprising fact about Jack Allyn."

Jack smiled. "What? That I have comics in my investment portfolio?"

"No. That you actually have an investment portfolio," said Samantha. Then after pausing, she commanded, "Tell me what happened."

Jack leaned back against the glass display case. "A few weeks ago, after that first murder outside of

Pulsar, Bryan tried to convince me that there was some ancient mythological creature running loose in the city. He kept going on and on about it, but I didn't pay much attention. The story he told was just too . . ."

"Incredulous?"

Jack smiled. "I was going to say stupid. But I guess incredulous is probably more appropriate. Said he had a contact in the police that was filling him in on the murders. At the time, it seemed insane to think it was true."

Folding her arms, Samantha replied, "When we spoke a few days ago, you said you didn't believe it, but it sounds like something's changed."

Jack hesitated, and then said, "Yeah. At the risk of sounding like a complete nut job, let me tell you what happened to me last night."

It only took Jack ten minutes to complete his narrative of the early morning events at the WPLX studios. He decided that it was best to hold nothing back, no matter how bad it made him look. At this point, he knew it would be folly to withhold any detail. Dried up dead bodies and floating naked women with burning red eyes were far beyond the realm of anything he had ever experienced. And as much as he would have liked to be passive and not get involved, it seemed that he was going to have little choice. Two of his friends were now dead. There was no longer any way to deny it, he was involved.

Samantha listened with interest to Jack's tale, and as much as she wanted to shrug the whole story off as being the ravings of a lunatic, she couldn't shake the feeling that there might be something in his dubious story. She had seen too much over the past few weeks to not give it serious consideration. As his words poured forth, her mind drifted back through each of the crime scenes she had seen during the investigation. The underground chamber. The parking garage. The alley alongside Pulsar. In her mind's eye, she vividly recalled the security camera footage from the club, and the horrifying scene it had recorded.

When Jack finished speaking, Samantha asked, "So, why'd you come here this morning?"

Gesturing back toward the office door, he replied, "Bryan called and left me a message, saying he had some info about these Seirenes. Besides, after everything that's happened, I needed to talk to somebody. He's the only person I could think of who wouldn't think I'm crazy."

Samantha sighed. She knew perfectly well how Jack felt. It was a feeling she had experienced during the Society Hill Serial Killer investigation. The vile and ghastly manner in which the killer had dispatched his victims had disturbed even the strongest detectives on the force, but Samantha even more so. Back then, she had been desperate to have someone to talk to, but there had been no one for her.

"Jack, I think your friend was right," said Samantha. "That woman you identified on Friday night killed two police officers on Saturday, leaving behind two corpses just like that one." She gestured back toward that small office. "We've been looking for her ever since."

"Shit!" replied Jack. "Wait . . . that doesn't make sense. The woman I saw Friday night at the club wasn't the same one I saw outside the radio station window! And she wasn't the one who attacked me!"

Samantha stared hard at Jack. "Are you sure?"

"Absolutely. There were some similarities, but they were definitely different women."

"Could she have been wearing a wig?" inquired Samantha.

Jack shook his head. "No way! Different women."

"Damn! That means there's more than one of them."

Jack gave Samantha a half-smile. "Sounds like you're starting to believe too."

Samantha hesitated before answering. She had fought so hard to keep a rational perspective on this investigation, and all of her rationality seemed to be crumbling before her eyes. To admit that there may be monsters stalking through the streets of Philadelphia was to admit that all of her intelligent reasoning had gone out the window. There was a time that she prided herself on her ability to maintain her grasp on reality, no matter how difficult or unusual the cases got. But now she was slowly watching herself believe in things that she would have outright criticized any fellow detective for even suggesting. Yet, she couldn't deny the evidence of her own eyes. She had seen the bodies of ordinary people reduced to nothing more than dried husks. Samantha had watched two healthy police officers walk into an elevator with a suspect and come out as shriveled corpses. There was little point in her trying to abnegate this theory any longer.

She nodded. "I believe it."

The door to the small comic shop swung open, and Peter Thornton stepped cautiously in. He glanced around the room before his eyes locked on Samantha. His dark face held a frown, causing his forehead to furrow. He crossed the space between them with a few long strides, and said, "Sorry I'm late. I rushed over here as fast as I could."

"We've got another body," said Samantha. She gestured toward the office door in the back of the shop. "He's back there."

Peter's eyes widened as he asked, "Bryan?"

Tilting her head, Samantha replied, "Yeah, Bryan Salisbury."

Pointing toward Jack, Peter inquired, "Why's he here?"

"He found the body," explained Samantha.

Turning toward Jack, Peter asked, "Did you know Bryan?"

Jack nodded.

"Apparently you knew him too," said Samantha. "Peter, is there anything I need to know before we start digging into this crime scene?"

Peter stared down at his feet, embarrassed, and avoiding eye contact with his partner. "I . . . I shop here occasionally."

Samantha raised her eyebrows. "You're into comic books?"

"I only read graphic novels. Not the regular monthly comics," admitted Peter.

Samantha smiled. "I think that's like saying you only read Playboy for the articles."

Suddenly, Jack interrupted with a revelation, "Ah, you must be Bryan's contact in the police force!"

Frowning, Samantha asked, "Were you feeding Bryan Salisbury sensitive information about our investigation?"

"I, ah, might have mentioned something here and there," muttered Peter.

"Did he tell you his theory about what was killing these people?" asked Jack.

Peter nodded his head. "Yeah, but it was all rubbish, right?"

When Samantha didn't respond, Peter said, "It's rubbish. It's total bullshit! It has to be!"

"Before we call in forensics, we need to find out everything Bryan knew about these creatures . . ." Turning to Jack, Samantha asked, "What are they called?"

"Seirenes. They're from Greek Mythology."

"Yeah, Seirenes. We need to find everything he had on them," said Samantha.

Peter scratched his head, and said, "He showed me a couple books on mythology, but . . ."

"I know he kept a lot of stuff on his laptop,"

interjected Jack. "In his message he said he'd been doing some research. Maybe there's something on his computer."

"It's worth a shot," replied Samantha, heading toward the back office door.

Chapter Twenty

With his face bathed in the pale blue illumination from the laptop's screen, Jack Allyn carefully scanned the words of the ninth document he had found during his search of Bryan Salisbury's computer. His bedroom was dark despite it being only five in the afternoon. Jack had pulled the drapes closed when he returned home several hours ago to safeguard himself from any further floating female apparitions. He had been surprised that Samantha had let him walk out of the comic book shop with the laptop under his arm, but the detective had stated that she didn't want it gathered up in evidence when forensics and the FBI arrived.

When they had examined the computer at the shop, it had been password protected, which, Samantha admitted, would mean having to hand it over to the police department's Cyber Crimes division. That was something, the detective stated, that she wanted to avoid at all costs. Her partner, Peter Thornton, had been quick to question her motives.

"Two reasons," she had replied. "One, there's no rushing the guys in Cyber Crimes. It could be several days before they return with anything. Second, we'd have to tell them what we're looking for. Do you want to be the one to tell them to look for information on a mythological monster?"

"Wilkinson's not gonna be happy," commented Peter.

"Wilkinson can kiss my ass," came Samantha's abrupt response.

Despite Peter's early reservations, Jack could tell that the detective was slowly beginning to open his mind to the possibility of the existence of these terrifying creatures. Like Samantha, the young detective had seen far too much to doubt the evidence before his own eyes. Although he couldn't be sure, Jack sensed that the death of the comic book shop owner had hit Peter Thornton harder than the detective was letting on.

Hindered by an unknown password, Samantha grew increasingly agitated and had shown no qualms about vocalizing her agitation. "Damn it!" she had shouted loudly after her fourth attempt at guessing the password had failed. She turned and glared at Jack and Peter, who had been standing behind her watching over her shoulders.

"Whatever happened to the days when everyone's password was *password123*?" she asked.

Glancing at his watch, Peter asked, "How much longer do you think we can sit on this without reporting it?"

Samantha's answer had been short and curt. "Until we crack this password."

"I've got an idea," said Jack. "I don't know if you'd go for this, but . . ."

The two detectives had turned to stare at Jack when he paused. After a moment, he continued, "I could take the laptop back to my apartment while you two get working with forensics. I can try to work on the password while you comb through the crime scene."

Samantha looked at Jack with dubious eyes. "Is this another of your hidden talents? Computer hacking?"

"I'm just trying to help," replied Jack. "I didn't know Bryan terribly well, but maybe I can have some luck at guessing the password. If I can't, there's no harm done."

Samantha said, "See what you can come up with. I'll swing by tonight around seven."

Ten minutes later, Jack was on his motorcycle with the laptop stashed in the black leather saddlebag hanging over the rear wheel. In another thirty minutes, he was in his darkened bedroom staring at the screen trying to decide where to start. Jack tried various comic book character names to no avail. Then Jack entered the names of characters from as many science fiction movies as he could think of without success. After that he tried superheroes, and then movie monster names. He wracked his brain trying to visualize the comic book shop in his mind, searching for clues to the right combination of letters and numbers that would open access to the files on the laptop.

After three hours, Jack had just about reached the point of giving up. With the laptop still sitting on his bed, he had been pacing back and forth across the bedroom floor. Jack had cursed out loud when he took his frustration out on a white tennis shoe that was resting on the floor by the bed. The kick had sent the shoe smashing into the wall with a loud bang, leaving a small dent in the drywall. That was when he had his epiphany. Jack could remember the conversation as if it were yesterday.

"It's one of his seminal works," Bryan had said. "A cult classic. My all-time favorite."

Jack's fingers danced across the keyboard as he entered "THX1138" into the password box. Smiling as the computer screen unlocked, Jack muttered, "Got it!"

After he finished reading the document, Jack closed the lid of the laptop and glanced at the clock on his bedside table. The aching in his stomach reminded him that he had not eaten lunch. He drew back the drapes slowly, just enough to look out upon the street below. The activity level below his apartment seemed normal for a Monday evening with a scattering of revelers heading down South Street to get an early start. He scrutinized the faces, looking for any sign of Adonia. Not finding the redhead among the pedestrians below, Jack decided it would be safe to venture forth for dinner.

With his meal from Geno's Pizza settling in his stomach, Jack Allyn was feeling particularly placid as he strolled up South Street toward his apartment. There had been something overly comforting about his chicken cheesesteak that evening, and Jack found himself pushing aside thoughts of mummified corpses and mythological creatures. Dusk had fallen across the city, bringing a cool breeze from the east, and the sky was clear and star-filled. It was a beautiful evening, which Jack didn't want to spoil with thoughts of impending danger or doom. He drew a deep breath and allowed the cool air to fill his lungs. Expecting Samantha Ballard's arrival at seven, he glanced at his watch, noting that he still had almost twenty minutes.

A block and a half from his apartment building, Jack barely noticed that he had passed a small alleyway between two buildings. The city was full of small alleys like it, most leading to side or back entrances of the buildings. A few even ended in small, perpetually shadowed courtyards, sheltered from the sun by looming brickwork on all sides. Some, like this one, were closed to the world outside by a rusting wrought iron gate. As he passed the shadow-filled passageway, Jack thought he heard the faint cry of a child.

"Help!"

He halted suddenly and looked behind him. Shrugging his shoulders, he took a step forward only to hear another faint cry. *It was definitely a child,* he thought.

"Somebody help me!"

Taking a step backward, Jack gazed between the bars of the gate into the shadowy darkness of the narrow ingress. Listening intently, he heard nothing but the sound of passing cars and the occasional pedestrian behind him.

"Hello?" he said.

"Help me! Please help me!" came the faint response of a young voice.

"What's wrong?" he replied.

"Please! Help!" was all he heard in reply.

Gripping the gate, he was surprised to find it unlatched. The rusty hinges creaked loudly as he swung the gate open, stepped into the passageway, and was enveloped in darkness instantly. The alley was narrower than he had realized with his shoulders gently brushing on the brickwork on either side. Ahead of him he could see the opposite end of the passageway, but the shadows surrounding him made it next to impossible to even see where to place his feet. He tread cautiously, feeling gingerly with his foot before taking each step forward. The sound of his footsteps impacting the cobblestones echoed so loudly off the walls that they seemed to block out any other noise.

When he had traversed halfway down the dark passage, he halted, having suddenly realized how foolish he had been. As his heart began to race, Jack watched as a shadowy figure rose from out of nowhere before him, blocking his forward progress. He could see nothing of the features in the darkness—just a dark apparition silhouetted against the dim light from the opposite end of the alleyway. Before he could move, something hard forcibly slammed into his chest, knocking Jack to the ground. The air rushed from his lungs as his back smashed onto the hard cobblestones below. He gasped for air as the black silhouette leaned forward and fiery red eyes appeared, filling the passage with a red iridescence.

"My sister let you off far too easy," said a husky female voice.

Still wrestling to draw oxygen into his lungs, Jack could say nothing in reply. He gazed up into the bright red balls of fire, and felt a hopelessness beyond all hopelessness. Knowing what he knew about the powers of these creatures, Jack was certain he had made the last mistake of his life by walking down the dark passageway. Now he was staring death itself in the face as retribution for that mistake. He had never been a religious man, but he began to recite in his head the only prayer he had ever known, the Lord's Prayer. It brought momentary comfort to him until he realized that he couldn't remember any of the prayer past the line "Thy kingdom come, thy will be done".

The burning eyes moved closer as the husky voice said, "It will be such a pleasure to take your life. Even more of a pleasure than your friend at the cartoon shop."

Waiting for death to descend on him, Jack was shocked when a white beam of light illuminated the figure before him. He could clearly see the face of the alluring woman who he had seen once before. The long black hair surrounded a face of exquisite complexion and beauty that was only hampered by the fiery red eyes and spike-like teeth. She jerked back and let out a loud ominous hiss. Suddenly, the narrow alleyway erupted with what seemed to Jack like three thundering explosions in rapid succession. The woman standing before him jerked backward as three crimson red spots appeared on her chest, sending a small splattering of red, viscous substance down upon Jack. Hissing with an indignant fury bordering on mania, the woman turned and fled toward the end of alleyway. Before he could move, rapidly approaching footsteps from behind him announced the arrival of another figure, which leapt over him in pursuit of the fleeing creature. Moments later, the figure returned and, grabbing his hand, pulled him up off the ground.

"Come on, Jack. Let's get out of here before I've got to write a twenty-page report on why I discharged my firearm," said Samantha.

Jack and Samantha had spent the next twenty minutes scurrying around corners and down side streets to ensure that no one from the growing crowd of gawkers, which had formed at the entrance of the alleyway, could identify where they had gone. When they had dashed out of the alley, Jack remembered hearing someone scream and felt at least one pair of hands try to grab him. But Samantha had simply bowled through the melee half-dragging Jack behind her. A precisely placed elbow and a few rigorous shoves with Samantha's free hand had driven a wedge through the people, creating a clear channel for their escape. They had even avoided entering through the front entrance to his apartment building, choosing a seldom-used fire exit in the alley behind the building.

When Jack finally closed the door of his apartment behind them, he leaned back against it to catch his breath. Samantha shed her grey overcoat and dropped it onto the sofa. Unclipping the leather holster from her belt, she dropped it on top of the overcoat, and then gave a long sigh.

Finally having caught his breath, Jack said, "That was the woman I saw at Pulsar."

Nodding, Samantha replied, "Her name is Calithea Panagakos, or so she claims."

"You saved my life."

Samantha nodded again. "Probably. At least for now."

Jack pushed off from the door, walked into the living room, and slid down into the Lazy Boy across from the sofa. "You make it sound like she'll be back."

"There was a small courtyard behind that building. The alley was the only way out. She wasn't in the courtyard. "

Jack gaped in surprise. "What?"

"It was empty."

Shaking his head, Jack replied, "That's not possible!"

"Neither is a naked woman floating twenty stories up, but you believe that."

"Don't remind me," replied Jack, holding up his hand as if to signal her to stop.

"I put three bullets straight into where her heart

should be, and she—that thing—ran off as if nothing had happened," said Samantha.

"How'd you find me?"

Samantha smiled. "I'd parked about a block up the street from that alley. You're lucky I caught sight of you when you started walking in. I ran up the street as fast as I could."

"How'd you know I was in trouble?"

Samantha laughed. "You were in a dark alley on South Street. Need I say more?"

Jack suddenly rose from his seat. "Do you want a drink? I can certainly use one."

"What've you got?"

"Same as I had last time you were here."

Samantha thought for a second back to her last visit, and finally replied, "A glass of wine."

Jack returned moments later from the kitchen carrying a bottle of Sam Adams Boston Lager and a glass of chilled Chardonnay. Taking the wine glass from Jack, she put the rim to her lips and took a long, slow sip, allowing the somewhat austere and tantalizing flavors to flow over her tongue.

"Mmm . . . This is very good. What is it?" she asked.

With a smile, Jack replied, "It's a Lynmar Estate 2010 La Sereinité Chardonnay. Only the best for the woman who saved my life."

Jack returned to his place in the Lazy Boy while Samantha took a seat on the sofa. They drank in silence, each deep in thought. Jack wondered why these creatures had suddenly taken such a deadly interest in him. He had never feared for his own safety before, but now he wondered if it was wise to even venture from his apartment. Yet, in light of what had happened at the radio station the previous evening, he was concerned that the perceived safety of his own apartment was an illusion. His brush with death drew his lifelong regrets once again to the surface, in the same manner as a quiet night with too much alcohol often did. Of all of them, one always seemed to overshadow all of his other regrets. And it always brought with it the underlying guilt that accompanied his regrets related to Emma. The guilt alone had kept him from returning to his hometown of Schenectady to visit his parents. He had allowed it to fester for so many years that it had simply become second nature to him, like the mild ache of arthritis that one simply grows to live with. Was it fair to deprive his parents of their own son's company because of what had happened? He often wondered if Emma's parents ever knew the truth. Jack had never spoken to them after that night, and he wondered if they would understand.

Samantha's mind had drifted into the recent past with thoughts of Faulkner and Anderson, the two officers who had died in the elevator at the hands of Calithea Panagakos. She couldn't help but cast the blame on herself for placing the two officers in the situation that had resulted in their deaths. With thoughts of what she should have done differently racing through her mind, she found her emotional barriers faltering at her own recriminations. She questioned her actions, asking herself why she hadn't ridden in the elevator with the two officers. Had it been prideful thinking that perhaps she thought that "suspect escort duties" were beneath a detective of her standing? No, she had always been willing to take on the most insignificant task if it needed to be done. Or perhaps, she thought, it was the way that Calithea Panagakos made her feel. She would never admit it publicly, but there was something about Calithea that intimidated Samantha in a way she had never experienced before. It was impossible for the detective to put her finger on exactly what it was. Perhaps it was the impossibly good looks the woman exuded, or the inexplicable persuasion that she had over her male counterparts. Whatever it was, it was unsettling Samantha to the extent that she could feel the cracks widening in her proverbial armor. The creature called Calithea had struck a ferocious blow by adding the death of two police officers to Samantha's tally. Now there were three for which the detective felt responsible.

"I've been kicked off the case," she suddenly said.

"Why?"

"I wasn't playing well with others. Particularly the FBI." Samantha paused, and then added, "Speaking of the feds, you're all they're talking about these days."

Raising his eyebrows in surprise, he simply said, "Huh?"

"Among their many theories, they think the killer has some kind of connection to you. It's a neat little theory, ties up the Pulsar murders as well as Bryan and Jason's deaths all in a neat little bow."

"They think I've got something to do with all this?"

"Not anymore . . . at least not directly. Perhaps it's someone who knows you, or an obsessed fan. At least, that's their theory. For now, I suggest we try to avoid running into Tweedle Dee and Tweedle Dum." Samantha emptied her wine glass with a long, slow sip and then said, "As good as the Chardonnay may be, I didn't come here to share small talk over a few drinks. Tell me you discovered something so I don't feel like I saved your life for nothing."

"As a matter of fact, I did. And you won't believe what I found."

Chapter Twenty-One

Carrying the laptop, Jack returned from the bedroom and sat down next to Samantha on the sofa. Tapping on the keyboard brought the dark screen to life, and Jack typed in the password at the prompt on the screen.

"What was the password?" inquired Samantha.

"THX1138" came Jack's reply.

Puzzled, Samantha asked, "What's that when it's at home? And, more to the point, how did you figure it out?"

Leaning back into the sofa, Jack smiled smugly. "About six months ago, Bryan was trying to get me to watch this movie. One of the all-time greats, he called it. It's the first feature film directed by George Lucas. You do know who George Lucas is, don't you?"

Frowning, Samantha replied, "Are you going to get on with this, or do I have to arrest you for obstruction?"

Smiling, Jack continued to explain. "Bryan wouldn't shut up about this film, calling it his personal favorite. The movie was called 'THX 1138'. I'd been racking my brain for hours without any success and then it came to me."

"Did you ever watch it?" asked Samantha.

"Yeah, but I just didn't get it."

Samantha leaned forward, gazing at the computer screen. "What'd you find? Anything helpful?"

"Quite a bit. Bryan's been busy over the past few weeks doing a lot of research on these creatures. There's a lot here, I'll just give you the highlights," explained Jack as he leaned over the laptop. "According to his notes, Seirenes are the real-life creatures that the Sirens of Greek mythology were based on. The difference being that the Seirenes are far more dangerous than their mythological counterparts."

"How dangerous?" questioned Samantha.

"I'll get to that in a minute. Sirens were mentioned in Greek mythology for centuries, one of the earliest references being in Homer's *Odyssey*. Bryan noted this as the classic representation that most people accept: their beauty and enchanting songs entice sailors to their deaths."

"That's a far cry from sucking corpses dry as a bone," remarked Samantha.

"Bryan's theory was that the real Seirenes were so terrifying that writers of that time didn't dare tell the truth of their nature, fearing it would cause widespread panic. But he also noted that Homer did try to convey some degree of the truth in the *Odyssey*. Let me find it," said Jack, as he tapped on the keyboard, searching the laptop for a particular file. Finding it, he continued, "Here it is. Circe—the Greek goddess of magic—is warning Odysseus about the Sirens. She says the Sirens 'sit in a meadow; men's corpses lie heaped up all round them, moldering upon the bones as the skin decays.' Mentions of the Sirens pop up all over Greek literature. They're in the *Odyssey*, a poem called "Argonautica", Ovid's poem "Metamorphoses", and even a play by Euripides called *Helen*. They're significant figures in Greek mythology."

"I get all that. But it doesn't explain how they ended up in Philadelphia."

"Bryan found other references," Jack explained. "He's noted some allusions to creatures called Seirenes in some obscure writings from the eighth century BCE. According to Bryan's notes, these writings pre-date the *Odyssey* by about fifty years. They tell a tale of a village on the island of Capri. Three women terrorized the village with their power to influence men, and strip them of their souls. What Bryan found interesting was these writings say that the Seirenes left the soulless empty shell of the men behind. Sound familiar?"

Samantha shook her head. "I'm not sure I buy it. All the talk about souls sounds more like religious superstition than fact."

"I know. But Bryan commented on the fact that in those days everything had a spiritual element to it. He theorized that they might have seen a dried up corpse left by a Seirene, and assumed this was what happened when the soul left the body."

"What else did he find?" asked Samantha.

"Some references in early first century documents alluding to an ancient text about Seirenes written by Aristotle—supposedly in the Ancient Library of Alexandria. Aristotle had written the manuscript, and gave it to his student, Demetrius of Phaleron, who has been attributed with initially organizing the ancient library. Whether it's true or not, no one knows. The library was destroyed by fire between 40 BCE and 400 CE."

"Fat load of good that does us," said Samantha.

"But Aristotle's manuscript supposedly theorizes that the Seirenes had some kind of mental ability to influence the minds of men and women, with men being more susceptible. That would appear, to the uneducated, as using their beauty to bewitch men."

Samantha laughed. "It's comforting to know that things haven't changed much. With big tits and a nice ass, you can get a man to do anything." She paused and then her face drew into a frown as she said, "That would explain Peter's behavior when we questioned Calithea. Damn, I came down on him pretty hard over that. It might also explains why I had such a feeling of . . ."

"Of what?"

Samantha shook her head. "Nothing. It's not important."

Jack continued. "According to Bryan's notes, there've been hints and references to Seirenes throughout history, mostly in private letters and journals. They always state that there are three Seirenes, working together to terrorize a small village or city. Most of the references were from Greece. The descriptions vary, but two things are always the same. They're very beautiful, and they use their beauty to entice men to their deaths. It's a recurring theme throughout all of the stories."

Shaking her head, Samantha said, "Hang on a minute. If these creatures were as terrorizing as you say, why are they relegated to obscure mentions in ancient texts? I'd have thought something this terrifying would've gotten a better mention than just a footnote in Homer's *Odyssey*."

"Bryan had a theory about that."

"Of course he did," interjected Samantha.

Smiling at her sarcasm, Jack continued to explain. "Their appearances, although terrifying, were not very frequent. The Seirenes would terrorize a village for a few months, and then disappear for a several decades, or even a century or more. Then they'd reappear in another village for a few months, only to disappear again for another century."

"That's one hell of a long hibernation period," joked Samantha.

"No one knew where they went, or why. The only consistency was that there were always three of them. A brunette, a redhead, and a blonde."

Samantha added, "Calithea, Adonia, and Kallista."

"Kallista? Can't these three have normal names, like Michelle, Amy, or Janet?" joked Jack.

Samantha laughed loudly. For the first time in weeks, she was beginning to relax. Was it the wine? She thought. Or . . . the company?

"There's a fairly descriptive tale about Laconia, a city in the southeastern part of the Peloponnese peninsula in Greece," continued Jack. "In the early 1270s, the city was a prosperous part of the Byzantine Empire. But there's a story that tells of a dark time when men and women were afraid to venture out at night, and it was ill advised to even walk alone during the day. They called them the 'Three Angels of Death.' It was said if you fell under their spell, you were as good as dead. The story describes how these angels would wander through the city enticing young men, old men, fathers, sons, and even a few women with their mysterious charms. Every day someone would be found missing. According to the story, this went on for months, until two soldiers patrolling the mountain region outside of the city stumbled into a cave. It contained over a hundred bodies, all with their souls damned for eternity . . . at least that was what they thought back then. Again, they lacked the understanding to know what had really happened. Everyone that had gone missing was in that cave. It created such a panic in the city that the soldiers were ordered to burn everything in the cave."

Samantha looked puzzled as she listened to the story. "How'd they know there were three of them?"

"Witnesses. There were people who had seen some of the victims walking away with a beautiful woman they didn't recognize," explained Jack. "Based on those descriptions, they made the assumption that there were three angels. But that's not the best part of the story. An artist named Sebastianos lived in Laconia at that time and wrote this obscure text. He added some illustrations based on the eyewitness accounts. Bryan found a picture of the illustrations." Opening another document on the screen, Jack handed the laptop to Samantha. "Take a look."

Samantha rested the laptop on her thighs, and peered at the screen in amazement. The artistic abilities of the medieval artist left quite a bit to be desired, and Samantha could understand why the world didn't rank the work of Sebastianos up there with that of Da Vinci and Picasso. But the illustrations were good enough for Samantha to see the resemblance. The detail in the crudely drawn face showed the now familiar oval shape, with the narrow chin and red lips. Although the style was different, Samantha immediately recognized the long strands of black hair falling on either side of a familiar countenance, which the artist had captured perfectly. Feeling a chill work its way up her spine, Samantha couldn't help but shiver. If she had not known any better, she would have sworn that the depiction had been created just a day or two ago. The resemblance was more than just uncanny; it was terrifying.

Jack leaned over, and pointed to the screen. "You may not recognize the other two, but I do. The redhead is Adonia, the woman I saw with Jason at Pulsar. And the blonde is the other woman I saw at the club. There are our three angels of death—our Seirenes."

Samantha, still staring at the images on the screen, mumbled, "Death's little angels. Is there anything in here that explains how they do what they do to their victims?"

Nodding, Jack replied, "You'll have to take this with the proverbial grain of salt. Bryan got some of his information from a roleplaying game called *Demons of the Myst*. He claimed the myths in the game were historically accurate. According to the game, the Seirenes had hundreds of microscopic hair-like fibers in their palms. When they feed, these fibers penetrate the skin of their victim like a thousand tiny needles. You can't see the fibers unless the Seirene is feeding. They can feed off just about any part of the body, but they prefer the neck."

"There's the handprints explained," remarked Samantha. "You realize I'd never believe a word of this if I hadn't seen it with my own eyes."

"There's one other thing you need to know. Among the numerous references in Bryan's notes, there were two of particular interest," Jack explained. "One was a letter dating back to December 1788 from William A. Doyle of Philadelphia to his sister, Esther, in New York. Apparently, this William Doyle was a constable in what would have been an early version of the city police department. In his letter, he described a string of baffling deaths around the city that the police were having no luck in solving. He told his sister that the mere sight of the victims frightened him and had to be the result of witchcraft. He didn't say much else, except that the one corpse he saw reminded him of something he had seen in the local tannery."

"They came to Philadelphia?" Samantha gasped.

Jack shrugged. "It would appear so. Here's the clincher. The final reference in Bryan's notes comes from the personal journal of none other than Benjamin Franklin himself. The entry was dated in March of 1789, a little over a year before he died. Here is the journal entry."

Samantha stared in amazement as she read the words on the laptop screen.

I have returned home from a night most terrifying. Perhaps the most terrifying of all my days, of which there are few left. I have this evening, in the company of many a good man, put to rest the three who have plagued us for so many months. The efforts of men have overcome those that would dare bring evil to this fair city of ours. To the city, the cost was high. But to see the iron cap lowered into place and the chains lay tight, brought relief to this weary heart. Entombed as the three are they shall never again bewitch this or any other soul. But weariness from the effort has brought me low and fear I do that this event has deprived me of some few years. Yet if it so happens that should I depart from these earthly bounds this night I do so content in the knowledge that the three have been subdued. And, God–willing, shall never walk these streets again.

She glanced at Jack and asked, "Is this for real?"

Shrugging his shoulders, Jack replied, "I'm just telling you what's on the laptop. I can't speak for the validity of the information. But Bryan seemed to believe it. And I think he died because of it."

Samantha rose from the sofa and began to pace around Jack's living room. Her head was spinning from all that she had heard, and now her mind was trying to put together all of the pieces.

"You're telling me that these three bitches terrorized this city in the seventeen hundreds, and now they've come back?"

Jack nodded. "It looks that way."

"And Benjamin Franklin defeated them?"

"Yep," replied Jack. "I'm still not sure where, though. Bryan didn't have any notes on that."

Samantha smiled. "Don't worry about that. I know where they were buried."

Jack leaned back into the cushions of the sofa as Samantha began to explain, "There's an old building being renovated over on Broad Street. Peter and I were called out there a few weeks ago to investigate three bodies that were found under the basement of the building. They were dried and shriveled corpses, just like all the others have been. But these were the first ones. I was certain someone had been playing a hoax on us. In the chamber with the bodies was a deep well, with an iron cap and a pile of chain. It was empty."

"Are you serious?" asked Jack.

"Yeah. The forensics team didn't find much, other than three sets of bare footprints, presumably women's feet based on the size and shape. I'm pretty confident this was probably where our little angels had been hiding for the past few centuries," explained

Samantha. Then, as an afterthought, she added, "I don't suppose he thought to put in his journal how he defeated them . . ."

Shaking his head, Jack responded, "No, unfortunately not."

"I guess the old bastard had no way of knowing they'd come back. But how did they get here?"

"It doesn't say," said Jack, shrugging his shoulders. "Those were the only two references in Bryan's notes to Philadelphia. Everything else was about Greece."

"Where could they be now? There's no way Calithea could return to her apartment. They must have another hideout somewhere in the city," theorized Samantha.

Glancing at his watch, Jack rose from the sofa and said, "I'd love to stay and talk about this all night, but it's just past eleven. I need to head into the station."

Samantha turned to face Jack. "I'll drive you over."

Shaking his head, Jack replied, "That's not necessary."

Folding her arms, Samantha stared at Jack. "I *am* driving you. Have you forgotten already what happened just a few hours ago? I'm not going to lose you to these creatures."

Smiling, Jack said, "I didn't know you cared."

"I don't. But you're the best resource I have right now. God knows nobody else would believe this shit. We'll leave the way we came in, just in case Wilkinson's got eyes on the building. I'll drop you off, and I'll pick you up tomorrow morning."

"If I say no, what're you going to do?" Jack jokingly asked.

"Slap the cuffs on you and drag your ass over there anyway."

"I guess I don't have much choice," remarked Jack.

Chapter Twenty-Two

The clock on her microwave told her it was close to one in the morning when Samantha finally arrived at her townhouse. The drive to the WPLX studios had been a quiet one. Neither occupant of her white Mini Cooper had felt like talking much after their lengthy discussion in Jack's apartment. She had never listened to the radio station before, but she had tuned in WPLX during her drive home. Samantha was surprised at how different Jack's disembodied voice sounded coming through her speakers. She had smiled as he, with his smoky voice, delivered the weather forecast, making it sound as if he was talking only to her.

Once she had removed her grey overcoat, Samantha poured herself a glass of wine from the half empty bottle of Pinot Noir in her refrigerator. She swirled the ruby liquid around in her glass before taking a long sip. Moving into the living room, Samantha slid down into the deep cushions of the chocolate microfiber sofa. The room was brightly illuminated with light coming from three floor lamps and a light in the ceiling fan above her head. The lights in the room had been strategically placed so as to not cast shadows—a practice she had initiated during the earlier Society Hill

Serial Killer investigation. Turning all the lights on had been a practice that had taken two years of therapy to break. Now, after the events of the past few weeks, she found herself returning to the behavior for comfort. She glanced around the room, taking a full inventory of each and every item. Each photo, piece of furniture, and every curio and knick-knack were right where they should be. That knowledge brought Samantha a great deal of comfort as she allowed herself to sink deeper into the sofa.

While sipping her wine, Samantha made a mental note to write letters to the families of Officers Faulkner and Anderson, expressing her deepest condolences. It wasn't something that was expected of her; she knew that the dead officers' captain would be sending letters. But Samantha felt compelled if for no other reason than to try to squelch the rising guilt she felt over their deaths. Her therapist would tell Samantha that their demise wasn't her fault. But, just like the last time, it wouldn't stop her from feeling guilty.

She tried to shift her mind toward reviewing what she had learned earlier in the evening from Jack Allyn. There was a lot of hearsay and not a lot of facts. Everything that they knew about these Seirenes was from ancient documents, whose veracity was doubtful to say the least. Even if the journal entry from Benjamin Franklin was utterly truthful, it had been far from helpful in nailing down a solution to the current situation. The question now became what to do next.

Samantha was certain that she couldn't present this information to her superior officer, let alone to the FBI. To walk into his office, and tell him they were looking for three creatures from Greek Mythology would be, in her own terms, a "résumé producing event." Her only ally at this juncture was Jack Allyn, and perhaps Peter Thornton. As far as Samantha was concerned, the jury was still out on whether or not Peter would believe any of it. He had seemed receptive when they were waiting for forensics to arrive at the comic book shop, but it was hard to tell if he was simply humoring her until he could speak to their boss.

Emptying her glass, Samantha turned the words of Franklin's journal over in her head. She thought again of the iron cap, and the old rusted chain she had seen beside it. The three Seirenes had been sealed away for eternity, or so it was thought at the time. The good folks of eighteenth century Philadelphia thought the creatures could never escape. If they had only known . . .

"Apparently, an iron cap and chain couldn't hold them forever," Samantha said aloud to no one but herself.

The white Mini Cooper was waiting in the alley behind the Flimm Building when Jack stepped out into the morning sunshine. Samantha had been correct about the FBI waiting for him at the entrance of the building. He had seen the black SUV pull up by the curb two hours before his shift was over. Luckily for

Jack, the building was only accessible after hours with a security keycard, and he doubted that the FBI could override the system. The doors wouldn't unlock for another half hour, so, figuring that they were hoping to stop him on his way out, Jack slipped down a little known stairwell into the alley where Samantha had agreed to meet him.

He pulled open the passenger door of the Mini Cooper and dropped into the seat next to Samantha, who was sipping from a Dunkin Doughnuts coffee cup.

"No sidekick this morning?" Jack asked as he slid into the car's passenger seat.

Samantha simply shook her head in reply.

"So, what's up with you two anyway? Have you been partners long?" inquired Jack.

"Only a few months. Peter's a rookie in the detective division. I'm supposed to be his mentor."

"You make it sound like a punishment."

"For me, it is. I'm not the mentoring type," said Samantha, smiling. "Truth be told, he's a good cop. He's got the smarts to go far as a detective. He's just a little rough around the edges."

"Have you eaten?" Jack asked.

Samantha shook her head in response.

"Great. I know the perfect place for breakfast."

While in the car, the only conversation between them was Jack providing Samantha with directions to Monk's Cafe. As she pulled her Mini Cooper into the only available spot in the small parking lot along the side of the grimy white-painted brick building,

Samantha turned and frowned at Jack.

"Here? Wasn't this place shut down by the health department once?" she asked.

Smiling, Jack replied, "Actually, it was shut down three times as far as I know."

As she pushed her door open, Samantha replied, "Great. If the Seirenes don't get me, breakfast will."

Jack led the detective into the small cafe and over to his usual table in the far corner. When the waitress, Meg, approached the table her eyes darted from Jack to Samantha, and then back to Jack. She raised her eyebrows at Jack, who simply smiled in return.

"Mornin' Jack. Do you want the usual?" the waitress asked.

"Yeah, Meg. That'd be great."

Turning to Samantha, Meg inquired, "And for you?"

"The largest cup of coffee you have, and eggs sunny side up with sausage on the side. And please hold the salmonella."

Meg smirked and then glanced at Jack. "A comedian? She's a comedian?" Turning back to Samantha, Meg scowled at her and added, "Since you're a friend of Jack's, I won't spit in your eggs before bringing them to you."

When the waitress had gone, Samantha looked across the table at Jack. "She doesn't have much of a sense of humor."

"They're a little touchy when it comes to the

subject of food poisoning," came his reply.

"Not to sound like I'm trying to pick you up, but do you come here often?"

Jack laughed. "Just about every morning. The place may not look like much, but the food's fantastic."

"I hope you're right. I'm placing my life in your hands by eating here," said Samantha.

"So, about this building you told me about . . . How old was it?"

"Not old enough to date back to Franklin's time, but the chamber was deep underneath the foundation of the building above," disclosed Samantha. "The building was probably simply built right over top of the subterranean chamber. I doubt that anyone knew it was there." She paused for a moment, and then added, "Something that dawned on me last night was that Calithea had been working with a lawyer who ended up dead the next day. He was working on some kind of legacy for her. I didn't dig any deeper at time because I didn't see a need to, but now . . ."

"You're going back to check it out," stated Jack.

Samantha replied, "Yeah. As soon as we're done with breakfast."

"Great. I'll tag along."

Samantha and Jack stood alone in the elevator of the Independence Capital building in downtown Philadelphia as they rode up to the twenty-fifth floor. The sound of soft music filled the interior, causing Jack to cringe. During the drive over from Monk's Cafe Samantha had called her partner, Peter Thornton, to provide him with an update on the previous evening. When she had ended the call, Samantha was still unsure about the state of her partner's belief in the mythological creatures. Now, she and Jack were approaching their first port of call for the morning, the law offices of Haskell, Seymour, and Meyers. As the elevator doors opened, she glanced at Jack for a moment. She knew that she was breaking department regulations by bringing him along during an investigation. There was no good reason for him to be accompanying her, other than the sense of comfort his presence seemed to give her. As they stepped off the elevator, Samantha was surprised to see an overweight man in grey overalls scraping at the lettering on the glass doors to the law offices. The "u" and the "r" in the name "Seymour" had already been removed, and the man was working diligently to remove the "o" from the glass. James Seymour had only been dead for a few weeks, but it seemed his old partners, Haskell and Meyers, were anxious to remove his name from the firm.

As they entered the office, Samantha noticed that the face behind the front desk was different, leading her to wonder if she had driven the previous receptionist to quit after her last visit. Samantha remembered that she had been a bit abrupt on her last visit. This young blonde receptionist seemed cold and unfazed when Samantha presented her badge along with her request to speak to Fredrick Haskell.

"Do you have an appointment?" the receptionist asked.

"No. Usually my badge is the only appointment I need," replied Samantha.

The receptionist replied, "Mr. Haskell doesn't see people without appointments. Perhaps I can schedule something for later this week?"

Placing her hands on the desk, Samantha leaned toward the young woman, and stared at her for a moment. "Look, sweetie. I don't have time for this. Please tell Mr. Haskell I'm here. He knows who I am, and he will see me."

As the receptionist stepped away from her desk, Samantha and Jack waited silently for her return. For the first time in this investigation, the detective was feeling as if she were getting somewhere. Her nerves had been frayed, and she was exhausted. But she was feeling the surge of adrenaline that she always got when a case started to come together. Samantha was banking everything on walking out of the law office with new information that would lead her to the three creatures. She hoped that she wouldn't walk out disappointed.

Jack, who had remained silent during the exchange between Samantha and the receptionist, had found humor in the detective's attitude toward the unfortunate young woman and was forced to stifle a laugh. Never in his life did Jack think that he would be involved in a police investigation, let alone one consisting of such bizarre and unimaginable circumstances. He considered how much had happened over the past couple of weeks and still found it all difficult to believe. Yet he couldn't deny his own eyes and his own memories. The sight of Jason Spinacker's body, the attack on Panama Street, and even the attempt on his life from the previous night were all far too vivid and fresh in his mind.

When the receptionist returned, she led Jack and Samantha to the same conference room where the detective had been during her previous visit. The receptionist closed the door behind them, leaving the pair alone to wait. Jack slid into one of the leather chairs surrounding the oval conference table while Samantha walked to the window and gazed out over the city.

"She's hiding out there somewhere," Samantha said quietly.

Before Jack could respond, the conference room door opened, and the elderly Fredrick Haskell stepped softly into the room. The man's blue eyes looked from Samantha to Jack, and then back again to Samantha; his face formed a deep grimace.

"Detective Ballard, I'm assuming that this is important to justify once again upsetting my receptionist," said Haskell.

"I'm sorry to intrude on your morning, but this is of the utmost importance." Gesturing to Jack, Samantha added, "This is my associate, Jack Allyn."

Haskell nodded toward Jack. "How can I help you both?"

Samantha gave Haskell the politest smile she could muster and said, "If you will remember, when

I was here last, it was in reference to James Seymour's death. You provided me information about one of his clients, Calithea Panagakos. You stated that Mr. Seymour was working on some kind of legacy for Ms. Panagakos. At the time, it didn't seem important to violate client confidentiality. But based on recent events, I'm going to have to request that you give me full access to the Panagakos file. I need to know everything that James Seymour was working on for her."

Taking a slow, deep breath, Haskell slowly shook his head. "Detective, as we discussed during your last visit, I will not violate confidentiality of my clients without a warrant or my client's written permission. Since you have not presented me with either of those items, I assume that you do not have them. Therefore, you are wasting your time as well as mine."

Samantha's eyes narrowed, and she stared across the room at the lawyer. "Mr. Haskell, your client is currently suspected of having killed two police officers, as well as being connected to numerous suspicious deaths in the city. Now, I understand how important client confidentiality is. But if you really want a warrant, I will get a warrant . . ." She paused for a moment, and then added, "to search every file on the premises, because you never know if someone may have made a mistake and filed a document in the wrong place. While I'm at it, I'll make sure the media are fully appraised of the situation. And, as an added bonus, I'll arrest you on charges of obstruction and harboring a fugitive."

Haskell glared at Samantha. "Are you

threatening me?"

The detective simply replied, "Yes."

Looking at Jack, Haskell exclaimed, "You're a witness! She can't do this!"

Shrugging his shoulders, Jack replied, "I'm just tagging along here."

Haskell puffed out his chest, and then gave a loud sigh. "Fine. I will get you our files on Ms. Panagakos."

As he turned to leave the room, Samantha spoke. "Mr. Haskell. I appreciate this. And I hope you know that I would never have followed through with my threats. But we've got no time to waste. This woman needs to be stopped before she kills again."

Haskell glanced over his shoulder. "I understand, detective. I'll be right back with those files."

When Haskell returned a few minutes later, he was carrying a thin manila folder under his arm. He set the folder down on the table and gently flipped open the lid, revealing a stack of documents inside. Haskell gestured for Samantha sit down as he pulled up a chair for himself.

"You may not be aware of this, but our small firm is quite an old one in the city. We've been in business in one form or another for well over two-hundred and fifty years," Haskell explained. "It's been a family business starting with our founder, Franklin F. Meyers, in the late 1780s. It's rare for us these days to have to dig into our files for anything dating that far back, but this one was one of those rare occasions." The elderly man drew an old piece of parchment from the bottom of the stack of documents and then continued to speak. "Very early in our founder's career, he was approached by a client wishing to draw up a will. According to Meyers' notes, this woman was leaving for a long voyage, and wished to leave provisions for the disposal of her property in the event something happened to her. Part of these provisions included the firm maintaining the property during our client's absence. For this service, a financial arrangement was provided from which we could draw a regular nominal fee, as well as any expenses incurred for said maintenance. Obviously, Meyers assumed that this would only be for a few months, but it turned out to last over two centuries."

"The money lasted that long?" questioned Jack.

Haskell nodded. "Oh, yes. The client provided the firm with a large amount of gold bullion, which we have used sparingly over the years to maintain the property in question, as well as pay our ongoing fee for the responsibility as originally agreed."

"Hang on a sec. Wasn't it illegal to own gold during World War II?" said Samantha.

Haskell blushed slightly. "Ah, yes. It was illegal for quite a number of years. Sometimes, we lawyers bend the rules a little in the best interest of our clients. In the 1970s we liquidated the gold and invested the funds, using mostly the interest to pay our ongoing legal fees."

"The history lesson is nice and all, but what does

all of this have to do with Calithea Panagakos?" asked the detective.

Laying the piece of parchment down on the table, Haskell said, "The property in question is a house over in Germantown. Ms. Panagakos arrived in our office claiming to be an ancestor of our client and the rightful heir. James Seymour was working with her to validate her claim and then transfer ownership of the property and the remaining funds to her."

Jack glanced at the yellowing palimpsest with its handwritten script, noting the signature at the bottom. Pointing toward the flared autograph, Jack asked, "Is that your client's signature?"

Haskell nodded. "Yes."

"It's the same name," observed Samantha.

"Yes, we thought that was interesting as well. But Ms. Panagakos explained that it was an old family name that's been passed down through the generations."

Samantha glanced at Jack and could tell that they were both thinking the same thing. Knowing what they did, they were both certain that this was not a coincidence. The signature on the parchment read, "Calithea Panagakos".

Samantha rose from her seat, and said, "Thank you, Mr. Haskell. If you can give us the address of that property, we should be on our way."

Chapter Twenty-Three

The house on the corner of W. Queen Lane and Knox Street was an old Georgian colonial-style home with broad white trim framing the pale yellow painted clapboard siding. The first floor windows, which were evenly spaced with two on each side of the large white door, were partnered with identical twins on the second floor. Each window was flanked by a set of black storm shutters which, at one time, may have served a purpose but now looked only decorative. The casing around the front door was broad, white, and topped with an oversized horizontal lintel. The three-paneled door itself was white as well, with a large, tarnished brass doorknocker. The house looked out of place between the nineteenth and twentieth century duplexes, which, over time, had been erected around it. But, as Frederick Haskell had said, the house had withstood the test of time with some help from the law firm. With no owner to consult, Haskell had disclosed, the lawyers at the firm had to make some decisions about what was best for maintaining the structure, including roofing, painting, and landscaping.

The white Mini Cooper was parked half a block from the house on the opposite side of the street. The two occupants sat quietly, gazing across at the old structure, as if admiring its beautifully maintained exterior. The house stood as a testament to an age that some might have called "simpler times." But neither Jack nor Samantha was thinking about the architectural significance of the old home. They were far more concerned about what might be waiting inside.

"It looks innocent enough," said Jack.

Samantha replied, "They always do."

"So, what do we do now?"

Never taking her eyes off of the old house, the detective replied, "Wait for Peter to get here."

On the drive over from the law firm, Samantha had called Peter Thornton, requesting that he meet them at the address provided by the lawyer. They had been waiting on W. Queen Lane for over fifteen minutes, and Samantha was growing impatient.

"When he gets here, we go in?" asked Jack.

Samantha turned toward him. "What do you mean 'we'? You're staying here. Peter and I will go in."

Jack shook his head. "Not a chance. I've come too far to be left out at the kill."

"I'll handcuff you to the steering wheel," stated Samantha.

"I'll honk the horn until the entire neighborhood knows we're here."

Shaking her head, Samantha replied, "Jack, I can't put your life at risk."

"You're not. *I'm* putting my life at risk."

"No. No. No. I can't take that risk," exclaimed

Samantha.

Jack gave her a half-smile. "I'm not giving you a choice. I'm going in with you."

Samantha began to plead with Jack. "Please don't put me in this position. I don't need four deaths on my conscience."

The words had just slipped out, and the moment she said them Samantha wished she could reach out and snatch them back. But it was too late. He had heard them and responded immediately.

"Four?" asked Jack.

Samantha hesitated, hoping that something would happen to draw his attention away from the question, but nothing did. It was something she didn't want to think about right now. It was something she never wanted to think about but she always did. She turned away from him and gazed out the window at the old house once again.

"I've been responsible for sending three officers to their deaths," Samantha explained. "Two died in the elevator on Saturday. I should've been with Faulkner and Anderson, maybe I could have stopped her."

"You might've died with them."

"Better that than . . ." Samantha's comment trailed off into silence.

Jack asked softly, "Who was the other?"

"Brad Peterson, a rookie fresh out of the academy for only about three months. I'd been investigating a string of murders in Society Hill," Samantha said, her voice quiet, almost a whisper. "You probably weren't living in the city at the time of the Society Hill Serial Killer case. It was gruesome. Sadistic doesn't even begin to describe the bastard. His name was Rodney Hillerman, and he was . . . a monster. He would kill his victims slowly, butcher the bodies, and then use a scalpel to carve messages in their flesh. We had already canvased the neighborhood twice, but I had some follow-up questions I wanted ask of the people who lived around the crime scenes. Our standard procedure is to always go out in pairs for that sort of thing, but we were shorthanded that day. I was too impatient. I wanted answers to my questions ASAP. So I bent the rules and sent Peterson out on his own. He never came back." Samantha paused, feeling the emotion trying to push its way out from within her. She hadn't spoken to anyone about this for a long time, and with all that happened over the past few weeks, Samantha had felt on the verge of breaking down. It had been a struggle in the evenings to keep from crying herself to sleep. Sometimes she lost the struggle. As a single tear rolled down her cheek, she managed to push the emotions back into the dark recesses of her mind and continue with her narrative. "We found him two days later. He became Hillerman's fifth victim. The bastard carved a message in Peterson's chest, which said 'He asked too many questions'."

"You couldn't have known—" Jack started to say.

"It doesn't matter," Samantha shot back. "I broke protocol. I was too focused on solving the case . . . and proving wrong all the people who didn't think I was good enough to be a detective. I sent him to his death."

Jack softly said, "I'm sorry."

"I don't want anyone else's death on my conscience. Three is enough."

"Look, you're not ordering me to go in there with you. I'm going of my own free will. If I die, you're not responsible," stated Jack.

Smiling, Samantha said, "That's not much comfort."

The car fell into silence again as they continued to wait for the absent Peter Thornton. Samantha thought about her partner, wondering if she had perhaps been a little too hard on him over the past couple of months. Peter Thornton was a good cop. She knew that. Although a little raw and inexperienced around the edges, Samantha knew he was a good detective too. He asked a lot of questions and came up with dozens of theories, not all of them good, but after all, wasn't that what being a detective was all about? Finding the theory that matched the evidence? Her mind drifted back to her first months as a detective. She wondered what her old partner, Eddie Murdock, had thought of her when she was a rookie. Was she just as impetuous back then as Peter was now? Samantha was still deep in thought when Jack broke the silence once again.

"You married?" he asked.

Samantha had been lost in thought, and the question took her by surprise. "What?"

"Are you married? It's an easy enough question,"

replied Jack.

"No. You?"

"Me neither. Couldn't find Mr. Right?"

"No. My father was a cop," Samantha explained. "He was . . . killed in the line of duty. It crushed my mom. I didn't want to put anyone I loved through that. So I really haven't dated much over the years. Tried not to get involved."

"Is your mom still alive?"

Samantha shook her head. "She passed away about a year ago."

Silence descended on the car once again. But, this time, it was Samantha who broke it.

"What about you? Your folks still alive?"

Jack nodded. "Yeah. They live up in Schenectady, New York."

"Do you get up there much?"

It was Jack's turn to hesitate. Her question was releasing a Pandora's box of memories from Jack's subconscious. He could see Emma's face as clear as day, looking so young and beautiful. Those vibrant blue eyes were what he remembered the most about her. That and her shoulder length hair, which he thought shone like golden honey in the summer sun. He vividly remembered their first kiss and the unique way it had felt so innocent yet so passionate at the same time. Recollections flitted through his mind of what seemed like a million nights spent together at that little Mexican restaurant two blocks from the community college where they had met. Jack was reminded of the evenings holding her in his arms as they danced in the moonlight on her back porch with the radio turned down low. He thought of the nights she would come to the studio at his first part-time job in broadcasting, and she would stay up all night while he played music on the weekend overnight shift. Then, out of the darkest corner of his memories, he remembered the night he had told her what he had done. Even now, he could count the tears that had fallen down her cheeks when he begged her for forgiveness over his unfaithfulness. He had taken one misstep and had pushed away the best thing that had ever happened to him. And he would never forgive himself.

"Jack? I asked you a question," said Samantha.

"Huh? Oh, no. I haven't been back in years."

Puzzled, Samantha asked, "Why not? You don't get along with your parents?"

"It's not that. I fell in love with this girl, Emma," explained Jack, turning his face away from Samantha to gaze out the passenger window. "We met in college, and I was certain that she was the one. Still am. It was the kind of love that you yearn for, the kind that hurts when you're apart. I'd asked her to marry me after only six months. She said she would after we graduated. We'd been together for a little over a year when I did something stupid. I had a one-night fling with someone else. The night I told Emma . . . we had met up at this little Mexican joint where we hung out. She was really upset." Jack paused, holding back his emotion. "She stormed out of the restaurant, and drove herself home that night, and . . . a drunk driver ran a stop sign. She probably didn't even see him coming . . . she died instantly."

Samantha frowned. "I don't know what say."

"Ever since that night, I can't help but wonder if she'd still be alive if she hadn't left early . . . if I hadn't said anything to her that night."

Samantha was silent. She knew there were never concrete answers to any of the proverbial "what if" questions. God only knew how many she had asked herself. She could have told Jack that it wasn't his fault, that he wasn't responsible for Emma's death. Samantha could have cited all the things that her therapist had told her during two years of weekly sessions. But she knew that those were all just words that never really wiped away the guilt. It continued to linger and fester in one's soul, never going away.

Jack added, "That's why all my relationships have been complete shit, I guess. It's why I haven't been back to New York. Her parents practically live next door to mine. I left for Allentown shortly after her death. I never told them what happened. They don't know why Emma was driving home so early. I can't bear to go home."

Glancing at her watch, Samantha said, "We've been here almost half an hour. I'm not waiting for Peter any longer."

Leaning forward, Samantha reached down toward her ankle. Jack heard the sound of Velcro separating and, seconds later, Samantha handed him a

Colt .38 snub nose revolver.

"Do you know how to fire one of these?" she asked.

"I lived in Texas. It was mandatory for residency."

Smiling, Samantha said, "This was my father's. Don't lose it."

Samantha pushed open her car door and stepped out into the street. Moments later, Jack was standing beside her, both of them staring at the old house on the corner. Before they could step forward, a Dodge Charger came around the corner two blocks down from them. Samantha gently elbowed Jack in the ribs.

"Just in time," she said, gesturing toward the slowing car.

The Charger pulled in behind the Mini Cooper, and Peter leapt from the driver's seat to join Samantha and Jack.

"Sorry I'm late. Traffic was a nightmare getting across town," he said.

"We almost started this party without you," said Jack.

Glancing at Samantha, Peter inquired, "We?"

Nodding toward Jack, Samantha clarified, "He didn't give me much choice."

Glancing at the old house, Peter said, "Seems awfully quiet. Do we know if anyone is inside?"

Samantha shook her head. "Been here for half an hour and haven't seen a soul."

"What's the plan?" inquired Peter.

"We'll knock and if no one answers—we'll just play it by ear," replied Samantha. "Did you bring them?"

Peter nodded and then reached into the pocket of his overcoat, extracting two small, square, black objects that looked to Jack like small portable radios. Samantha handed one to Jack, saying "Body cams."

As Jack turned the object over in his hand, he could see the small lens on the front along with a small grill-like opening that he assumed was the microphone. The outer shell appeared to be constructed from an industrial strength polymer which, Jack thought, could probably withstand a bullet strike. The back contained a large black clip which Peter was already using to attach his body cam to the collar of his overcoat. Handing the body cam back to Samantha, Jack watched as she followed Peter's action by attaching the camera to her coat as well.

The trio crossed the street single file with Samantha in the lead like, Jack thought, three gunfighters at the O.K. Corral. Their steps were slow and steady, and Samantha's eyes darted right and left in a constant vigil for anything suspicious. Her hand rested on her hip, close to the bulge from her holster. Jack, who was bringing up the rear of the small parade, could feel the adrenaline coursing through his veins with every step they took. He could feel the cold steel hammer of the revolver pressed against his stomach where he had slipped it into his waistband. The palms of his hands were sweating, and a brief wave of nausea passed through him. He wouldn't admit it to his companions, but Jack had never felt so scared in his life.

There were three steps leading up to the door, and Samantha mounted them in a single stride. She stood to the side of the door and rapped loudly on its white-painted wood surface with her knuckles. Jack stood silently at the bottom of the stairs, with his eyes alternating between Samantha and Peter. While Samantha rapped again on the door, Jack noticed that Peter kept glancing up and down the street, as if expecting something to happen. After her third knock on the door went unanswered, Samantha's hand slowly reached for the tarnished brass doorknob. She grasped the knob gently and slowly turned. The trio was surprised to hear the soft click of the latch as it disengaged and the door started to swing open.

"I don't like this," whispered Samantha.

Beyond the doorway, they could see very little of the dimly lit interior; the only light source appeared to be from the open door itself. Samantha reached into her coat pocket in search of her flashlight, but she cursed when she found the pocket void of anything other than her keys. Gesturing back toward his car, Peter stated, "I've got a flashlight in the car."

Shaking her head, Samantha replied, "Don't worry about it."

She glanced around the immediate area and then, finding no witnesses, drew her Glock from its holster. Jack, having caught sight of Peter's firearm as it was withdrawn from its resting place on his hip, followed suit by pulling the small revolver from his waistband. Glancing over her shoulder at her two companions, Samantha said, "Let's do this. Watch yourselves. We know what they can do."

Samantha moved through the doorway, and Jack watched as she was swallowed by the darkness. In two easy strides, Peter followed on Samantha's heels and vanished as well through the darkened doorway. Jack made a quick glance around, and then shrugged his shoulders. He tightened his grip on the grip of the revolver, feeling reassured by its presence in his hand. Then he took three quick treads up the stairs, stepped through like his companions before him, and then pushed the door closed behind him.

Chapter Twenty-Four

As he waited for his eyes to adjust to the dark, Jack remained still just inside the threshold of the house. He inhaled deeply only to find the air around him was dust-filled and stale. Faint strips of light shone through the edges of the heavily curtained windows, giving him his first glimpse of the room in which he was standing. Furniture was arranged around the room, each enveloped with a white sheet. Some held the distinct shapes of end tables, a sofa, and chairs, while one in the far corner resembled, Jack thought, a harp with its tall triangular form rising toward the low ceiling. Dark paneling covered the walls and surrounded the fireplace, and a rectangular area rug was centered in the room atop the hardwood floor. It looked like it was covered with two centuries of dust. Thick cobwebs hung from the walls and stretched across the covered furniture. Along the wall opposite the front door, Jack could just make out a narrow stairwell leading to the second floor, and next to that was a dark opening leading further into the house. The wall to his left held a set of oak double doors, which were closed. The room reminded Jack of an old set from almost any 1940s horror film.

Samantha was scanning the room a few feet from Jack while Peter took slow strides around the perimeter. She eyeballed the various shapes covered in white sheets and felt uncomfortable. Any of them could disguise an ambush. She cautiously stepped forward, and slid the sheet off of the nearest object. The antique rocking chair underneath softly creaked as it gently rocked back and forth. Peter returned to her side after completing his circuit of the room.

"There's no light switches," he said quietly.

Samantha replied, "There's no power lines outside running to the house. I thought that was odd, but it makes sense now. No one's lived here for more than two centuries. Why go to the expense of wiring the house for electricity?"

Jack cautiously moved forward to join them, only half listening to their conversation. The extraordinary silence in the house seemed unreal, and he found himself straining to hear anything past the four walls. It seemed unbelievable to Jack that, in a world where there was always a hum or buzz from some form of electronics or HVAC, there would be utter silence in this house. There was not a single background sound to be heard, not even from outside.

"Let's split up. Peter, you check the upstairs. Jack and I will see what else is down here," directed Samantha.

Peter nodded his acquiescence, and turned toward the narrow stairway as Jack said, "In horror films, this is how everyone dies. They split up."

Samantha frowned. "I wish I'd left you in the car."

Peter cautiously climbed the stairs, trying in vain not to cause the old wood beneath his feet to creak with each step, and Samantha led Jack through the open doorway into the dark room beyond. As they entered, Jack noticed a long table centered in the room over which hung, from four black chains, a black iron pot rack. From the curved hooks of the rack dangled an assortment of tarnished copper pots, each looking as if it had not been used in many a long year. To his right, a huge stone fireplace stood along the wall adjoining the living room, and Jack assumed that it probably shared a chimney with its companion in the other room. Thick cobwebs lined the interior of the fireplace, hung down from the pot rack, and even extended out from the fireplace to the center table. Along the far wall, underneath two shuttered windows, was a long row of old cabinets topped with a wooden butcher block, the wood cracked and split from age. Jack was surprised, at first, by the lack of modern day appliances, such as a stove, refrigerator, or dishwasher, but then he remembered what Samantha had said about the absence of electricity. Along the wall to his left was an oak door followed by an archway, which led into what Jack assumed was the dining room, based on the shapes of the objects covered in white sheets.

Samantha stepped into the dining room long enough to give it a cursory survey, and then she returned to the old kitchen. She could tell that Jack was going to speak, and she gestured with her finger for him to remain silent. With slow, deliberate steps, she approached the oak door, tightening her grip on her firearm as she did. Gently grasping the black iron door latch, she slowly pressed her thumb down and heard the latch click. The hinges creaked as she pulled the door open and gazed at a precarious flight of stairs leading downward. Considering how dark the rest of the house had been, Jack and Samantha were surprised to find flickering illumination drifting up from below.

Samantha guardedly made her way down the old stairs, which rocked and swayed beneath her feet. She was comforted to find that on her left was a stone wall, against which she could lean as she scanned the chamber below for danger. When she reached the bottom, she signaled for Jack to follow her down. They both stood in a cold, stonewalled cellar with an uneven, damp stone floor beneath their feet. Across from the stairs were four stacks of wooden crates each stacked five high. The lid of one of the topmost crates stood open. In the far corner of the cold cellar were half a dozen propane tanks, similar in size to those Jack would expect to find fueling a barbecue. The flickering light, which they had noticed earlier, came from lighted candles that hung from black iron sconces on the walls.

Jack approached the open crate and quickly beckoned Samantha to his side. He dipped his hand into the crate and pulled out a handful of gold coins unlike any that he had ever seen before. Some glimmered brightly in the flickering candlelight, while others were tarnished and dull. The style of the coins varied greatly, most emblazoned with text that Jack couldn't read. He recognized some as being Spanish, and he saw others that he thought might be Latin.

"Holy shit! Is this real? Some of these coins look ancient. There's thousands in here," he said.

Jack allowed the coins to fall back into the crate, and then he grabbed one between his fingers, holding it up to get a closer look at the impression molded into the precious metal.

"Does this look like Julius Caesar to you?" he asked his companion.

With her eyes opened wide at the sight, Samantha's lips parted to reply. But the words were halted by a sound from across the room. She spun around quickly and leveled her Glock in the direction of the noise. Along the wall by the propane tanks was a jagged opening, which appeared to have been chiseled out of the stone wall. They could see a line of sconces with burning candles disappear into the darkened passageway. As they approached, Jack tapped Samantha on the shoulder and gestured toward the propane tanks. A long hose, which was connected to the nearest tank, snaked along the floor into the passageway and disappeared into the darkness.

"Maybe they're having a cookout," whispered Jack.

Samantha quietly responded, "Not funny."

Inching forward, Samantha moved toward the passageway until she stood on the precipice.

The opening itself looked as if it had been recently excavated, but the uneven stone stairs on the other side looked ancient. The narrow stone corridor sloped downward and to the right, making it impossible to see where it led. As she took her first step, Samantha could hear the faint echo of her footfall as it bounced off the aged masonry. *So much for sneaking up on anyone,* she thought.

The pair moved down the twisting stone passage, carefully watching every footstep on the damp stone treads beneath their feet. Jack guessed that they had dropped an additional eight to ten feet underground when they stepped out into a vast underground chamber. The first thing they noticed was the immediate foul combination of odors that greeted them. A moldy odor of damp had intermixed with the scent of human excrement to form an offensive smell that made Jack gag as they entered.

With only a few candles burning, the chamber was shrouded in shadows. The narrow propane gas hose, which they had followed down the stone stairway, attached to a small space heater on the floor near their feet, providing a minuscule amount of heat to the otherwise chilly stone cell. A simple twin bed sat against the far wall, with its arched wrought iron headboard showing signs of dilapidation; a white chamber pot rested on the floor at the foot of the bed. Across the corridor that they had just entered from was another passageway leading into further darkness. Jack took a few steps into the darkened passage ahead of them, while Samantha moved further into the chamber.

As extraordinary as the dark room was, the occupant of the bed made it almost surreal and a little terrifying at the same time. She was chained to the headboard by one wrist, while the other was attached to an IV bag, which hung above the bed. The young woman's chocolate hair was matted and knotty, looking as if it had not been washed in a few weeks. The color of her heart-shaped face was pale, and her thin lips were a faded pink. Samantha thought she might be in her early twenties, but in her current state she looked ten years older. Deep in slumber, the woman's eyes were closed, and her chest rose and fell with each shallow breath. A dingy white sheet covered her body, but it couldn't hide the bulge of her abdomen.

"Jack!" exclaimed Samantha.

When he didn't return, Samantha called out again, "Jack!"

Jack quickly returned from the darkened corridor and, gesturing behind him, said, "There's another chamber back there. The old door's got a barred window. Someone's in there. I could just see him over in the corner."

"What'd he look like?" inquired Samantha.

"I couldn't see him well. Tall, thin, with white hair."

"Could be Hardwick," replied Samantha.

"The fertility doctor?"'"

Samantha gestured toward the bed, and "She's pregnant."

Quickly moving to the side of the bed, Samantha slid her firearm into its holster, and she leaned over the sleeping woman. The detective touched the woman's shoulder and tried, unsuccessfully, to wake her. Samantha nudged a little harder, receiving only a faint moan in response.

Looking up at Jack, who was standing on the opposite side of the bed, Samantha quietly said, "She's sedated. We've got to get her out of here."

"If we can get this chain off, we could carry her out with the sheet," Jack suggested.

"Look, Adonia. We have visitors," echoed a disembodied voice throughout the chamber.

Samantha's hand flashed to her holster, and her Glock was suddenly in her hand and sweeping the room in search of a target. From out of the shadows appeared the naked form of Adonia, with her fiery red hair flowing down to her shoulders. In an equal state of undress stood another woman who Jack, even though he had only seen her from afar, recognized from her brief appearances at Pulsar. In such close proximity, Jack was struck by her beauty, which was equaled only by that of her companion. Their shapely bodies looked almost identical, with the only visible difference between the two being their facial structure and hair color. He was mesmerized by the sight of her blonde hair flowing off her shoulders, like a golden waterfall stirring his memories of Emma. He now understood the power that the two could hold over men.

Smiling, Adonia asked, "What shall we do with

them, Kallista?"

The one called Kallista replied, "Is this the little man you were telling me about?"

Adonia nodded her head in silent reply.

As she glared at the bare flesh of the two Seirenes, a flood of conflicting emotions and thoughts filled Samantha's head. She hated them for what they had done in her city. Samantha was angry about the trail of bodies that these creatures had left in their wake and the seemingly easy manner with which they disregarded human life. Yet, to her surprise, Samantha found a streak of jealousy emerge from her subconscious. She had always thought of herself as being attractive, but Samantha had to admit that these two were the most beautiful women she had ever seen. The two naked creatures standing before her would put every Playboy model to shame. It was this jealousy that sent an even greater sense of hatred bursting from her psyche. The past few days had been an emotional roller coaster ride, and keeping her emotions in check was siphoning off all of Samantha's reserves.

Samantha, who was swinging her gun from one to the other, glanced at Jack for only a moment. The snub-nosed revolver was still tucked away in his waistband. His eyes were focused on the exposed bodies of Adonia and Kallista, and they were not wavering. She suddenly felt very much alone.

"So, what's the deal? You're nudists, is that it?" Samantha asked, trying to make light of her precarious situation.

Kallista smiled. "Such simple minds. We find clothing to be abhorrent. To restrict one's body with flimsy fabric is so distasteful."

Adonia added, "One's beauty should be worshipped and held aloft for all to see. Even you, detective, must admit that ours is a beauty far beyond any other on this earth."

"But your modest conventions do not allow us to wander free without covering our beauty," finished Kallista.

Glancing around the chamber, Samantha said, "Nice place you have here. Very rustic."

Adonia raised her hands, and with a sweeping gesture, said, "You like our refuge? This shall one day be heralded as sacred ground."

"It took three of your strongest men to unseal the chamber. We didn't want to—what do women say these days? Break a nail?" added Kallista.

Gesturing toward the unconscious woman in the bed, Samantha demanded, "What have you done to her?"

"She is our vessel, our carrier," replied Kallista.

"She shall be exalted for all eternity as the First Mother," added Adonia.

Glancing between the Seirenes and the woman in the bed, Samantha struggled to understand the meaning of what they were saying. Their unusual expressions combined with their strong Greek accents made it difficult to follow the conversation. With her mind clouded and conflicted, Samantha was finding it difficult to not be blinded by admiration of their beauty. As much as she hated these two creatures, Samantha couldn't help but feel a sense of appreciation bordering on reverence. She wondered if this was just another of the Seirenes' mind tricks.

Samantha shook her head, hoping it would clear her thoughts. "If there's anyone in this room that's a mother, it's you two. Just a pair of mothe—"

"Now, now. There's no need to be uncivil, detective," interrupted Adonia. "It is our destiny to thrive, to break beyond the three and become those adored and worshipped for our beauty."

Samantha laughed. "Worshipped? I don't see anything worth worshipping. All I see are enormous egos."

"It's such a pity, detective. You don't understand beauty that can transcend time when you see it. We are the ones who are irresistible. Men and even women are entranced by our beauty," said Adonia.

Samantha chuckled. "Transcend time? All beauty eventually fades."

Kallista tossed her head back and laughed. "Our beauty has remained for centuries. You can't deny your admiration and wonderment of our beauty. I can see it in your eyes. I can see it in your mind. Look at your companion. Even he's in awe over what's before him, despite his broken heart."

Samantha glanced at Jack once again. He hadn't moved since the two Seirenes appeared. She tried to seem relaxed and unconcerned by the situation, but she could feel the fear building up inside her. Holding onto the hope that Peter would find his way down to the cellar was becoming the only hope she had left.

"What'd you expect? He's a man, and you're naked. Of course he's in awe," Samantha said.

"Oh, it's far more than that. Far more," said Kallista. Then she stared at Jack, and her eyes began to glow. At first, it started as a pale red incandescence but quickly increased in intensity until her eyes burned like an out-of-control forest fire. "Jack, kill Samantha Ballard."

Chapter Twenty-Five

Jack had not been paying attention to the conversation up to that point and had found it difficult to focus on anything but Adonia and Kallista. His mind had become a hazy fog from which he couldn't seem to escape. Faint whisperings had been echoing through his subconscious that Jack could hear but not understand. It was a feeling far different from that which he experienced during Adonia's appearance at the radio station. Where that had been an overwhelming lust for the Seirene's nakedness, this was more like an emptiness that hindered all conscious thought. He had been vaguely aware that a conversation was occurring around him, but Jack had no capacity to participate until the command had been issued.

The single command echoed through his mind, not so much as one that he should obey, but one that he was unable to disobey. Every fiber of his being said that he must disregard the mandate, but every one of those fibers seemed to be overridden by his mind. Jack's arm slowly reached for the revolver tucked in his waistband.

Samantha watched helplessly as Jack's arm moved like an automaton, slowly gripping the handle of her father's Colt .38 revolver, and drawing it from his waistband. She swung her body toward Jack, aiming her Glock in his direction, and then, concerned about leaving the Seirenes unchecked, swung back toward them.

"Jack!" she shouted.

With the revolver gripped firmly in his hand, he slowly lifted his arm and turned to face Samantha. In desperation, she spun back toward him and took aim at Jack's chest.

"Damn it! Jack! Snap out of it!" she exclaimed.

Leveling his firearm at Samantha, he heard nothing but the whispering voices repeating the command over and over, "Kill Samantha Ballard."

Samantha looked deep into Jack's empty eyes, and felt utterly helpless. She knew she would have no choice but to shoot him before he could pull the trigger. It was an agonizing decision, which she knew had only one outcome. She stared down the barrel of her father's gun and fought back the tears, which threatened to pour down her cheeks. Being a police officer always came with the risk of looking down the wrong end of a gun, but she never thought it would be her father's own gun that might take her life.

It was like playing chicken as Samantha desperately tried to judge when Jack would pull the trigger. She was hoping that Jack would suddenly snap out of his trance or that Peter would swoop in to save the day. The man across the bed from her had quickly become a friend, and even a confidant, in the inexplicable events of the past few weeks. Who else did she have who believed the reality that these creatures existed, and were a threat to the city?

"Jack! Please don't make me shoot you! Jack!" she shouted, as she watched his finger tighten on the trigger.

Samantha's eye had sighted the center of Jack's chest down the barrel of her Glock, and felt the cold trigger pressed against her finger. It would be an easy shot at such a short distance, and Samantha had no doubt that she could put Jack down quickly. But she was finding it difficult to pull the trigger. Although not a religious woman, she found herself praying for some kind of reprieve. Not knowing how powerful the Seirenes' influence was on Jack, Samantha was desperate for anything that could break the spell.

"Jack!" she shouted again. Then, as a desperate thought crossed her mind, "Jack, think about Emma! Emma, Jack! Think about Emma!"

The name echoed in his head, intermingling with the command "Kill Samantha Ballard". The hazy fog in his mind had been burning a fiery red ever since the command had been issued from Kallista's ruby lips. But as he sighted his target down the barrel of the revolver, something changed. Amidst the fiery haze, two tiny pinpricks of blue appeared, at first minuscule when compared to the burning red brightness, but growing in intensity. The vibrant blue orbs swelled, rapidly encompassing the fiery haze until it had vanished, leaving behind only a vision of two crisp, blue eyes, so beautiful and lovely that Jack couldn't help but shed a tear. Lowering his arm, Jack slid the revolver back into his waistband, and weakly smiled at Samantha.

"I'm okay," he said quietly.

Samantha returned his smile, nodded her head, and then replied, "Good."

Before Jack could interpret the meaning of the nod, the detective swiftly swung her arm around, and the chamber filled with two booming echoes as Samantha's finger pulled the trigger on her Glock twice in rapid succession. Her arm shifted again quickly, and two more loud concussions followed the first pair. In the enclosed space, the gunshots reverberated off the walls like a crushing cannonade, making Jack's ears ring. He caught a glimpse of the two Seirenes reeling back as each took the full blast of the shots in their chests. Small crimson holes showed Samantha's bullets had found their mark. But his glimpse was only momentary as Samantha rushed past, grabbed his hand, and dragged him toward the exit.

They stumbled up the stairs of the dimly lit passageway and burst out into the upper cellar of the old house. They could hear the two Seirenes behind them roaring with a bloodcurdling fury. Neither Jack nor Samantha believed that the bullets would stop them. Samantha halted momentarily, spun around, and fired two more shots down the darkened corridor, hoping to slow the Seirenes down, if nothing else. When she turned back to make her escape, she was surprised to run straight into the back of Jack, who had halted near the rickety old staircase that led up to freedom. Samantha followed his gaze up the stairs and felt her hopes dashed.

Standing in the middle of the stairs towered Calithea Panagakos, looking like an Amazon goddess. She, like her companions, was unclothed with her black hair draped delicately on her shoulders. However, where the bodies of the other two Seirenes had been perfection incarnate, Calithea's body bordered on the divine. Adonia and Kallista had physical beauty that was unimaginable, but Calithea had something else. She had a poise and sophistication that elevated her beauty above that of the other two Seirenes. As intense as Calithea's beauty may have been, Samantha found her attention drawn more to the limp body within the woman's grasp. The face was drooped away from view, but the detective instantly recognized her partner, his arms and legs dangling like a lifeless doll. Samantha's only consolation was that he appeared to still be alive, barely.

"I found this pathetic creature roaming around the second floor," Calithea said.

With a quick thrust of her arms, she expelled Peter's slack body over the railing, sending it crashing against the stacked wooden crates. The jangle of gold coins and jewelry echoed through the cellar as the crates shifted with the impact, and Peter's torso came to rest hard on the cold floor. Samantha felt torn between rushing to her partner's side to assess his injuries, and emptying the remaining bullets from her Glock into Calithea Panagakos. But she didn't have time to do either. In the mayhem of the past few seconds, she had forgotten the other two Seirenes, who emerged from the dark passage behind Jack and Samantha. With a swift swing of her arm, Adonia made her presence felt when the back of her hand impacted the side of Samantha's head. The detective hit the ground hard and slid across the floor into the stone wall. Losing grip on her gun, the firearm clattered onto the floor, out of Samantha's reach. Jack spun and ducked in time to avoid Kallista's fist, which was aimed at his head. But the Seirene quickly compensated for the missed opportunity by driving her knee into Jack's groin, sending him to the floor writhing in pain.

Calithea, watching from the top of the stairs, tilted her head back and laughed out loud. Slowly, she descended the stairs; her bare feet didn't make a sound. Samantha rolled onto her side, grimacing in pain as Calithea approached and then knelt down at the detective's side.

"Was my sister a little rough? I should apologize. Neither of them are quite as cultured and refined as I am. They still rely more on their baser instincts and tend to lean more toward violence," Calithea said. She paused for a moment, and then added, "Having said that, I must admit that I do occasionally enjoy inflicting pain and suffering on others."

As her final word exited her mouth, the Seirene grabbed a fist full of Samantha's auburn hair. With a savage jerk of her hand, she yanked the detective's head backward, forcing Samantha to look the Seirene in the eyes.

"I hope you understand," hissed Calithea.

A groan from across the room prompted the black-haired Seirene to release her grip, rise, and then walk toward Jack. With hands on her hips, she stood over him, and gazed down at his huddled mass, watching as he rolled over on his back still cupping his groin with his hands.

Through gritted teeth, Jack said, "Damn it. If you don't want people to come in, lock your damn door."

He regretted the jest almost as soon as the words had left his mouth for Kallista drove her foot into the side of his head with a swift kick. His ears were ringing and his vision blurred as he tried to shake off the vicious attack. Jack tried to focus across the room to see if Samantha was still alive, and felt relieved to see a hazy figure struggling to rise to her knees.

"I'm impressed," Calithea said. "I wasn't expecting you to find us so quickly, but my sisters have been a bit overzealous with their feeding. I tried to stop them, but they do so love a good meal, particularly after starving for so long in that pit." She looked toward Samantha. "You do know about the pit, don't you? Of course, you do. You know, detective, I told you once before that you didn't know with whom you were dealing. Do you know now?"

Samantha wiped the back of her hand across her nose and found a streak of bright red blood left on the skin. Her back ached and her head pounded. She rose to her knees, steadying herself on the wall behind her. She glanced at Peter's barely conscious body, lying amidst a pile of scattered gold coins on the floor. His face was swollen, and black and blue. His left arm was twisted in a way that she knew wasn't natural, making her wonder how many broken bones Peter had. Blood trickled from his ear and the side of his mouth. His jacket had been torn, and she could see at least three distinct bloodstains on the front of his shirt. She knew he wasn't dead, but Samantha wondered if it would have been better if he were.

She glanced over at Jack, who had been able to lift himself up, and was now seated on the floor rubbing the side of his head. The Seirenes stood over Samantha and her companions like the victors gloating over the spoils of war. Samantha glanced at Adonia and felt an overwhelming discouragement to see only a faint discoloration on the skin where she had earlier placed two precisely aimed bullets.

Spitting blood from her mouth, Samantha said, "I know who you are—an arrogant bitch. But I don't understand how you got here. This isn't Greece. Why the hell are you here?"

As Kallista smiled in response, Samantha watched in horror as the Seirene's mouth morphed from luscious lips and perfectly white teeth to a broad, sinister row of hideous dagger-like incisors. Hissing, the serene said, "So, the detective doesn't have it all figured out. Should we tell her?"

Calithea replied, "Why not?"

The three Seirenes began to circle around the chamber with slow predatory steps; their heads slowly oscillated like animals of prey. Samantha couldn't help but be reminded of vultures as they circle a carcass, and she wondered if that was what she would soon be.

"We are as old as time, and have lived for more centuries than you can imagine," said Adonia.

Calithea continued, "We were considered an abomination to nature, and cast out with the expectation that we would die."

"But we lived, feeding on the very ones who had cast us out," added Kallista.

"And then our reign of terror began," said Calithea.

Adonia said, "We sought out villages and feasted on their nectar. But this wasn't enough."

"We wanted more. We wanted wealth and, with that, power," stated Kallista.

Calithea added to the narrative with, "We found that some villages would pay us handsomely to leave them alone."

"But we gorged ourselves on those that refused," said Adonia.

Samantha, still on her knees, shook her head. "Enough with the synchronized sentences. How the hell did you get here?"

Calithea halted and then turned to face the detective. As her eyes burned bright, and her mouth contorted into a line of sharp fangs, she said, "We had heard much about this new world. Its potential seemed far too good to pass up. We booked passage on a schooner heading for your city of brotherly love. Your historians have been diligent to excise from the historical record the name of our vessel, the Zephryia. It was the only vessel in 1788 to arrive without its crew. They, shall we say, each met with their demise during the voyage."

"You killed them," clarified Samantha.

"We killed them all . . . for the sheer pleasure of it. One by one over the course of our journey. You should have seen the faces of the last three shipmen. Even as Zephryia drifted into dock, we were enjoying our last meal. Three hapless souls who became our celebratory feast. Would you have preferred we starve?" responded Kallista.

"If I had my choice . . ." started Samantha.

Jack slowly rose to his feet, cautiously, so as to not provoke a response from the three Seirenes. A wave of nausea came over him, as his abdomen ached from the blow he had received. He leaned forward, placing his hands on his knees for support as he struggled to keep from dry heaving in front of his attackers.

Feigning pity, Kallista said, "The poor man seems to be ill."

Between deep breaths, Jack asked, "People didn't take too kindly to your presence here, did they?"

Hissing with venomous hatred, Adonia exclaimed, "Franklin!"

Calithea explained, "The people of Philadelphia were happy enough to have three beautiful, wealthy women spending money in their city. We were invited to some of the finest homes by some of the wealthiest members of society. They were so stupid and so inept. They had no idea what they had let into their homes. Sheep can be so easily led, and they were such good sheep. But Franklin . . . Benjamin Franklin was different."

"The old man began to assist the city constabulary with their investigation into what they called murders. We had been feasting on the city's population for months before he finally subdued us. One would never have expected such fight and vigor from the old man, but he succeeded where most had failed. It won't happen again," added Kallista.

Rising to her feet, Samantha grimaced at the ache, which seemed to encompass her entire body. She tried to brush some of the dirt and dust from her clothing but quickly determined that it was an exercise in futility.

"How did he stop you?" she asked.

Calithea's head tilted back, and she let out a loud laugh, which was quickly imitated by the other two Seirenes. "Do you think us foolish? Is your opinion of our intelligence so low that you think we would so easily tell you of our weaknesses?"

Samantha's smirked antagonistically. "Yeah, actually it is."

Before she knew what had happened, Kallista had swiftly crossed the room, and delivered a fierce backhanded blow across Samantha's face. Stumbling back, Samantha clutched the wall for support, but refused to fall to the ground. The Seirene raised her hand into the air to strike out again at the detective.

"Sister, stop this," commanded Calithea. "There is no need to inflict such senseless violence on the good detective. She was just expressing her . . . objections to our raison d'être."

As Kallista backed away, Samantha could taste blood in her mouth. Her mind was racing, and she was filled with a combination of uncontrollable rage and utter fear. She wanted nothing more than to get her hands around the neck of any one of the three and throttle them to death. But she knew from experience that their strength was far superior to hers. Samantha considered herself more than efficient when it came to close quarter hand-to-hand fighting, but she doubted she would last more than a minute against any of the three Seirenes. Their strength and violent nature would be far too difficult to overcome.

"You won't tell me how to defeat you. At least tell me what you've done to that poor girl in your underground chamber of horrors," said Samantha.

"Her? Oh, she is very special to us. She will be our, how can I say it? Our Virgin Mary," said Adonia.

Samantha stared blankly at the Seirene. "What the hell does that mean?"

Calithea responded, "She is our child bearer. That young girl is carrying the first of a new breed of Seirene."

Chapter Twenty-Six

With her eyes wide open and her mouth gaping, Samantha could barely contain her shock and disbelief. It was an idea that had never crossed her mind, and now it came crashing into her conscious thought like a runaway freight train. She had simply assumed that there were three, and only three, and never gave any consideration to the fact that they could reproduce. *Three of these creatures are hard enough to deal with,* she thought. Her head was whirling with the possibilities and none of them were pleasant. She stared at the three Seirenes, each looking calm and relaxed at first glance, but a closer examination showed the tautness in their muscles as a sign of their readiness to strike at a moment's notice. She turned her gaze toward Jack, who looked as aghast as she felt.

"Hang on a second. You three can reproduce with another woman? How the hell does that work?" inquired Jack.

Calithea turned toward Jack. "We've tried for centuries to reproduce, but our bodies are incapable of carrying a child. Although we can produce eggs, all of our attempts to become pregnant ourselves have failed in the most painful and debilitating manner."

Jack stole a quick glance toward Peter's limp body as Adonia added, "When one of us would fall ill, the other two would dedicate themselves to the care and protection of the fallen one. It takes years of isolation, constant care to recover from such a traumatic event."

Samantha, trying to maintain a calm composure despite her ever increasing fear, let out a laugh, and said, "Hey Jack, did you hear that? All we got to do is get them knocked up, and then we can defeat them. For the sake of the city, would you mind obliging?"

No sooner had the words exited Samantha's mouth than Kallista had her hand around the detective's throat and shoved her back against the cold stone wall. Samantha struggled to breathe with the vise-like grip crushing her windpipe.

"You dare to mock us!" exclaimed the blonde Seirene.

Samantha, unable to answer, felt her feet lift away from the floor as her back was dragged up the rough stone of the wall. Grasping Kallista's wrist with both of her hands, the detective tried to free herself from the tightening grip to no avail. Her head was beginning to spin, and her vision was becoming blurry from the lack of oxygen.

More out of instinct than courage or valor, Jack lunged forward to try and help Samantha. He had only taken two steps when Adonia's fist smashed into his abdomen. As he doubled over in pain, his face met her knee as it raced upward, snapping his head back and sending him crashing against the crates filled with gold. The jangle of coins echoed through the cellar as the top crate broke open, spilling its contents all over the floor. The gold coins, some shiny and some dull, scattered across the cold stone surface, creating a carpet of metallic yellow that shifted easily underneath Jack's weight as he impacted the ground. When his huddled mass finished sliding across the coin-littered floor, Jack was lying still in front of Peter's unmoving body.

"Enough!" shouted Calithea, resulting in the release of the iron grip on Samantha's neck.

As she dropped down to the floor, Samantha struggled to keep her knees from giving out under the weight. She pressed her back against the stone wall behind her for support. Stroking her sore neck, Samantha gasped for air. From where she stood, she couldn't tell if Jack was alive or dead. She was feeling an overwhelming sense of hopelessness as she summed up the odds and found them to be greatly lacking in her favor. She had done exactly what her father had always told her not to do; she had gone in without backup. It had crossed her mind as she drove across the city that morning, but what choice did she have? How could she have called for backup? She was entering a house without a search warrant under the suspicion that the owner was some kind of mythological killer. And, even if she had applied for a search warrant, would she ever have succeeded in convincing a judge of the facts? She had taken a risk, and the gamble had failed. Now she was facing imminent death. Samantha assumed that it would only be a matter of time before they grew tired of her presence and simply killed her. The only thing she could do was bide her time.

"If you can't get pregnant, then how are you going to reproduce?" she asked.

Calithea smugly replied, "Humans have made such great strides since we were entombed. I believe the good doctor called it . . . in vitro fertilization. We provided the egg, as well as the sperm from a . . . let's just call him a healthy donor."

"Doctor Hardwick?" inquired Samantha.

"Yes," Calithea explained. "He's resting in the chamber next to our mother-to-be. Dr. Hardwick was considerably shocked at how fast the fetus has grown. It seems that our genetic makeup, when combined with that of a human, has somehow accelerated the growth rate. He's anticipating that we shall be happy parents within a month."

Samantha thought about Susan and Jessica Hardwick and shuddered as she recalled the sight of their bodies in their home on Thirteenth Street. The doctor's wife and daughter had died in the most horrible and, Samantha had little doubt, most painful manner possible. Death at the hands of these creatures was a terrifying proposition that Samantha feared she would soon experience.

"You killed his family? And kidnapped him?" Samantha asked.

Kallista smiled. "We . . . borrowed him."

"You kidnapped him," Samantha stated.

"Let's not bandy words. You say kidnapped, and we say borrowed. Does it really matter? After all, the end result will be the same," said Calithea.

Feeling increasingly frantic, Samantha exclaimed, "The ends justify the means? Is that it? What about that woman? Let me guess . . . you found her jogging alone in the park, and just decided to help yourself to her uterus."

Calithea tossed her head back and laughed. "You have such a way with words, detective."

"You're putting her through this hell! Does she even know what you've done to her?" exclaimed Samantha.

"It doesn't matter. When she gives birth, she'll be too close to death to care, and won't survive very long after. The fetus is feeding off her as it grows. There'll be hardly anything left of her at birth. And what is left will make a nice first meal for our newborn," replied Calithea.

The Seirene's nonchalant manner when speaking of the young girl's inevitable death infuriated Samantha. There was no compassion, no remorse, and no emotion at all. The Seirenes were treating the young woman, whoever she was, like nothing more than an incubator. She was just a thing to be discarded when her usefulness was over.

"Why now?" asked Jack suddenly as he slowly rolled onto his back and tried to lift himself to his feet.

Samantha shuddered at the state of his battered face, with its swollen cheek, bloody nose, and a deep

306

cut above his left eye. He also, she noted, was favoring his left leg. His last scuffle with the Seirenes must have been worse than it had appeared. Samantha's hopes for escape continued to plummet.

Pointing at him, Calithea commanded, "Bring him over here."

Adonia approached Jack, grabbed him by the arm, and jerked him forward till he was standing against the wall beside Samantha. Reaching forward, Samantha wiped a trickle of blood away from his eye.

"Are you all right?" she asked.

Jack nodded, and then looked at Calithea. "Answer my question. Why did you decide to reproduce? You've been content for centuries. Why now?"

Adonia, who was still standing beside Jack, leaned closer, placing her face inches from his. "Because we want to rule."

Calithea added, "We are the superior species. We are only three, yet we could easily dominate this city. But just imagine what an entire race of Seirenes could do. We could dominate the world. All of the human race would be under our thumb."

"Superior race? One man already tried that and failed. Look it up on the Internet. His name was Hitler," said Samantha.

"Genetics can be a complicated thing. What if this baby doesn't turn out to be the superior child that you're hoping for?" Jack inquired.

Kallista replied, "We shall kill it and start again."

Samantha said, "You'll have to find another surrogate mother."

"Yes, we will. Care to volunteer?" said Calithea.

"Why's Hardwick helping you?" the detective asked.

"He has no choice. His mind is easily influenced," Adonia replied.

"You're controlling him, just like you controlled everyone else," Samantha exclaimed.

"Sisters, I grow tired of this. We have things to attend to," Calithea said. "Who would like to feast on the detective?"

Kallista rubbed her hands together, and her eyes began to burn a bright fiery red. The bright eyes looked Samantha up and down like a ravenous animal.

"Adonia, you may have the man," Calithea stated.

Adonia smiled at Jack. "I've waited quite long enough to taste your nectar, Jack Allyn. You should feel special. There are few who have made me wait."

The three Seirenes stood before Jack and Samantha in all their naked glory. Their visage had transformed into a hideous nightmare of deadly saliva-covered fangs, and the eyes of all three were glowing, casting the cellar in bright hues of orange and red. Samantha stepped backward until her back touched the wall. She had nowhere left to go, nowhere left to run. During the Society Hill Serial Killer investigation, Samantha had felt fear. It had been a fear of failure, a fear of allowing a monster to continue to terrorize the city—her city. The beast had taunted her and had filled her nightmares. Yet she had overcome. It had taken a long time for the emotional scars to heal, but she did heal. But now she felt something far worse than fear. Her heart pounded with utter terror at the sight of the three creatures advancing toward her. She wanted to scream and cower back against the wall, but no matter how terrified Samantha was, she would never give them the satisfaction. She knew deep in her soul that there was only one chance to act, and one chance was all she was going to get.

Jack stood helpless as the creatures slowly stalked forward toward them as a lifetime of regrets surfaced in his mind. His heart raced as his subconscious took the opportunity to flaunt his mistakes before him, like some twisted form of *This is Your Life*. The blazing red eyes of the Seirenes only helped to punctuate each regret as being final. He had never imagined that he would die at the hands of such terrifying creatures, but then he realized that none of the other victims probably had either. He glanced toward Peter and thought he saw movement, but Jack knew that there would be no hope. Even if they had all been healthy, there would be no way to fight off these creatures. He knew they were all doomed to die.

When Samantha's hand darted toward his belt, Jack had been taken completely by surprise. He felt her extract the revolver from his waistband and heard the first blast as Samantha placed a bullet in Kallista's face, causing a small spattering of crimson fluid. The second bullet to burst from the gun smashed a small hole into Calithea's knee, causing the Seirene's leg to buckle.

"Grab Peter! Get out of here!" Samantha shouted as she fired a third shot at Adonia's heart, sending the Seirene reeling backward.

Jack was across the room in an instant, grabbing Peter and trying to lift him off the cold stone floor. Wrapping his arm around Peter's waist, Jack heaved the detective up, and half-dragged him toward the steps. As another shot rattled from the Samantha's gun, Jack struggled to haul Peter's dead weight up the swaying staircase. His shoulder and arm muscles burned, and he stumbled more than once, slamming his shins into the hard edge of the steps. Jack glanced down into the basement and caught sight of Samantha lunging across the chamber below toward the Glock she had lost earlier. The screams of the Seirenes echoed through the stone chamber, and pierced Jack's ears with their loud shrieks.

Two more shots from her father's revolver had emptied the gun, and Samantha's hand scooped up the Glock. She couldn't remember how many shots she had fired earlier, and hoped that the magazine wasn't empty when she pulled the trigger. She was rewarded by another ear-shattering blast, which sent Calithea to the ground. As elated as Samantha was to watch the Seirene crash into the stone floor, she knew it would only be a few moments before the creature rose again. Glancing toward the stairs, she watched as Jack struggled to lug Peter upward. *I've just got to buy them a little time,* she thought as she pulled the trigger again, sending Adonia falling backward with a bullet to the face.

Jack had been struggling with Peter's feet getting caught on the lip of each step, and had to halt his progress momentarily to roll the unconscious detective over on his back. Now, with his arms under Peter's armpits and around his chest, Jack pulled toward the door at the top of the stairs. As he backed his way upward, Jack's heel caught on the step, and he fell back, hitting his head on the door. The impact swung the door open, and Jack glanced over his shoulder into the dark kitchen. His arms were searing with pain as he heaved Peter's body through the door, and onto the kitchen floor beyond. But as Jack began to lift himself up, a vise-like grip clamped around his ankle and began to drag him back down the stairs. He spun around to find Kallista's glistening dagger-like teeth and flaming red eyes glaring up at him. Jack lashed out with his other foot, kicking the Seirene in the face over and over to no avail. Her iron grip only tightened on his ankle. She pulled hard on his leg, and he slid further down, hitting his head against the step. Another loud boom suddenly echoed through the chamber, and a crimson hole shattered through the Seirene's wrist, forcing her to release her grip. Jack heard Samantha scream, "Go! Damn it! Go!" as he scrambled up the stairs and into the kitchen.

Falling through the door, Jack spun around quickly and slammed it shut, blocking out the majority of the Seirenes' screams from below. Peter lay huddled on the floor, taking slow, shallow breaths. Jack heard another gunshot from below, climbed to his feet, and, wrapping his arms around Peter's chest, lifted the detective and dragged him toward the front door of the house. As Jack struggled to carry Peter's weight, he could feel his own strength being quickly drained. He gasped for air with each step forward, and sweat was pouring down into his eyes, causing them to sting. The screams and gunshots from the basement below faded as Jack drew closer to the entrance of the house. But each step forward seemed slower and sapped more and more of his energy. Jack and Peter passed through the front room, which was still shrouded in darkness. Jack flung open the front door, and a burst of sunlight ripped through the gloom.

As he stumbled down the three front steps, Jack hadn't realized how long he had been below ground until the glaring sunlight blinded him. His foot landed on the soft ground, and Jack fell to his knee; his elbow stopped him from falling face down into the grass. Despite the adrenaline coursing through his veins, Jack's bruised left thigh ached as he rolled over on the ground. Gritting his teeth in pain, he glanced toward the door of the house. Peter's comatose body lay huddled in the doorway. Jack rose to his feet, grabbed one of Peter's limp arms, and dragged him down the front steps into the grass.

He had barely dragged the unconscious detective's body more than a few yards when the explosion erupted behind them, throwing Jack back down onto the ground with the force of the blast. Glass shattered around them as the explosion blew out the windows on the first floor of the house. Intense flames and heat were expelled from the doorway and threatened to burn Jack and Peter alive. Blown off its hinges, the old front door shattered into pieces and rocketed out into the yard.

When the initial shock of the blast subsided, Jack rolled over and gazed at the house behind him. The centuries old timbers had ignited, and the house was an inferno. Blazing orange flames and dark black smoke poured from every window, and smoldering debris covered the grassy lawn on all sides of the house. Finding the heat to be too intense, Jack scrambled to his feet, grabbed Peter's arm once again, and lugged him away from the house toward the street. The intensity of the fire seemed to lessen as he slowly crept further from the house. A few feet from the sidewalk, Jack could go no further and dropped Peter's arm, and then he fell to the ground in exhaustion. Lying on the cool grass, Jack glanced up at the burning house and watched as a section of the roof collapsed into the fiery structure. In the distance, he could hear the faint sound of sirens echoing through the streets of the city, signaling that help was on the way.

Chapter Twenty-Seven

When the door to the Den of Heroes opened, Jack looked up from the comic book he was reading to see Peter Thornton limp through the doorway. The detective's arm was hanging in a cast and sling, and his face still held the fresh scars left from recently removed stitches. When Jack last saw Peter, the paramedics were loading the unconscious detective into an ambulance. The Philadelphia Fire Department had responded quickly, but not fast enough to save the structure. The old wood framed house had collapsed in on itself. The centuries old timbers had ignited fast and burned even faster, leaving little more than a pile of charred rubble when finally extinguished. The four weeks that had followed had come and gone like a whirlwind, and Jack was only now beginning to settle into his new life.

"You look like hell," Jack said as the detective limped over to the glass display case.

"Thanks. Coming from you, I'll assume that's a compliment."

Jack laughed. "You look better than you did the last time I saw you. At least now you can open your eyes."

"Yeah. The doctor says it'll be another few months before I have the full use of my hand again."

"You out on disability?" asked Jack.

Nodding, Peter replied, "For now. But I'm planning to return to active duty as soon as I can."

"I figured you were still in pretty bad shape when I didn't see you at Samantha's funeral."

Peter's head hung low for a moment, and then he said, "I really wanted to go, but I was still laid up in the hospital."

"It was a good service. I'd say half the police force was there."

An awkward silence fell between them as they both contemplated their own thoughts about Samantha Ballard and the events leading up to her death. Jack had only known her for a few weeks, but he still felt a twinge of pain at her memory. Theirs had been a friendship forged out of circumstance, but Jack still found himself grieving her loss. The events of that fateful day were still fresh in his memory. He could remember his trip to the hospital, with a police officer sitting beside him in the ambulance. Then there were the hours of interrogation, repeating his story over and over again to disbelieving officers and FBI agents. Jack had lost track of how many different detectives, officers, and special agents he had spoken with, and he never could tell who was playing the good cop and who was playing the bad cop. They all seemed pissed at him. When the police commissioner himself entered the room, Jack was tired, hungry, and sore. He didn't want to be asked any more questions, and he had expressed his thoughts in as loud and rude a manner as he could possibly muster. The commissioner sat quietly and listened to every word. When his tirade had ended, Jack was surprised by the calm manner in which the commissioner apologized for his treatment and told him he was free to go. The next morning, the headlines in all the city newspapers declared that the city's serial killer had died, along with a police detective, in a house explosion in Germantown. There was no mention of the Seirenes. A lawyer from city hall had shown up later that day with some papers for Jack to sign, silencing his version of the story in perpetuity.

Peter broke the silence. "Jack, I never got the chance to thank you for dragging me out of that house. You saved my life."

"No," said Jack, shaking his head. "Samantha saved our lives. We'd never have made it if not for her."

Wistfully, Peter said, "I don't think she really liked me. Or maybe it was just that I was a rookie. I got the impression she didn't want me as a partner. I can't blame her. But I did learn a hell of a lot from her. I don't think she ever realized it."

After another awkward silence, Peter said, "I hope my boss didn't come down too hard on you."

Jack smiled. "It was a little touch and go for a while. They weren't sure if I was telling the truth or just a lunatic."

"Consider yourself lucky we took those body cams in with us. If it wasn't for those they would have locked you up and thrown away the key."

"Did they find Samantha's?" asked Jack.

Nodding, Peter replied, "Yes. They found it that day while they were searching the rubble for any remains. The footage pretty much spoke for itself. Between my cam and Samantha's, the police commissioner got to see more of those creatures than he probably ever wanted to."

"You've seen the footage?"

"Yeah. All of it," replied Peter.

"What happened?"

Peter went silent for a second, composing himself before replying. "The shots she was firing at the Seirenes weren't keeping them down for very long. They seemed to have incredible recovery time. They were back on their feet in seconds. Samantha did what she could, but they charged her all at once. She couldn't stop them." Peter paused, fighting to hold back his emotions. "They, uh . . . pounced on her, and then began to beat her . . . and tear her to shreds. She must have saved a round in her gun. The footage caught Samantha setting off the explosion. She put a bullet through one of the propane tanks."

"Damn," was all Jack could say.

"The last image from the camera was the Seirenes being engulfed in flames. It was pretty disturbing to watch."

"Did they find her body, or did they bury an empty coffin?"

Shaking his head, Peter replied, "They didn't

find much, just a few bones. That was about it. The medical examiner wasn't even sure whose they were. The heat from the fire incinerated just about everything."

"I'm surprised the body cam survived."

"Yeah. Those things are built to last. I've seen one take a bullet and still record."

"I guess there's no way to know if they survived," said Jack.

Peter shook his head. "Don't know how they could. They must have been incinerated like everything else."

"I guess that doctor and the pregnant woman didn't make it either." Jack bowed his head. "So many dead. It's just so hard to believe. If I hadn't lived through it—"

"I know," interjected Peter. "Over the past few days, we've turned up a few more bodies, scattered throughout the city. They were well hidden, but didn't seem freshly killed. Probably some of their early victims."

"There's one thing I haven't figured out. How did they know about in vitro fertilization? They'd been buried for centuries."

"They probably got that from one of their early victims. Robert Crosse and his fiancé were patients of Dr. Hardwick, trying to have a baby."

"Minds are open when they feed," muttered Jack.

"What?"

"It was something Adonia said to me," explained

Jack. "Her victim's mind was open to her when she fed."

Another long moment of silence fell across the shop, until Peter spoke up. "Saw the banner over the door of the shop. Under new management?"

Jack tried to smile, only half succeeding. "Yeah. It was time for a change. Bryan's parents accepted my offer. They didn't know what to do with the shop after Bryan was killed, so I'm buying it from them. We're still waiting for all the legal mumbo jumbo to be taken care of, but they let me open the place, and keep it running until the sale's complete."

"No more Pulsar or WPLX?"

"No more Pulsar. But, I'll still be on the air at WPLX, at least for a little while longer," Jack replied.

"I'll still come in. Will I get a discount?" said Peter, smiling.

"Discount? Hell, you're going to pay a premium. I'm the one who saved your life, remember?"

As the two men laughed, they continued to converse for a few more minutes, talking about mundane things like the weather and the upcoming baseball season, until another awkward silence led Peter to say his farewell and head toward the door of the shop. When the detective's hand was on the doorknob, Jack called out his name. Peter turned back to look at Jack.

"She thought you were a good detective. She really did. I just thought you should know," Jack said.

Peter nodded. "Thanks."

As Jack watched the door close behind the

detective, he glanced down at the comic he had been reading. Wedged between the pages, acting as a bookmark, was a single round-trip airline ticket. Philly to Albany, New York. Then, a rental car to Schenectady. Jack Allyn was going home.

Somewhere along US Route 96, between the interchange of US Route 96 and US Route 183, near the small Kansas town of Nekoma, Sheriff's Deputy William Albright pulled his police cruiser over to the side of the road. The tires of the Ford Crown Victoria crunched on the gravel along the shoulder. To his right and left were the telltale signs of autumn; the crops in the fields, which lined either side of the road, had browned with the change of seasons and rustled in the October breeze. The late model Honda Accord in front of him sat quietly on the side of the road. The deputy could see the driver's head through the rear window. It was slouched toward the driver's door. William Albright, a five year veteran of the Rush County Sheriff's department, switched on the blue light bar atop his car and grabbed for his radio.

"Base, this is Albright," he said.

The radio speaker crackled a reply with a soft-spoken feminine tone. "Hey, Billy. What's up?"

He gritted his teeth, and sighed loudly. He hated to be called Billy, especially by the likes of Brenda Hoffman. She was only two years younger than him, but they had both graduated from the same high school.

He had been the local high school football star, and she had been the love-struck teenager that went to every game just to see him play. Albright, however, had a long list of girlfriends that didn't include Brenda. Now, years later, her focus was not so much on catching his eye, but riling him up every chance she got.

"Brenda! It's Deputy Albright. Show some professionalism over the radio."

"Ok, Billy. What's going on?"

Deciding to ignore it, the deputy replied, "I got myself a sleeper out on Ninety-six. Just going to check it out."

"Roger that, Billy," came Brenda's reply, with extra emphasis on his name.

Pushing open the car door, William Albright stepped from his cruiser and slid his hat onto his head. Pushing the door closed with one hand, he casually undid the thumb snap on his holster with the other. *There was no sense in not being cautious,* he thought.

The cool evening breeze blew hard across the Kansas plains, reminding him that he had left his jacket in the car. His broad shoulders shivered momentarily with the chill before he put the cold out of his mind. *This will only take a few minutes,* he thought. With the sun slowly setting in the distance, he walked with evenly spaced strides to the Honda. As he drew closer, he could see the full head of black hair leaning against the driver's side window. It wasn't too unusual for Deputy Albright to find someone, tired from driving through the miles and miles of monotonous farm fields, sleeping on the side of the road. It happened at least once a week, and Albright would nudge them along, pointing out the nearest motel.

He reached the driver's door, and, without paying much attention to the occupant, gently tapped on the glass of the window. "Wake up."

He glanced up and down the deserted road. When there was no response, he tapped on the window harder. "Wake up."

When he looked down at the unmoving figure in the car, his heart stopped. Stepping back into the deserted road, he stared wide-eyed at the Honda, and drew his gun from the holster on his hip. Slowly stepping toward the car again, he reached for the door handle. As the car door opened, the body in the car fell out onto the road with a soft thud. As the corpse rocked gently on the asphalt surface, the cracked leathery skin seemed to shine in the setting sun. The young deputy leaned forward for a moment, looking closely at the body. Then he swiftly rushed back toward his police cruiser. Flinging the car door open, Deputy Albright reached for his radio again.

"Brenda!" he exclaimed.

"Hey Billy, back so soon? Did you wake up your sleeper?" came the reply.

The deputy responded, "Shut up and listen, Brenda. Call the sheriff, and get him out here right away! Tell him I've got some really weird shit to show him!"

Sirens in the Night

Acknowledgements

Special thanks to Christine Schulden, Alicia Downs, and Paul Popiel for their efforts and feedback as early readers of this little tale. Your feedback was invaluable.

Thanks also to my editor, Cherrita, who was instrumental in helping to turn a disjointed, error-filled manuscript into a book. You rock!

Finally, thanks to all students of Greek Mythology for allowing me to take some literary license with some of the great mythological creatures from ancient Greece. When it comes to creating fiction, sometimes one must stretch the myths a little for the sake of the story.

About The Author

Born and raised in southern New Jersey, Michael Bradley is an author and software consultant whose frequent travels have brought him in touch with a variety of people throughout the United States. In his day job, he has presented on a variety of subjects at several IT conferences, both in America and Europe. When he isn't on the road, working, or writing, Michael hits the waterways in one of his three kayaks, paddling all over Delaware, Pennsylvania, Maryland, and New Jersey.

Before working in information technology, Michael spent eight years in radio broadcasting, working for stations in New Jersey and West Virginia, including the Marconi Award winning WVAQ in Morgantown. He has been "up and down the dial" working as on air personality, promotions director, and even program director. This experience has provided a wealth of fond, enduring, and, sometimes, scandalous memories that he hopes to someday write about.

Among the writers in which he finds inspiration, Michael favors P.D. James, Raymond Chandler, Leslie Charteris, Simon Brett, Terry Pratchett, and Ian Fleming. He lives in Delaware with his wife, Diane, and their three furry four-legged "kids", Simon, Brandy, and Preaya.

CPSIA information can be obtained
at www.ICGtesting.com
Printed in the USA
LVOW01s1143130416
483361LV00002B/3/P